A Council of Betrayal
Kim Bair

Facebook: kimbairauthor
Instagram: KimBairAuthor
Email: kimbair@proton.me
Website: www.kimbair.com
Telegram: kimbairauthor
Copyright © Kim Bair 2016
Ebook Cover Design by http://www.ebooklaunch.com

More books by Kim Bair:
Dead Shifter Walking, The Succubus Executioner Book 1
Demigod Down, The Succubus Executioner Book 2
A Witch's Fury, The Succubus Executioner Book 3
A Council of Betrayal, The Succubus Executioner Book 4
Death of a Succubus, The Succubus Executioner Book 5
Legacy of the Succubus, The Succubus Executioner Book 6
Creation of the Dual Shifter, The Dual Shifter Executioner
The Mel Files
Andy's Origin, The Andromalius Chronicles

Table of Contents

Chapter 1

"How do you want to do this?" Logan asked, resting his raw sienna gaze on me.

I chewed on my bottom lip, meeting his intrigued look with my own sea green gaze. So many options lingered on my tongue, none of them appropriate for our current situation.

I smiled at my own internal joke, turning my attention to the window of the violet-eyed mage's shop. It looked the same as when I had been here with Blake. This time I had an irritated shifter with me who had suffered the effects of Mae's magically enhanced silver cuffs firsthand. We both had. He had felt the power of the cuffs pushing him to pure beast, and I had knocked myself against a concrete basement floor sucking the magic in to save him.

I drummed my fingers against my bottom lip, catching Logan's intent interest at the movement. "I'll go in first."

"How long do you want me to wait?" he questioned, with a knowing glance.

"Once I stop breaking things." I knew my smile was unhinged, can't say I gave a shit. I was done not being allowed in the backrooms of witches' shops, or hell, not being allowed in their shops at all. I was also done being tied down with magical silver fucking chains.

The door chimed as I crossed the threshold, announcing that the party was about to get started. I reached behind me, slipping the lock home. Anticipation threaded through my veins, putting a bounce in my step.

The silver haired mage pushed through the beaded curtain separating the store from her private backroom. Her greeting caught in her throat, her beautiful violet eyes widening as she took a step back, mouth still hanging open.

I wasn't sure if it was the throwing knives secured around my thigh, or my open leather duster revealing the dual guns resting against my sides.

I was betting on my off balanced smile.

"What do you want?" She took another step back, into the safety of her backroom. I took several toward her. I stopped at the counter, giving her the small illusion of safety.

"Answers, Mae."

1

"I won't help you. You killed an entire coven." Disgust laced her words, giving her confidence as she stepped forward, her arms crossed stiffly across her middle.

I shrugged. Technically, that wasn't me, but I'd take the compliment. The Fae, whom the coven had called forth, claimed the witches' lives as payment for being bothered. If Destiny and her crew of flunkies were lucky, they were dead. The Fae beat me hands down for finding creative ways to torture.

I'd admit to being jealous, but I was too damn scared of those bastards.

I straightened up, drumming my fingers against the glass counter.

"Let's be honest, Mae. The witches aren't strong enough to put up a fight if I decide to kill you. And at this point, I'm not sure I give a fuck."

Her expression blanked, matching a mind that had nothing intelligent to say.

The smile left my face. "You are a threat to me and those I protect. I need to send a message, and it will be sent brutally on your flesh."

Stepping back, keeping my eyes trained on Mae, I kicked over her impressive display case. She moved instinctively closer to stop me.

"What is wrong with you?" she screamed. "Do you have any idea how expensive those items are?"

I pulled off my leather duster, resting it over the untouched cash register on top of a filing cabinet.

It was a new addition to my ensemble and I was still weighing its merits.

Her hands clenched and unclenched as her plum gaze swung around the shop, frantic.

"Looking for how to take down a pissed off succubus, Mae?"

Her panicked stare landed back on me. "The witches will protect me." She was grasping at straws, and we both knew it.

I laughed, a deep, roaring belly laugh. It was totally misplaced there, but I didn't give a fuck.

"Oh Mae, you are a fool. I'll be honest, I hadn't pegged you for such easy prey." I drew out the last word, moving closer to her.

Her eyes widened, watching my progress with trepidation.

"You can't hurt me," she repeated, trying to convince herself, not me.

I laughed again, a silken sound this time. "You going to stop me?" I asked, tilting my head.

She floundered backwards, displacing the annoying hanging beads, finally attempting to escape.

I cleared the distance between us in an instant, landing a hand on her shoulder with all the force of my irritation. She spun, bringing a hand to her mouth and blowing a dust at me. I coughed, caught off guard.

"Fucking witches," I grunted, blinking rapidly to clear my gaze.

Mae chanted words I didn't understand, drawing strength and conviction as I stayed still. Her arms rose from her sides as her cadence quickened.

I spat out chunks of unknown shit, waiting until my tears cleared the crap out of my eyes before moving.

Based on her terrified response, that wasn't what she was going for. "I — what — I don't understand, you shouldn't be able to move!" She screamed the last word at me, desperation forcing her voice up a few octaves.

I brushed off my shoulder before turning to her.

"Now would be a good time to run."

She took my advice, heading to the back door. I smiled as I stalked after her. I wasn't expecting Logan to toss her back into the room.

"Oh come on! You are ruining all my fun," I scolded him.

He rolled his eyes. "You've had enough time to play; we need answers. In case you don't remember, I was the one chained up with the magic restraints."

I huffed, pulling out the chair Mae used for customers.

"Sit her here. It's sturdy enough." Indeed it was. Thick arms arched up from the seat in hand carved designs, melting solidly into the high back.

I pulled out rope and a worn leather case from my duster pocket.

"I have to say, the duster does allow me to stash more," I informed Logan, tying Mae into the chair securely.

"I'm glad you like it."

"I haven't decided if I like it, or if I'm accepting it."

It was Logan's turn to chuckle as he watched me unroll my toys. Destiny had a knack for flare and it wasn't lost on me. Oftentimes the anticipation of pain is a greater motivator than pain itself.

I caressed my blades, secured with leather bindings, my fingers knowing each groove and ridge. I wasn't ready to slice at her though. I had some aggression I needed to work out, brutally.

Logan's lips at my ear had me jumping slightly. "It was a gift, Olivia, accept it."

I huffed, turned on by the violence running through my veins and the warmth of his breath on my skin. I cracked my neck, turning to look at him. He certainly was different lately. I mean, the man got me a random birthday present. I didn't even know when my birthday was. He had just shrugged and assured me that would only help him surprise me. As in, he planned to do it again. A small part of my still-healing heart liked that, a lot. The remainder, fuck, didn't know how to feel about it.

For now, I'd settle for hurting Mae.

I pulled a chair in front of her, leaving my pretty tools on the counter, for now.

"Answers, Mae. Answers."

"No," she hissed at me.

I smiled, my shoulder relaxing. "I was hoping you'd say that."

My fist cracked against her delicate nose, smashing the cartilage. Her head snapped against the plush chair as she cried out in pain. She hung her head, whimpering, blood dripping onto her silk dress.

I caressed the side of her face. "I want to hurt you, Mae. I need to. But I'll give you an out. Tell me what I want to know, and I'll make it quick," I whispered into her ear.

Sitting down, I braced my elbows on my knees, tensely awaiting her decision.

"Since when is it a crime to fabricate an item for a client?" she asked softly.

"Since I said so. You created two very unique sets of chains. One designed specifically to drive a shifter to pure beast, and one to restrain rogue vampires. You've played both sides with two powerful groups. This visit cannot be a surprise."

She grimaced, looking up at me. "Go back to the hell that spawned you."

I smiled. "Right answer."

...

"I'd like to play a game," I told my violet-eyed mage, twirling a blade around my finger as I leisurely sat in front of her.

She wheezed, keeping her gaze trained on the blood-stained carpeting in front of her. I had to give her credit, she had taken a full twenty minutes of my beating before blacking out.

"You're insane," Mae rasped.

I gave her a soft laugh. "Probably," I admitted, with a nonchalant shrug of my shoulders. "I want to know who you made the spelled chains for."

"A client," she huffed out, her back vibrating with the effort.

I gave her a weary look. "Are you certain you want to continue?"

She coughed, blood spilling down her chin as she finally looked up at me again. Her silver hair was matted with blood, her formerly pristine skin bruised, her left eye swollen shut.

So I might have gone a little overboard on the beating. The bitch had tried to fry me with her magic.

"Vampires," she wheezed.

I looked sharply up at Logan. We had ended up in the clutches of a Fae-loving witch and a magically enhanced, crazy shifter. That was not the answer I was expecting.

I looked back down at Mae, wondering if perhaps she wasn't lying.

Even Nari, the demigod who had a horde of rogue vampires tied up with the magical chains, would have been an acceptable answer. It was interesting to note, though, that she was with the vampires called to release said magical chains. Perhaps the vampire answer made sense?

"More," I demanded, pushing on her dislocated shoulder.

She cried out, blood bubbling down her chin. "I don't know!" she screamed. Her tortured cry turned into sobbing.

"He put me on retainer for a million dollars to make chains on demand for a year," she finally muttered, her head hung low, her bound body the only thing keeping her upright.

"How did he pay you?" Logan asked.

"Wire transfer," Mae exhaled.

"Paper trail?" I asked hopefully.

Mae shook her head. "I hope they get you," she sneered at me.

I laughed before snapping her neck.

"Hey, can you call Tommy? Last time I got blood on my phone he was super pissed at me."

5

"Yep." Logan dialed as I found the small bathroom, warming the water up to wash off my hands.

"Your reigning champion is online," Tommy answered on speakerphone. I snorted in amusement, opening my mouth to respond.

"You beat me at that racing game once, Tommy. You can't claim that title yet," Logan grunted.

I looked at Logan, shocked. When was he at the manor?

"Anyway, we need you to check a wire for us," he continued, clearing his throat.

...

"Just because a vampire approached her, that doesn't mean the vampires as a whole sought the creation of the chains."

"I agree," I told Logan, shifting positions in the SUV and staring at the open road.

"Nor does it mean that one person is behind all the recent attacks."

"I know, Logan," I groaned at him.

"I wonder how difficult chains like those are to create."

I groaned, "We can ask Jerry."

"I suppose we will have to, since you killed her already!" Logan raised his voice in irritation, hitting the steering wheel.

I flipped him off.

He rubbed the back of his neck wearily. "You need to work on your control."

"Bite me."

Logan dropped me off at the manor, sighing, "Stay out of trouble."

I laughed, "That's my middle name."

I plodded up the stairs and dropped my bags off, rubbing the back of my neck.

"So Olie, you up for a game?" Tommy asked, leaning in my doorway.

I laughed, "Yeah, let me shower and get some rest. Shouldn't you be getting some sleep also?"

He shrugged with a sly smile.

I grunted. A teenager was not outdoing me in my ability to stay up late. "Fine, just let me shower."

...

A full night and half a day later I claimed one victory against Tommy. One.

"I'm tempted to revoke your video games," I groaned, rubbing my eyes as I sat on his floor.

"Olivia, don't speak those words!" he teased me.

"Alright, kid, I gotta get some sleep."

"It's the middle of the day."

"I know. I still haven't slept from last night." I pulled him into a side hug before retreating into my own room.

...

"OLIE!" a gaggle of teenagers screamed from the bottom of the stairs. I rolled over, cracking my door open.

"What?" I yelled back.

"Logan's here to see you!"

I grumbled, tossing off the covers from my midday nap. I ambled down the stairs while throwing my mess of hair up. I had just seen the fucker yesterday, but the paternity test results had come in and we needed to talk about it, since I was keeping the bitch safe.

He raised an eyebrow at my rumpled shirt as I plodded down the stairs. "Come on, the walls have ears," I grumbled, leading him to the conference room as the girls giggled around the corner.

"Lorraine still wants to attend The Conferences," Logan said, slipping off his jacket and resting it on the back of a leather chair. I closed the door with a huff.

"She can't come, Logan," I told him yet again. I sat on the polished wood of the conference room table.

He leaned against the window overlooking the front yard.

"I know, that's what I've been telling her every, single, time she calls."

I laughed, "Who gave her a phone?"

"I think Blue is upset at me."

I laughed harder, "Gee, ya think?"

"I'm not the one who assigned Blue to watch Lorraine."

"I'm not the one who knocked her up."

He groaned before sitting next to me on the table, our thighs touching. I felt his scorching heat through the thin fabric of my yoga pants. I wasn't thinking about it.

"I'd think she'd be taking this a little more seriously after the last attack."

Logan exhaled forcefully, leaning back, his arms behind him. "Don't remind me."

"We're lucky Blue and Victoria were both there. According to Blue, she is actually listening without having to be manipulated. It's not our fault she didn't take our warnings seriously. Your unborn baby is a hot commodity." I tried at humor, pretty sure I failed.

His eyes cut to me. "Blue is an incubus?"

I nodded, "One of the more powerful."

He shrugged. "I guess that is for the best."

I toyed with the envelope under my right hand, on the opposite side from Logan. There was a reason he was here and it wasn't just to complain about Lorraine, his pregnant ex-fiancée.

"I have the results."

He didn't look at me, but I caught the clenching of his jaw and the narrowing of his eyes.

"She's yours," I whispered, a small smile on my lips. I may not like Lorraine—okay, fine, I hate the bitch—but the thought of Logan being a dad made me go all gooey inside. Not that I'd admit it to him.

He didn't breathe for a moment, before looking at me with a mix of wonder and fear stealing his features.

"She?" he asked, his voice soft.

"You are having a girl," I whispered, my smile growing.

"A girl," he repeated on an exhale.

I reached behind our bodies, covering his hand. "Do you want to see the ultrasound?" I asked tentatively.

He shook his head, clearing it, not moving his hand under mine. "I'd love to."

I handed him the envelope, removing my hand. I watched closely as he opened it, noting his slight tremble. He squinted, rotating the small black and white photo.

I laughed, "That's her head." I pointed.

"Is it supposed to be that large?"

I laughed again, "Yes, the doctor says she is perfectly healthy." I waited a moment before asking, "Do you want to go to her next appointment?"

He sighed, the joy of finding out the child was his now overshadowed by Lorraine and her betrayal, or maybe just her general unpleasant behavior. I found her fucking insufferable.

"I don't know. As much as I'd like to see our unborn child, I don't want to upset Lorraine."

"I've been at every appointment. Trust me, the bitch is worked up plenty on her own.

"I'll think about it. Have you heard from Blake?"

It was my turn to groan. "I got a thank you note."

Logan scoffed, "You're joking?"

"I wish I was."

"What did it say?"

"I love you. I'm sorry. Please help me."

"You're joking!" he repeated, shocked.

I shook my head, looking over at him. "Nope."

"What are you going to do?"

"Let the fucker lie in the bed he made. His problems are not mine, and I have plenty of my own."

He grunted his approval.

"OLIE!" Tommy called out, banging on the door.

"It's open, you banshee!" I called out.

"I have arrived!" he announced, parading in his Halloween costume. He was going as an executioner.

"How do I look?" he asked eagerly, twirling around in his ensemble.

"Do I usually wear that much leather?" I asked, tilting my head.

"Yes." They both answered, emphatically, in unison.

"Fine, but you clearly need more weapons." I waved a dismissive hand.

"That's what I told Grams, but she said my costume was offensive as it was."

"I'll talk to her," I promised. "Where's Mindy?"

He rolled his eyes, coming to sit next to Logan but leaning forward so I could see him.

"Learning how to hack into the police department."

"She's like eleven!" I scolded.

"And your point is?" Tommy asked, an eyebrow raised.

"Shouldn't she be playing with dolls or something?" I questioned.

9

"Not after the shit she went through. She needs a destructive hobby and since she is too young to kill people I thought this would be an acceptable replacement."

"How very scientific of you," Logan commented.

"I know, right?" Tommy agreed.

"I should be going. I have to stop at Darren's before we fly out," Logan said, standing. Did I imagine his brush over my hand? Probably.

"He isn't still trying to come?" I asked, trying to prolong his visit.

"He is," Logan answered, slipping his jacket back on.

"No way. I need Kass and him here to watch Tommy and the army of hackers he is training." I gave Tommy a playful shove.

"I'll be sure to inform him. You flying out with us?" Logan asked, adjusting the collar of his jacket.

"Yeah, Grams has vetoed my driving to Vegas."

"She's probably worried you wouldn't show up again." He lingered at the doorway, his eyes lingering on my own.

"I was there for a full day. It's not my fault I had to deal with traffic ... for a week. Besides, what do all those self-important asses do other than make big plans and fail to follow though? I don't even understand why we have to go."

"Careful, Olie. I think Logan is considered one of those self-important asses," Tommy muttered to me, leaning closer.

I laughed and Logan did as well. "I'll see you on the plane," he said. "Oh, and Tommy, I want a rematch."

"Anytime, Logan. Anytime!"

I slung an arm around Tommy's shoulders. I meant what I had said: The Conferences were just a glorified dick-measuring contest. The only value was that my defenses and fighting skills were tested.

...

I had a full day between Logan's visit and our flight to Vegas. I decided to take a look at our security cameras, not that I didn't trust Becky to handle everything. Okay, let's be real. I have deep-seated trust issues, and something was nagging at my awareness.

I pulled up Grams's cameras.

Yeah, I'm a distrustful bitch. The cameras were everywhere in the house save the bathrooms, but they were set up for our protection. This was not their intended purpose.

I had been absent for maybe a week and a half. I wanted to see what she was up to.

I went back two full weeks and started watching. I saw myself come in and out of her office. I watched the kids bound gleefully in, the younger ones going behind her desk to seek her comforting touch.

The older ones sat across the desk from her. I watched Grams's body language as she listened to the kids, leaning forward, laughing together with them. She spent time with all of them, never rushing them out.

Fast forwarding three days later on the videos, I watched Hash walk into Grams's office. I aggressively hit the play button, wanting to see this visit in real time.

I sat forward on the edge of my chair, slowing down the feed. Hitting—okay, maybe smashing—a few buttons, I had sound.

Grams sat behind her desk and indicated to Hash to take a seat.

"What can I do for you?" she asked sweetly.

I watched Hash settle into the chair, crossing his legs.

"I've come to speak with you regarding a new position," Hash stated.

Grams had the decency to look confused. "Do you need another liaison for the police files?"

Hash leaned forward. "I want to offer you a position with the human government."

Grams laughed, "Why would I want a new position?"

"Because you are human, you aren't like these freaks here."

Grams's jaw tightened. "They are not freaks. They are children, children I am charged with protecting."

Hash shrugged. "Let's be honest, if you could have your own wage, your own house, wouldn't you prefer that?"

Grams paused, her perfectly polished nails tapping her desk. Hash read her body language perfectly, leaning forward.

"I can offer you all of that. I can give you a life that is your own. No one's orders to listen to. No one to dictate how much you spend or on what. You,

Mercer and Mindy can build a normal life away from the controversy facing Olivia."

Grams was still watching him. "What makes you think I want that?"

Hash shrugged, and while I couldn't see his face, I knew he was smiling.

"Who doesn't want to control their own destiny? You are tied to Olivia right now, protected only as long as she lives."

Grams swallowed. How the fuck did Hash know that? Why the fuck didn't I know she was worried about that?

I sunk back in my chair, feeling I had failed her. If she was confident in my skills, as I had always thought she was, Hash couldn't have touched her.

Grams's gaze flicked to the camera I was watching. She wrote something down and slid it over to Hash. He read it, nodding, and tucked it into his pocket before leaving.

Why wouldn't she tell me she wanted out? Should I approach her about it? I chewed on my thumbnail. No, I'd let this play out. I couldn't force her to stay and I wouldn't.

I was, however, going shopping. It had been too long since I had seen my favorite troll and her impressive array of weapons.

...

I was loading my car up at Myrtle's, a smile on my lips easing the tightness in my chest at the thought of Grams leaving, when my phone rang.

"Bloody hell, woman, get your gun toting assets down to The Roasted Onion on 5th! That imbecile just made an escape attempt," Blue yelled at me.

The phone went dead at my ear. I was running, sliding to the driver's door, using the handle to stabilize myself as I wrenched it open. Fucking hell. I was going to kill Lorraine, you know, after she had safely delivered Logan's baby.

I pulled my phone back out hazardously from the pocket I had shoved it in. It took me two tries to get the keys in the ignition and crank the engine. I paused only long enough to dial Logan. Once my SUV picked up the call over its speakers, I tossed the phone and slammed the gas.

"What's up, Olie?" Logan answered.

"The Roasted Onion on 5th, Lorraine, escape attempt," I barked out.

"WHAT?" he roared.

Horns blared as I skidded across an intersection at a speed recommended only for movies.

"Shit, I'm ten minutes away—" I yelled at him.

"I'm shifting." That ended our call. Ever seen a lion with a phone? Me, either.

It took me seven minutes, three red lights, and one damaged fender from taking the sidewalk and running into a stop sign.

I flung myself out of the car, parked in a clearly marked no parking zone. Whatever. They could tow my car, I'd just steal it back later.

Blue was screaming and I ran to his voice around the corner and down the dirty, smelly ally. I couldn't believe the bitch, she was not worth it at all.

A giant lion sideswiped me. "Ouch!" I went down with a grunt, slamming my shoulder on the dirty brick wall.

"Asshole!" I yelled, flailing in a pile of garbage. Disgusting. Seriously, not worth it.

I lost track of the lion when he turned a corner. I was hard pressed to match his speed. Barreling around the corner, I slammed into Blue. "She's got help," he panted at me.

"Who?" I growled. Yes, someone I can kill!

Blue shook his head. "Witch."

Fucking witches, I really should have known.

Logan roared a sound that struck terror into everyone close by. Except for us, as we kept running straight into the lion's den. Haha, I'm a riot.

Blue shoved his shoulder against a worn blue door and we both tumbled into the boarded-up shop.

A terrible wailing had us sprinting around the corner. The witch lay dead, thick slices cutting her body into multiple pieces. Good fucking riddance.

My gaze shifted to Lorraine and away from Logan, who was shifting back into a naked man.

"You're too late," she wheezed, smiling at me triumphantly, a hand clutched over her stomach. Fear drained the blood from my face.

"Salt," I whispered, my eyes darting frantically around the warehouse. "Bring her back to the diner!" I yelled, slamming into the same worn door and breaking it off the hinges. I shielded my pretty face, my feet not slowing. I turned the corner quickly, clobbering my shoulder against the brick wall.

That was going to leave a mark.

My feet couldn't carry me fast enough to save that little, unborn baby girl. I barreled through the glass doors of The Roasted Onion. Diving over patrons, I gathered three glass salt shakers to my chest.

"Call an ambulance! The pregnant woman just OD'd on drugs!" I bellowed, letting my guards fall and pushing urgent compliance into the room.

Forks and knives clattered onto tables as multiple people spoke rapidly on the phone. I snagged a glass of water from a table, not giving a damn about the possible germs. I kicked the doors open, my hands full, turned the corner and ran into Logan, still naked, carrying Lorraine.

I twisted open the salt shakers and dumped all three into the glass, using my fingers to mix the solution.

"Hold her mouth open!" I yelled, my fear growing with each passing second.

Logan pulled her jaws open and Lorraine struggled, her teeth leaving bloody imprints in the tender flesh of his fingers. I forced the salt water solution into her mouth and down her throat.

She tried not to swallow it, but it was either that or drown. Her body made the right decision, and I kept the steady steam down her throat until the entire glass was emptied, chunks of ice falling over both of us.

I heard the sirens in the distance.

"Logan, clothing," I commanded. He looked from me to Lorraine, clearly torn.

"We got this, mate." Blue wrapped a hand around Logan's corded bicep, and I knew he was pushing confidence in our abilities.

With a nod Logan handed Lorraine over to us, turning to disappear into the alley.

"I won't carry her. I won't be a mother, you can't make me!" Lorraine rasped between ragged breaths.

I leaned forward and whispered into her ear, "This child will live Lorraine, your life depends on it. What did you really think would happen if you killed Logan's child?"

I pulled back and she vomited all over me.

I'd have been disgusted if I wasn't so fucking relieved. My shoulders slumped as I turned her onto her side, her body convulsing with dry heaves.

The ambulance was music to my ears.

"How we playing this, luv?" Blue asked softly.

"Drug overdose. We are her support group," I whispered.

"What's going on?" I heard the voices and pounding feet behind me. I stepped back, letting them next to Lorraine.

"She took some pills. I don't know what, but we made her drink salt water and, as you can see, we got her to throw up." I summarized.

"How far along?" one of the paramedics asked.

"Twenty-six and a half weeks," Blue answered. Dammit, we were both attached to this kid.

"Alright, let's get her vitals and move her to the hospital. Is one of you coming with us?"

"Yes, I will." Blue moved forward. "Olie, get cleaned up and get Logan."

I nodded, watching them wheel her away, hoping I had gotten to her in time. Please, let me have gotten there in time.

Drawing a ragged breath, I turned, seeing Logan in front of me, wearing the same terrified and helpless expression. Clamping down on my emotions, I pointed him over to my SUV. He nodded, his gaze shifting to where Lorraine was strapped down and being loaded into the ambulance.

We waited a breath until they pulled away before Logan ventured out, wearing a cardboard box. If it wasn't such a serious situation, I totally would have teased him about it.

Getting into the SUV, Logan left the dirty box on the ground.

"Where do we get you clothing at?" I asked, throwing the vehicle into drive.

"Go to my place, we both need to clean up."

I nodded.

...

After the fastest showers ever, Logan was driving us to the hospital.

"Blue texted, they're asking questions," I relayed to Logan as I cringed at wearing Lorraine's too-tight top and yoga pants.

"How are we going to explain why we didn't allow her to get an abortion?" he asked softly.

"Drugs. She was so distraught that she asked us to help her bring the baby to term cleanly."

"What about her medical records?"

"Our doctor is already on site. She can corroborate that Lorraine has had exceptional medical treatment."

"Will she corroborate our drug story?"

"Only if she wants to live." I smiled.

Logan grunted, pulling into a parking place in front of the ER.

We weaved our way through the busy bodies, not needing to stop for directions, Logan's nose able to seek out his ex-fiancée and unborn child.

We crossed the threshold to see Lorraine in restraints on the hospital bed, "That's her! She is the one who has kept me kidnapped. Please, you have to believe me! I don't want this baby, but they are forcing it on me."

Blue was on the sidelines, arms crossed over his middle.

The doctor and police officer both turned to us. "I'm Olivia," I began. "Part of what she is saying is true. This is Logan, the father."

The officer turned to Logan, "Can you explain why the mother of your child is making such insane accusations?"

Logan took a long inhale. "Unfortunately, she is not well. In order to keep both her person and our unborn child safe, we had to place her in a very well monitored environment."

That was impressive; he actually didn't lie.

"Did you keep her from an abortion?"

"Only because she asked us to. She knew the lure of the drugs would be so great that she would do anything to get back to them," I answered. I had zero problems lying.

"They're lying!" Lorraine screamed, sobbing. "I don't want this horrible creature!"

"I do." Logan's rough voice cut right to the heart of the matter.

I walked forward, kindness in my gaze, and sat next to Lorraine. She pulled and flailed, yelling incoherently.

I took her restrained hand gently, folding both of mine over hers.

"It's okay, Lorraine, we are here now," I cooed to her as she flung her head violently from side to side. I dumped contentment, peace and gratefulness into her. The bitch could use the latter in huge, heaping amounts.

Slowly, her wailing calmed. "Easy," I continued my ministrations. She relented into soft sobbing.

I looked over at the doctor and the officer before I turned to Blue. "Has her doctor been here yet?"

"Yes, she is running a second set of tests personally," Blue responded.

I nodded.

The doctor cleared his throat, holding his metal clipboard under his arm. "All our preliminary tests show the baby is doing fine, but we want to keep her for overnight monitoring."

"Can we get the restraints off?" I asked.

Blue pushed off the wall and even Logan fidgeted, looking at me with worry. I'd been tied down before, and it's not a good feeling. The doctor looked at the officer, who shrugged. "That's your call, Doc. This seems to have taken care of itself."

The doctor turned his gaze back to us. "I suppose we can give it a try."

I nodded. "Thank you. We will be leaving Blue and another one of my associates here to help watch over her."

"What exactly do you do?" The officer turned to me. Fucking hell, associate was not the right word.

"I specialize in protection for unique situations, like this, for example." The officer still watched me closely.

"I can have my files sent over, for vetting those who will be here," I added.

He nodded, fucker was way too attentive for my liking. "I'd appreciate it. Here's my card."

I took it. I was stomping down very hard on my urge to sneer.

Logan moved past me, undoing Lorraine's restraints, and I eased back. I turned along with everyone else, watching him. How would it feel to have the woman carrying your child trying to kill it? I couldn't even imagine. His hands were gentle, though, and she rolled over to her side, still sobbing.

I exhaled a trapped breath as the doctor and police officer left us.

"I'm going to stay for a while, Blue," Logan said, sitting down next to Lorraine.

Blue's eyes flashed to me, silently asking if he should stay. I tried for a discreet shake of my head no.

"I'm capable of watching her," Logan grunted. Like I said, I tried, didn't mean it was successful.

17

I rested a hand on Logan's shoulder, squeezing gently. "Call if you need anything."

Logan nodded, his attention riveted to Lorraine. I walked out with Blue, releasing a pent-up sigh as he closed the door.

The officer spoke behind us. "So tell me, what do you do again?"

I flicked my eyes down to his name badge. "Officer Bacco, as I stated previously, I provide security for unique situations."

"And Lorraine asked you to help her?"

"She did, once she knew of the baby," I agreed.

He watched me shrewdly. "Why didn't you let her have an abortion when she changed her mind?"

My brows drew down. "She would have hated herself for it."

"How does the ex-fiancée of the Shifter Nation get attached to drugs?"

"The same way anyone does." My answers were getting clipped.

"And no one bothered to get her cleaned up until after she was pregnant?"

"Correct."

"But now that she is carrying precious cargo, you care?"

I tilted my head, stepping closer to him. "All life is important, Officer Bacco, especially the unwanted. I won't lie: Have there been times when I wondered if Lorraine was sincere in wanting to be rid of the child, for more reasons than just the drugs? Yes. But you saw him." I pointed toward Logan, who we couldn't see at that moment. "If she doesn't want to have the baby, she can pretend it never happened and walk out of the kid's life forever. Logan will take care of the child and we will take care of Logan."

Bacco watched me and I wasn't backing down. Okay, sure, did I feel a little, and I mean a very small, insignificant amount of uncertainty about forcing Lorraine to carry the baby to term? Yes.

Did a small part of me think Logan's life would be better without Lorraine and the baby? Yes.

But I meant what I had said: all life is precious. Especially to Supernaturals, who struggle with fertility. And yes, I will admit it, not being able to have children myself made this little baby's life that much more important.

Bacco nodded, stepping back. "I'd still like those files."

"Of course." I smiled sweetly. I wasn't sending them.

Bacco turned and walked down the hall, and I released a pent-up breath.

"So Blue, what's on the agenda next?"

"You, my dear girl, need to get ready to leave tomorrow," Blue kindly reminded me.

"If Logan stays, I'm staying with him."

"Is this a tit for tat? Logan has his unborn child to concern himself with, and he undoubtedly will need his right-hand woman to assist in his absence."

I groaned, "Blue, do you have to be so damn logical?"

He laughed. Fucking logical asshole.

...

The next day, I was analyzing the contents of my trunk when Jerry pulled up in front of the manor.

"Are you ready?" Jerry asked, rubbing his dark-skinned hands together excitedly. I was glad he was excited, and equally glad he hadn't heard of Lorraine's thwarted attempt at an abortion. I needed a little joy.

"I think so."

Looking down to the bags at my feet, Jerry laughed. "Olivia, I know all three of those bags are not yours."

I toed a bag before looking back into my empty trunk. "Two are weapons, one is clothing."

Jerry raised a mocha eyebrow at me. "You need two bags of weapons?"

I turned, leaning against the tailgate. "I was debating if I had time to get to Myrtle's to buy more."

"Olivia, it's a meeting, not a war!" Jerry laughed, pushing me away from the trunk and towards the car, hoisting a bag.

I pulled the other two over my shoulders.

"It's a war. It's always a fucking war when that much power gets together."

Jerry deposited one of my duffle bags into his SUV trunk with a thud.

"You need to focus on slot machines, tanned bodies, and dirty dancing." Jerry wrapped his arm around my shoulders, his other arm extended in front of him as he attempted to convey his daydream to me.

Not wanting to burst it, I leaned into him. "So, you're pretty excited about your first vacation with Mark?"

His smile revealed all the starkly white teeth in his dark-skinned head. "It is that obvious?"

"Naw, just a lucky guess." I leaned back, bumping his shoulder good-naturedly.

He nudged me back. We both turned, hearing the clatter on the cobblestones. Grams exited with Mercer in tow with her three suitcases, none of which contained weapons. My smile fell watching her.

"Everyone set?" she asked merrily. I wished I knew what was going on behind her slate gaze. It was possible there was nothing.

"Where are Ali and Grant?" I asked, helping stow her and Mercer's luggage. He, like me, only had a duffle bag of clothing, which was good since the back was starting to look a little crowded.

Ali and Grant were next in line to rule the Supernatural Council should anything happen to Grams, or when she chose to retire. They helped run the day-to-day activities of the Council and each had their own special brand of unique powers.

That was the sole purpose of the Council, to protect those who lacked the strength of a shifter clan or the resources of a vampire House. Granted, when I had taken over, some 7 or 8 years ago, its power had been grossly misused. I like to think I brought back clarity, justice, and protection for those like my succubus and incubus brethren.

The reality was I probably just scared the Council into obedience. Whatever. I'm not picky.

It helped that I was the most powerful succubus I had yet met. I'll have to pay credit where it is due, at the dead feet of Selena, my own personal monster who had pushed me beyond my limits. Most of our kind went unnoticed in the human population until our power manifested, usually after a traumatic event. At that point, unless controlled, the emotions would be felt by all.

You'd be amazed how many I liberated from mental health institutions.

"They are meeting us at the airport," Grams replied, bringing me back. "Grant had to drop his cat off at his sister's." She settled her leather purse pristinely over her shoulder.

"Jerry, you need three bags?" Mercer asked, closing the trunk with a thud.

"I only have one suitcase; those three bags belong to Olivia," Jerry informed him. The conversation halted as we got seated.

"Weapons?" Mercer asked, sitting in the backseat with me. Powder blue eyes twinkled with approval. His hair had grown out since he was no longer with the police department, and I liked the look on him.

"Weapons," I confirmed with a nod and a grin. "I got some new toys you are going to love."

"Is that the opening line of a badly-planned porno?" Jerry asked in the front seat.

I slipped a hand around his shoulder from the back seat, "Do you want it to be?"

"Eww! Get your female hands off of me."

I laughed, his easy mood catching. Or perhaps I was just getting better at faking it.

The drive to the airport made me nervous. The Fae fucking terrified me, and so did flying. Probably for the same reason: lack of control was not something I handled well. I didn't know how to kill the Fae and I couldn't fly a plane.

...

Logan was arguing with airport security when we pulled up to his private jet.

"Shit," I groaned, getting out of the car. It really probably wasn't for the best that he was here right now, given everything that had happened.

I debated. Offering help might only throw the unhinged shifter into more of an angry tailspin. Not getting involved could lead to the small human getting ground into the asphalt.

Jerry gave me a look, knowing what was going through my mind as we met at the trunk.

"Sir, you cannot—" began the security guard again.

"Tell me I can't again," Logan growled, stepping forward, leering over the smaller man.

I watched the man step back, seeing the fear in his widening eyes, the flare of his nostrils. Logan's tall form arched over him. His eyes began to shift, his lion pressing against his control.

I hesitated, grabbing my bags, moving to the side to let Jerry, Grams and Mercer take their bags to the plane.

"I'm going to call for back up," the human squeaked, shaking.

21

"Logan," I began softly, moving between the two of them. Placing a hand against Logan's chest, I pushed gently before turning to the security officer.

"What appears to be the problem?" I asked, flashing my best smile.

Straightening at having the threat of the Alpha removed, he pointed to the plane. "The safety checklist hasn't been completed."

"I signed off on the checklist," Logan growled, directly into my ear. I can't lie, that was kind of hot. The fact he kept picking inopportune times to flirt with me was annoying.

I watched the man shift in front of me ever so slightly, his shoulders slumping almost imperceptibly, a nervous twitch on the side of his lip.

"Where is your identification?" I asked, all kindness gone from my voice.

His eyes widened slightly. I pushed forward from the balls of my feet, my left hand slamming down on his wrist, connecting to the skin not covered by his jacket.

"Tell me who you are," I demanded again, my voice low with the persuasion I was pumping though his body.

He sucked in air as I pushed compliance, the pleasure of obeying, into his body. His eyes glassed over. "Tony."

"Who do you work for, Tony?" I asked, softly drawing my power back slightly as his knees wobbled.

"The Herald."

I released him, disgusted I had even touched him. My lips curled in repugnance.

"Why did you want on the plane?" Logan asked behind me, his shifter warmth seeping into me.

"One of the spy cameras on the plane needs new batteries," Tony admitted, swaying slightly, his head lolling on his shoulders.

"WHAT?" Logan bellowed.

I reached down and steadied Tony.

"Olivia." Logan said my name between clenched teeth.

"If there are cameras in the plane, Logan, we are undoubtedly on camera now." I wanted to kill Tony, too, but now wasn't the time or the place.

He moved to Tony's other side, roughly helping him stand. I reached in my back pocket, calling my favorite troll.

"Olivia," Myrtle answered. "What can I do for my best client?"

22

I like guns, knives, swords, crossbows—okay, so anything that can kill or maim. Some women collect shoes. I collect weapons.

"Hi Myrtle, I was wondering if you'd consider delivery for your favorite customer?"

"What do you need and where?"

"I need equipment that can detect cameras and listening equipment."

The noise on Myrtle's end died. Apparently, I had her attention. "Do I even want to—actually, no. I don't want to know."

I laughed, "We are on Airmark Field outside of St Ann."

"Give me twenty minutes. I'm also charging you a delivery fee."

"Twenty minutes, that is impressive," Logan commented as we entered an empty hanger, following Tony.

I sat Tony down gingerly, though Logan did not mirror my actions. Tony sat dazed.

"What is wrong with him?" Logan asked, turning to survey the area with his superior hearing.

"Humans react differently to my powers. Unlike Supernaturals, they take a few hours to rebound."

Logan twitched his head toward the far left corner. So we weren't alone.

"Come and get Tony," I called out.

Even I heard the shuffling and muffled voices.

"Seriously assholes, we don't have all fucking day," I grunted.

Still no one came out.

Logan tilted his head, listening, before he laughed. "They're scared."

"I suppose they aren't completely idiotic, then," I muttered.

"Maybe they were after another X-rated video of you, Olie," Logan joked.

I turned to him, hands on my hips, mouth hanging open in shock.

"Too soon?" He cringed.

I could have been mad at him. It would have been easy to let my humiliation at that video overshadow everything. Instead I rolled my eyes. "And who do you think I was going to be giving a repeat performance with?"

His gaze met mine with an alluring half-smile, and I couldn't help the flashback to the kiss he had given me, my cheeks warming.

I wasn't claiming my heart had healed up perfectly from the devastation known as Blake. Hell, just the thought of him had my smile slipping. Logan was dangerous. He wasn't a quick fuck to get my rocks off, he was an emotional attachment and I wasn't sure I was ready for that again.

"Are you going to kill us?" a small voice squeaked out, breaking our moment.

"No, but we are going to sue you," Logan replied evenly, arms crossing over his broad chest.

A red head peeked out from a door in the back, his stature hunched and meek.

"Technically, you can't since your status as a citizen hasn't been approved," Meek replied.

"Mine was never in question," I replied.

He pushed his glasses up, taking a few steps forward. "After that little demonstration, I'm doubtful of your species."

I narrowed my eyes.

Logan rummaged through Tony's pockets, pulling out his ID and sticking it in his own pocket.

"Any video gets leaked of this event, and we will find you and make you pay. Legally," he added as an after-thought.

I'd make him pay in blood, but let's not put that on tape to come back and haunt my ass.

I shrugged. "I'm agreeable to that."

A car horn honked behind us.

"Supplies are here," I announced. Casting a look at Logan, I turned my back on Tony and his friend. In the Supernatural community, turning a back on an enemy was disrespectful. It was a sign that we didn't perceive them as a threat.

Logan and I moved away. Neither of us was comfortable that the situation had been handled, but we had things to do, and scaring the daylights out of two feeble humans wasn't high on the list.

Myrtle's lilac hair glowed in the morning sun, her dark sunglasses protecting her delicate eyes.

"Olivia, your fans not satisfied with only one sex tape?" she joked.

I groaned. This wasn't going away for a while.

"I'm pretty sure they just want to steal my moves," I informed her, trying to make the best of a crappy situation.

Behind her, Jerry was getting instructions from another troll on how to sweep for bugs.

Logan, Myrtle, and I talked for a bit. Ali and Grant arrived in a rush. They were lucky we were delayed.

Ali sent a look at Grant before her cheeks flushed and he took her hand, bringing it to his lips.

"Aww!" I yelled, happy to shift the attention off of me. "You guys got back together."

They shrugged uncomfortably before heading into the plane.

Jerry moved in front of us. "Alright, we are good, the bugs have been destroyed."

"Wonderful," Logan grunted, following Jerry up the short flight of stairs to the plane.

I blew out a breath, feeling Myrtle's eyes on me. "Not a fan of flying, Olie?" she asked gently.

"Not too much." I turned to face her, putting off climbing into the flying machine. "Are you going to the Conferences?"

She shook her head. "I prefer to stay out of politics. Besides, with our limited numbers, we fall under your protection."

"Does that earn me a discount?"

She laughed, "Not with your expensive taste. Take care, Olie." She patted my arm in farewell.

I made myself climb the stairs, finding someone had already put my bags in the plane. I gripped the white handrail with a venom that suggested it alone could save me.

The interior was dimly lit and the ceiling was far too close to the top of my head. The flight attendant closed up the hatch upon my arrival. I swallowed loudly, taking the first available seat. It faced Logan and Mark. Alec sat on the bench seat with me.

With shaky hands, I secured the seatbelt against my torso, although it seemed silly. If the plane crashed, the seatbelt's only function would be to identify my body, and since we didn't have assigned seats, even that was pointless.

Blowing out a breath, I closed my eyes, willing my insides to relax and my breakfast to stay down.

I grunted, screwing my eyes closed as the plane began moving. I clenched my jaw. This was going to be a long fucking flight.

Our speed increased. My heart rate did as well, my fingers digging into the soft leather seating. It was five hours. I could survive five hours.

The seat next to me dipped down and Logan's scent filled my nostrils, wild woods and pine trees. I opened my eyes, watching him continue his conversation. He handed me whisky on the rocks.

I smiled up at him, taking the drink gratefully.

"What's the game plan, Olivia?" Alec asked. "Darren told me to come prepared."

I cleared my throat, having downed half my drink. "Grams is to be protected at all cost. She is not to be alone at any time. Ali, Grant, and you are charged with keeping her safe."

"Safe from what?" Jerry asked, realizing this wasn't the social vacation he had originally thought.

"Everyone," Logan answered. "Olivia is the head of the Supernatural Council for the Eastern United States, plus she holds an honorary place next to me. Many will use Grams to try bring down Olivia, who, in her death, would relinquish that power."

"Wait, you mean to tell me that if someone kills Olie, they take her power?" Jerry asked from the grouping of seats behind us.

I chuckled. "Guess we have more in common with the witches than I originally thought." I took a long sip.

"The same goes for Logan. He isn't to be alone, Mark will be with him constantly, and you as well, Jerry."

"Who the hell is going to guard you?" Mark asked.

I was about to answer that I didn't need a guard, but Logan interrupted me. "Olie will be attending many of the same meetings we will. Only the meetings with Garrick will need to be covered."

I shook my head, signaling the flight attendant for another drink. "Garrick has a small army with him. I'll be fine."

He grunted a displeased answer, but I didn't care. I was too busy drowning my nerves in alcohol. The Conferences were always a disaster. I had no doubt this year wouldn't be any different. That much power in one hotel was guaranteed to leave a few dead bodies. Just as long as they weren't any of mine.

Chapter 2

The flight passed, or rather I passed out on the flight. Apparently, the high altitude made me a lightweight. I awoke with Logan stroking my hair, my head nestled on a pillow in his lap.

I sat up quickly, fighting the head rush.

"We've arrived," he announced, his fingers still trailing through my hair.

I nodded, rubbing sleep from my eyes as everyone gathered their belongings and headed off.

We were loaded up into a long limo. I leaned back against the seat, blowing out a breath, gearing up.

"You ready for this?" Logan asked softly.

I smiled, patting his knee. "Don't worry, I'll protect you."

He huffed his amusement.

I turned to our group. "You've probably heard this speech before, but pay attention. You are not to be alone. Making that foolish decision puts not only you but our entire organization in danger. If someone attacks you physically, kill them. If they verbally assault you, hurt them. We cannot appear too strong or too confident. Weakness will be preyed upon, so release you inner asshole. And if you need help with that, you can have some of mine."

Grams clapped and said with a laugh, "Well said, Olie."

"Questions?" Grams asked, far kinder than me.

Everyone shook their heads no, while surreptitiously checking their concealed weapons. Glad I wasn't the only one who was packing.

"Grant is handing out your schedules. While the attacks will undoubtedly come, these meetings are designed as information sharing sessions. This year we even have a full day of new tech products."

I didn't pay attention to the paper Grant handed me.

"Logan, you will need to be sure she keeps to the schedule," Grant said. "Since you two are a power duo, you will be attending most of the functions together."

I grunted, leaning back against the leather seat.

I was tied to Logan the entire weekend? So much for having vacation sex with Garrick.

Our limo pulled up in front of the extravagant hotel, towering above the heart of the Las Vegas Strip. There is no better way to hide the Supernatural than in plain sight.

Piling out, I whistled. "I probably don't want to know what this costs."

Grams smoothed down her powder blue suit and I mentally clicked off my weapons. I had traded in my trademark leather pants for soft jeans. My steel-toed boots had made the trip, though, hiding a dagger each.

Under my fitted suede jacket, I had a small pistol secured against my ribs at my side. The idea was to look like we didn't have a care in the world, but be able to handle whatever these assholes threw at us. Most of them would keep it clean in hand-to-hand combat, but I wasn't betting on anyone's morals keeping me alive.

The entire lobby was a whirlwind of activity. Shifters, vampires and witches were the dominant forces, and everyone turned upon our arrival.

Logan came to stand next to me at the front of our group.

A hotel clerk moved in front of us, careful to keep his eyes on his tablet in front of him.

"Welcome to The Bellagio, I'm Luke and I will be getting you checked in." Luke had excellent timing. "If I can get your party's name and everyone's fingerprint, please."

"Fingerprint?" I questioned.

Luke gave a small bow. "Yes, our systems have been upgraded. We no longer use keys, but fingerprints, to allow our guests access to their rooms."

"Huh, that's slick," I muttered.

"Didn't Tommy program your phone to unlock with your fingerprint?" Logan asked as I swiped my finger where Luke indicated.

I shrugged, "I suppose it's possible."

Once Luke finished checking us in, a bellhop came to gather our impressive luggage. I kept my weapons bags with me. He could take the clothing.

Alec also kept the surveillance detection equipment.

"If you will follow me, please. I will show you to your private elevators," Luke announced, scurrying away to lead us.

"Private elevators?" I muttered.

"Only the best for you, Olie," Logan muttered back.

We passed the bank of six black elevators and continued down the marble hallway to a set of gold elevator doors.

"To activate the elevator, just press your finger here." Luke indicated the pad where a call button usually was. "If you have any problems or questions, please do not hesitate to contact the front desk. We welcome you to Las Vegas."

With that, Luke left, probably to check in other arriving guests. The poor human.

Resting against the elevator wall, sandwiched between Logan and Alec, I asked, "Do we have anything scheduled tonight?

Logan pulled out his phone, checking our schedule electronically, I assumed.

"We have a mixer that begins in three hours," he announced.

"Do we all have said mixer?"

"Yes," the entire cabin informed me.

"Don't even think about missing it," Grams warned me.

I sighed, "Wouldn't dream of it."

Grams, Mercer, Ali, Grant and I were sharing a three-room suite. It was a good thing they had recently made up, or maybe they had made up a while ago and I was just behind. Either way it was beneficial for the arrangement.

Logan, Jerry, Mark and Alec were across the hall in a suite exactly like ours. I closed the door behind me, and sunk face first into the soft mattress with a groan.

A knock on the door had me yelling into the pillow, "It has not been three hours!"

Grams poked her head in, "It's been two hours and the makeup artist is here to get you ready."

I flopped to my back with a groan, staring at the ceiling. "Go shower," she instructed with a chuckle.

I huffed and puffed into the shower, keeping up the annoyance to an audience of no one. I was grateful Grams was taking care of details like this. I didn't think twice about my image.

Once I was out of the shower, it took another half hour before I was freed from the hair and makeup chair.

I twirled in my new dress again.

"Well? Olivia, the suspense is killing me!" Jerry cried in the living room.

With a laugh I opened the door, taking a spin as I stepped forward.

"Wow," he and Mark said together.

I smiled, running my hands over the black satin skirt. My midriff was covered by see-through black lace, climbing upward to the satin triangles that covered the girls, before tying behind my neck.

"Jerry, it is amazing!" I cried. "Where did you find it?"

"I had it custom made," he admitted with a satisfied smile.

I should have probably taken issue with the cost, but I couldn't bring myself to care. I strapped on my throwing knives around my upper thigh. The slight ruffling of the dress hid them perfectly.

Grams and Mercer exited their room, equally dressed up.

"Oh, Olie, you look lovely." She smiled, touching my arm before making her way out, her arm linked in Mercer's. Jerry and Mark went next and I was last, slipping into my matching black satin ballerina flats.

I doubted I would ever wear high heels again, for the simple reason that the last time I wore them, Blake ripped out my heart.

I was over that. Mainly, mostly.

I sighed, closing the door behind me. The conversation in the hallway died. My hands instantly went to my hidden daggers, my body crouching down as I assessed the threat.

Jerry chuckled, shaking his head. "Darlin', conversation stopped for you."

I narrowed my eyes at him, straightening and smoothing down the dress.

"Whatever, let's get this show on the road. Pay attention everyone, just because we are dressed up does not mean blood won't be spilled."

...

The atmosphere was relaxed in the elevator ride down. I was actually feeling rested after my drunken nap on the plane and another few hours here. It was an unusual feeling, but not unwelcome.

The doors opened at the lobby and I couldn't help my smile as we cleared out.

His eyes found mine, and while he might have been able to repress his smile, his eyes gave his glee away.

"Garrick," I greeted him, stepping into his personal space.

"Olivia." He inclined his head in greeting. He wasn't tall, only an inch or so above my own 5' 8", with chestnut hair and coffee-colored eyes. His body was forever etched in hard lines from his work as a slave before he was accidentally made into a vampire.

"It has been some time, my lady," he whispered, his eyes roving over my outfit.

My smile widened. "Heard you got yourself a selkie problem."

The spell was broken and we moved next to each other, my group in front, his behind, to the restaurant.

"You heard about that?" he asked, taking my hand and wrapping it around his upper arm.

"I heard you spent three days marooned on an island while they bargained their terms." I laughed, noticing Logan slowing down to walk next to us.

"The little shits. I have to give them credit for their negotiating tactics, but really, who does that anymore?"

I laughed, watching his intense gaze rove over my outfit.

"I've heard things about you as well," he said. "By the raw desire of the Alpha's gaze, it seems those rumors are not unfounded."

I debated, knowing any answer I gave would be heard by most here. "You can't deny the allure of my dress," I decided on, nudging him.

Garrick nodded, taking my hand in his and pressing a gentle kiss to my knuckle. "You are always alluring, no matter the clothing." He nodded his leave, but not before warmth spread upward from my hand.

I flexed my hand, surprised by his comment, turning to Logan as we felt the flow of Garrick's party and my own separating.

"I'm starved. Please tell me they have vegetarian food here."

He smiled, resting his hand on my lower back and guiding me to our table. "I'm sure we can find you a salad."

"Gag, how about a pie?"

Grams touched my elbow and I turned to her. "You are sitting with Logan and the Compass Alphas for dinner," she instructed. "Do be sure to socialize with others after dinner."

I nodded, watching as she moved away with Mercer, her gold gown flowing exquisitely with her steps.

Logan offered his elbow and I took it, our bodies gently brushing up against each other.

"Are you still down a Compass Alpha due to Darren?" I asked softly.

The Compass Alphas each patrolled a compass point: North, South, East and West, dividing the country and the packs into four large groups under Logan's reign.

"I was going to talk to you about that," he murmured to me. So many listening ears.

I nodded, understanding it needed to happen later. I thought Alec would be a good replacement, but Logan might need him for other duties.

We made our way over the wooden dance floor to the tables adorned with cream linens and blood red roses as centerpieces. Logan pulled out the black leather chair for me. I sat, surprisingly gracefully.

Logan took the seat next to me, and the empty table suddenly had other shifters sitting down as well. There were six in addition to Logan and me, each muscular, with eyes darting constantly around the room.

There was only one other woman at the table besides me, and she sat regally. "Alpha," she bowed her head respectfully. "We are happy to be in your presence."

Okay, that was a little much, but whatever, this was Logan's show, not mine.

"Sage, how are you faring?"

"Well, thank you," she replied, inclining her head respectfully. She turned to me. "We haven't been introduced. I am Sage, Compass Alpha of the North."

"It's a pleasure. I'm Olie, Head Executioner for the Supernatural Council of the Eastern U.S." Gah, that was a mouthful.

"Please let me introduce you to my second, Nathaniel." She touched the shoulder of a gentleman in a gray suit and he also nodded his polite acknowledgement.

A belch from the shifter next to him had all eyes turning. The belcher shrugged a broad shoulder, his blond hair mussed and his olive green eyes dancing with mirth. "Sorry, Sage, but we're about done with the pleasantries."

He turned to me with a winning grin that boasted of trouble.

"Meet my cousin, Hudson," Logan introduced us.

I smirked and nodded.

"He takes care of the West, his beta is Andy. Across form him is Riley. He patrols the South, and his beta is Henry," Logan finished.

A waiter set a drink down in front of me. "Hi, I'm Olie and I like to kill stuff," I said with a smile, lifting my glass up in toast.

"To Olie!" Hudson rang out. I laughed. The tension drained as the others lifted their glasses. I was certain I'd have to prove myself to these shifters, but hopefully not before dinner.

Dinner was bland. I made a face at Logan as I picked at my vegetables.

"Here," he offered, pushing his plate to me. "Try the risotto."

I dug my fork in while he picked at the mush known as squash.

He made a face, putting the rest of the uneaten bite down.

"I suppose this means you will just have to eat more dessert," Logan teased.

"Read my mind."

"So Olivia, we heard about that terrible sex tape that your ex-boyfriend released." Sage gave me sad, understanding eyes.

I pursed my lips. "I rather thought it was some of my better work, you know, being without proper tools." I took a long pull of my drink, smiling at her.

She shifted in her chair, stabbing a bite of strawberry shortcake. "Really? I actually hadn't watched it." She lifted the bite to her painted cherry lips.

"How long do you anticipate keeping your place with us?" Nathaniel asked, dabbing his mouth delicately with a napkin.

I tilted my head. "Until it's pried from my cold, dead hands."

Nathaniel swallowed and I smiled, showing all my teeth.

"Or if Logan gets hitched," I amended with a half shrug.

Hudson slung a heavy arm over my shoulders. "I for one am happy to welcome you to the fold, dear Olivia. Aside from needing more attractive females, it sets my weary heart at rest knowing Logan has someone to keep him from getting stale."

Logan's fork landed so forcefully it chipped his plate.

Hudson released my shoulders, flashing a smile. "I watched the sex tape."

I tried to inhale my next sip of alcohol, choking as I looked up at Hudson. He pounded on my back as the liquid fire tried to fry my lungs.

Pulling an unencumbered breath, I laughed, "Glad you are a fan."

He waggled his eyebrows. "I'd love a—"

"Enough," Logan growled lowly.

Hudson took the hint, turning back to his dessert, but not before flashing me a sly smile.

The waiter delivered another dessert to me. I smiled, slipping him more money with one hand while using the other to fork half the chocolate pie into my mouth.

"I am impressed at your appetite," Sage commented.

"Enough," Logan commanded again.

I drew my eyebrows down at him. I'm not a baby, I didn't need to be protected, especially from one jealous bitch.

The band, which had been playing low-key background music, changed to an upbeat tune. That appeared to be the sign for us to stop playing human.

A hand brushed over my shoulder gently and I turned.

Garrick kept his eyes carefully on me. "May I have this dance?"

I took his extended hand, scooting off my chair. "If you will excuse me," I said to the group, following Garrick onto the empty dance floor.

"What did you have in mind?" I asked him. His hand rested on the delicate lace on my hip.

"I was thinking we should really get this party started."

"Did you intentionally just quote P!nk?" I laughed.

He smiled. "Just because I'm older than you, that does not mean I haven't kept current with the times."

I laughed, "Think the band is taking requests?"

"Darling girl, I expect you to know me better by now. The band is waiting for my signal." He rotated us toward the stage. The woman playing the harp saw his nod and quickly spoke to the other band members.

After a brief pause while the harpist counted them off, they burst out with a swinging fifties song.

I laughed, throwing my head back as Garrick's eye glittered with an unspoken challenge. "I forgot this was your favorite era."

He shrugged, spinning me out with an excellent snap, holding my hand as both our feet made the quick steps to the beat. Coincidently enough, the skirt gave a perfect flare for the hippy, toe-tapping kicking we were doing.

Narrowing my eyes, I decided to give Garrick a challenge. He spun me again and instead of tapping my feet as usual for a few counts, I rebounded, quickly charging him for a jump. With quick vampire reflexes, he caught me in midair, twisting my body around his neck. I locked my knees, pressing my arms straight out as he spun my body down his own.

A peal of laugher bubbled up my throat as he slowed the spin down, pinning my knees behind his back. I took his offered hand before he released my knees and I landed on my feet, kicking to the beat that I swear had increased in pace.

Garrick smiled and moved gracefully, thanks to perfect reflexes and years of honing his dance skills. I kept up easily, although I was sporting a thin sheen of sweat from my exertion, to his cool complexion.

He used an impressive, one-handed move, swinging me over his shoulder. We had the entire dance floor to work with. We were acquiring a growing audience, since no one had yet ventured onto the floor with us. Garrick slowed the dance down, and I looked to him for a clue as to what had caused the change.

His dark brow furrowed and I followed his gaze. I could no longer see Grams or Logan through the crowd of people. Without a word, I released his hand, changing directions and tunneling through the crowd.

I didn't make it very far. Those I had assumed to be idle spectators were actually thugs for hire. Strong arms swooped around my waist before I snapped both bones with a crisp sound. He went down, harder than a shifter should. His skin was warm where my hands gripped his wrist.

I inhaled deeply. "Fucking djinn," I hissed, before throwing my weight into getting to Grams.

Garrick wouldn't help me. I was on my own. I didn't fault him for not lending a hand. In that public place, it would be seen as siding with me, and my enemies would be his, his would become mine. I appreciated his staying out of it.

He had slowed the dance to allow me to realize something was amiss. Even that might be enough to throw his lot in with me. Neutrality was important at the Conferences; picking sides with a group made you as vulnerable as them to attacks.

Let's face it, folks, I have quite a few enemies. Another djinn, a clone of the first, landed a blocky fist against my head. I staggered into a third body. They closed in on me, their fallen companion at my feet, writhing in pain. I kicked him for good measure.

My right hand slid to my hidden daggers. I fisted two and sliced through their business suits and into the gray flesh of their bodies. More grayish substances oozed from the wounds, forcing me to grip my blades tighter. Given how closely they were gathered around me, I wouldn't be given the opportunity to draw new blades now that my hidden gems had been revealed.

One flunky landed an impressive jab to my kidney and I sliced the offending hand off, not cleanly. It dangled as he yelled in pain. The last djinn standing bear hugged me from behind, lifting me off my feet and spinning toward the exit.

I finally had a clear view of Logan and Grams. She was fine, protected by Jerry, who had constructed an impressive shield around the group. How did he do that?

My brief glance at Logan had me smiling. Hudson was holding him back, sweating profusely at trying to out alpha the Alpha. I used the upward momentum, flipping myself over the djinn's head onto his back. He reached back a clumsy hand, trying to get me off, succeeding in grabbing my hair. Gripping both blades hard, I slammed them through the flesh of his back. His hand in my hair jerked and I felt chunks of my scalp trying to break free.

I really liked that haircut. I was not going to lose pieces of it to that piece of shit.

I pressed the blades in farther, my hands going through the gray flesh with a sick sliding. The smell had me gagging, my face too close to the wounds. I continued to carve, though, with the asshole still pulling on my hair.

I dropped my left blade and shoved my hand through the muscle I had just damaged, searching for his heart. Realizing what I was after, he let go of my hair, stumbling to the nearest gold and chestnut post and slamming my body into the metal and wood construction. I tightened my grip on my right blade, pointing the tip downward as he tried again.

Everyone was watching now. Some had stood up, others still relaxed in their chairs, enjoying the show.

The djinn twisted and I saw Garrick surrounded by his entourage, watching my fight intently. My searching fingers finally clenched down on the throbbing heart muscle I was searching for.

With the djinn still under my touch, I gave a final yank and pulled my left hand and forearm out of his back, using my teeth to rip the gray flesh of his heart open, watching the red blood inside surrender to gray mush.

I landed on my knees in a pile of gray goo that all three bodies had left behind.

Spitting, I leaned heavily on my knees, pulling my spine straight, not giving away how badly my side or head hurt. I turned to Garrick, shaking off my blades. "Thanks for the dance, but it appears my dance card is full for the night. Unless you'd like it dirty."

Garrick inclined his head slightly. "Always a pleasure, Executioner."

I nodded my head, turning to Grams. She stood up gracefully and our table stood with her. Logan finally relaxed enough that Hudson didn't have to physically restrain him. I smiled and winked at him before heading to the exit.

I was going to drop gray goop everywhere and it didn't seem right to make the humans clean up our mess. They were already going to have a hell of a time getting the giant gray blob cleaned up.

At the trash can at our private elevator, I stopped. "Mercer, can I have your jacket?"

"Of course." He slipped the garment off quickly, removing his arm from Grams's shoulders.

"Goodbye, beautiful dress," I said sorrowfully, peeling the material and shoes off before depositing them into the trash, using the material to try and scrape off the large chunks of goop.

Slipped over my shoulders, the jacket hid the fact that I wasn't wearing a bra.

"Sorry about the dress, Jerry," I lamented.

He smiled, reaching over to squeeze my shoulder, wrinkling his nose. "I'm glad you are okay. The dress is replaceable."

Mercer kept touching his gun nervously, now that it was revealed with my taking his jacket. "What the fuck were those?" he asked, doing a good job of handling the unknown.

"Djinn," Jerry answered, his arms crossed in front of him. I could guess he was missing Mark about now, but as a shifter Mark had to stay with his pack.

"Gin? Like the alcohol?" Mercer asked, adjusting his tie.

"It's pronounced the same, but spelled differently," Jerry agreed, undoing his own tie.

"What are they?" Grams asked me.

I groaned, gingerly touching my bruised kidney. "In human lore they are the genie in a bottle. The truth is they are very rare, very powerful, and very expensive. The three I killed weren't the actual djinn, but short term clones, for lack of a better word."

"You are telling me this djinn is able to clone himself with enough intelligence to attack you?" Mercer asked, pulling on his shit tie again, then giving up on the damn thing and loosening it entirely.

"Yes, but they are exceptionally weak. The more clones they create, the weaker each one is," Jerry offered.

"So how did you know to eat the heart?" Ali asked in the corner. I had forgotten about her and Grant.

That was a gross visual. I needed to spit. "I wasn't trying to eat it. I just didn't have a free hand to slice it. The heart of a clone contains the blood of the djinn. Spilling it kills all the clones created with that blood source."

"What happens if they give each clone its own blood source, and how did you know that one had the blood in it?" Grant asked.

"I didn't, it was a lucky guess. As to the other, I don't know. I've never met a djinn that powerful," I answered, grateful when the doors to the elevator opened.

Grams swiped her finger over the print reader and I headed to the shower. As I closed the door behind me, I spied my phone blinking at me. I swiped it off the nightstand before going to stand next to the tub, turning on the faucet to warm the water up.

Are you okay? Logan asked.

I'm good, just a little sore, I replied.

We are leaving, came the instant reply.

NO! I sent back quickly, before drafting another message. You already showed how important I am to you by needing to have Hudson restrain you.

He did NOT restrain me, he replied.

I laughed. By having him talk sense into you? Better, Alpha?

Mildly.

I rolled my eyes at him. The water was warm on my feet. I flipped the lever to start the shower, resting my phone on the top of the toilet.

Who had I pissed off badly enough that they would find and make a deal with the djinn?

My stomach dropped away. Zachariah. Shit. I slammed my fist against the tile. Of course, he did tell me he was coming after me and mine for killing his vampire, Gabrielle. He deserved it for kidnapping Tommy, and I would make the same decision again if I had to.

I had to admire Zachariah's timing. Attacking me at the Conferences was smart. Violence was expected, and if I was weak enough to be killed or allow members under my protection to be killed, then I didn't deserve my post and should be replaced.

There would be no retribution by my allies, and they couldn't help me here.

I sighed. Zachariah was just one in a long list of Supernaturals I had pissed off. It might be him, it might not. Either way, someone was after my ass, and not in a fun, let's-play-all-night kind of way.

I massaged my head, wincing as my fingers brushed over the goose egg forming there. The gray goop ruined the washcloth and was in danger of clogging the drain when I finally stepped out to dry off. Wrapping myself in a towel, with another in my hair, I padded into my room and threw on clean yoga pants and a pink tank top.

Making my way out of the room, I collapsed into the navy chair, closing my eyes. "Jerry, any chance you have that healing potion for head injuries?"

"I do. But are you sure you want a witch's potion?"

I smiled, keeping my eyes closed, leaning my head against the high arms, "You're a mage, Jerry, and my friend. That makes you far superior to the fucking witches."

He laughed, "Don't let them hear you say that."

"Ugh, I guess that's one benefit of being attacked so soon. All my mingling time got canceled."

Jerry pressed the mixture into my hand and I gulped it down, cringing at the taste.

"Thanks," I muttered, before heading back to my room. I needed sleep for my body to heal, especially given there was a very high probability that tomorrow I'd be fighting for my life or the lives I was responsible for.

...

I was being shoved over in the soft cocoon of blankets. I huffed, blinking up at Logan, surprised I hadn't woken up instantly when my door opened. Either I had misjudged my injuries, or the potion Jerry gave me was more powerful than I realized.

"What are you doing?" I grunted.

"Checking to be sure you are alive," Mark announced.

"Mark, what are you doing here?" I asked, refusing to open my eyes, letting Logan check the bump on my head.

"I think I gave you the wrong potion," Jerry admitted.

"Fuck, how many of you are in here?" I hissed, pulling away from Logan's hands.

"You've been asleep for 14 hours, Olie. It's time for the first meetings," Logan informed me, running a hand through my hair.

I groaned, "My head still hurts. Fucking hell, Jerry."

I fought for control to open my eyes, feeling pretty sure sand should be pouring out given how dry they felt.

"Sorry," he offered meekly.

I huffed, "What did you give me, anyway?" I sat up with help from Logan.

"A heavy relaxation aid. I made it for myself in case I was too stressed." He shrugged.

I huffed, "I feel confident in saying it works."

He smiled before putting his hands in his black pants pockets.

"Fuck, you all are dressed? How much time do I have?"

"Twenty minutes," Grams announced at the open doorway. "Breakfast is waiting until you smell better."

I pulled my hair down, giving it a sniff. "Fucking Dijnn," I muttered, before heading to the shower again.

Fifteen minutes later I was inhaling a cream filled donut while Jerry tried to blow dry my hair into something presentable. Grams had laid out a pinstriped pant suit for me with a silk shirt. Apparently I was no longer dressing myself, either. Whatever, there was food.

"Look up, Olie," Jerry instructed, coating my lashes with mascara. "There, that's all the time we have."

I nodded. "So help me if you wipe your hands on your pants!" he scolded me, throwing several napkins at me. I smiled, carefully cleaning my hands. "Gah!" He complained.

Mark smiled in the corner. "What's on the agenda today?" I asked, checking the clock. It was approaching noon, but since most Supernaturals were more active at night, this was our morning.

"Meet and greet," Logan announced.

I groaned, "Didn't I miss that last night?"

Logan laughed, "No one stayed around last night. The smell was hard to handle for many."

"You'll get to say hello to the witches, Olie," Jerry informed me with glee.

"Fucking hell," I groaned.

...

The ride down the elevator was a silent one. I was still half asleep, as evidenced by my head lolling on Logan's shoulder. The sudden jerk at the lobby had me wiping my drool away. I wasn't even looking at the asshole for a comment.

Jerry led the way, winding past the restaurant from last night, which still had a very distinctive odor coming from it, past the lobby, down another hallway, until we finally arrived at a massive conference room. Tables had been set up similar to last night and there was a breakfast buffet.

"Mmm, come to mama sugar goodness," I crooned, making a beeline for the food.

Logan laughed, corralling me easily against his body and leading me to a seat. The tables were larger than last night and our entire group was able to sit together, shifters and council members.

We had just made it. The speaker in the middle of the room watched us settle with a disapproving gaze. I lifted my arm to flip him off, but Logan covered my hand, smoothing a laugh under a cough. The speaker raised an eyebrow and I glared at him, trying to pull away from Logan.

The speaker cleared his throat, averting his gaze as he began to speak.

"Thank you everyone for attending this year's Conferences. We are pleased to announce this year the human government has decided to send an ambassador. Governor Hash, will you please stand?"

Ice ran through my veins as I turned sharply, staring holes into Grams. Son of a bitch! Is this what the no good, twisted asshole had been doing in her office when I arrived with Mindy, Mercer's granddaughter?

Logan's fingers clamped down around my hand, currently gripping my dinner knife in a chokehold. I cut a glance to him. I didn't appreciate the slight shake of his head telling me to calm the fuck down. Grams had lied, monumentally, and I wasn't sure our relationship could be repaired. I wasn't sure I wanted it to be.

Hash stood, raising a hand, buttoning his jacket as he gave a princess waive.

The speaker continued, "Governor Hash has been sent here to assist the government in drafting their legislation regarding our rights in the human realm as Supernaturals."

Several individuals shifted uncomfortably in their seats, watching Hash closely. He was off limits and any death matches would have to be conducted behind closed doors. I wondered where he was last night.

I let my gaze wander from Hash, anger pressing against my shields, wanting an outlet, wanting to destroy Grams. Pain was a close second. She knew he was going to be here and said nothing—hell, she might even be the reason he was here in the first place. It was another strike against her and while I was willing to forgive a lot, it had to stop. We had to be on the same page.

When my brain started registering what my eyes were seeing, I almost laughed at the protection he had gathered. From my vantage point I counted ten humans packing heat and high tech earpieces, watching the group of killers surrounding them.

I blew out a breath. At least while in Hash's company I was safe. Too bad I wouldn't be staying there.

The speaker was still going on when I tuned back in, "...please enjoy breakfast and continue the meet and greet that last night's unfortunate sewage leak called a stop to early."

I laughed. "Sewage leak?" I asked Logan.

He shrugged. My gaze cut to Grams, seated three seats down from me. She met my gaze this time, her steel gray eyes against my own sea green ones.

I wanted to ask her what she had done, what she had used my organization to do, but there were far too many ears listening.

Jerry broke the tension at our table. "Let's eat before the witches take all the good food."

I nodded, following him and Logan to the already growing line. The vampires had little use for food, and the drink being served to them was undoubtedly warm blood. I touched my neck absently, thinking back to Blake.

Hudson slung an arm over my shoulders, leaning down to whisper in my ear, "Now that you're cleaned up, my dear, I'd be happy to help you over those anger issues."

I watched Logan's shoulders stiffen, but he didn't turn around.

I moved forward with the crowd, picking up a warm plate with gold trim. "You watch the video again?"

He had the decency to pretend to be slightly ashamed, and I do mean ever so slightly with that wide-mouthed grin. "Let's just say it's not every day one gets to try out the succubus who ruined a vampire."

I piled donuts, waffles, maple syrup and a giant glob of butter before I answered him. I gave thought to being an asshole and denying once again the claim that Blake needed my blood to sleep with Angelina, but I was done carrying around that shame and that pain.

Instead, I smiled. "I'm thinking of making my own web series. 'How to Fuck Like a Succubus.'"

Hudson roared laughing, throwing his head back and almost upsetting his precarious stack of bacon and sausage. He unapologetically bumped into the witch behind him. She sent him a murderous glare before clearing her throat and turning to me.

"Actually, I'd like to discuss a business opportunity with you," she began.

My mouth hung open and Logan turned, raising an eyebrow.

"Um, what opportunity would that be?" I asked, moving aside from the table with my full plate.

Logan and Hudson followed me closely.

"I'm aware of your dance establishment, Kitten, and I'm opening a similar business venue. It's a hotel, and the rooms are magically charged to enhance a couple's pleasure."

My eyes widened. "That's kinda brilliant, but it would need to be well controlled."

She smiled under my unintentional praise. She was a witch, and I had no love for that brand of Supernatural after my run in with Destiny and her brand of crazy. I couldn't help but agree, though, it was a good idea. I kinda wish I had thought of it myself.

"Our grand opening is Thursday. I was hopeful you would be able to attend. If you like what you see, I'd love to discuss teaming up to build a location in St. Ann."

I nodded, "I'd like that." I wasn't averse to branching out to additional sources of income. Jerry would be an excellent choice to manage it.

She pulled a business card from her pocket. "I'm Gretchen."

I took the card and muttered, "Olivia." Shit, was I supposed to be carrying business cards around?

"I know who you are. After the trouble with Destiny, I think everyone does." She smiled and I groaned. "Do you have any free time Thursday?" she asked.

I turned to Logan with a shrug. "Do I?"

Logan gave me a half smile. "Yes, we have time around 11 p.m."

"Wonderful, I'll text you the address," Gretchen beamed as Logan handed her his card.

I turned and Logan walked next to me. "So, branching out into brothels?

"Hmm, hotels, I believe. Enhanced hotels. But for you, Logan, I'll throw in company if you can't find your own." I winked, smirking at my own joke.

I wanted to call him Kitty. Since Becky had outed me about calling him that behind his back, I found immense joy in it. However, he had made it very clear that I was not to do that in public. Besides, I didn't really feel like having to get into yet another fight this early. The day was young, it would happen.

Hudson covered his laugh in a cough when Logan sent him a glare. I shrugged, digging into breakfast.

I hadn't forgotten Grams's betrayal, but this public setting was not the time to confront her.

"Okay, Logan, what's on the schedule for today?" I turned to him, sipping coffee.

"Hudson, get her a to-go cup," Logan asked, as my cup was pulled from my hands.

I huffed, "You are all fucking lucky I am tired."

Logan nodded, checking his phone. He laughed, not looking at me. "Actually, this needs to be a surprise."

Hudson slipped the coffee back into my waiting hand. I glared at him. "Logan, I do not like surprises."

He slipped a hand behind my back, guiding me.

I grunted, following his lead.

...

The day and evening passed quickly. Logan and I met with the European packs, and while everyone had been introduced to me, I wasn't remembering names, aside from Hudson. He was much-needed comic relief amid the veiled threats and fake smiles.

I cracked my back while waiting in our suite for Grams. Logan had checked her schedule; she would be coming back. I shouldn't have been there, but didn't care for the hair and nail appointment she had made for me. I let Jerry go instead.

"You sure about confronting her now?" Logan asked around a mouthful of rice as he sat on the couch.

"Yes," I told him yet again, crunching down on a delicious bowlful of fake orange chicken. I had expected tofu, but the fake chicken was actually deep fried cauliflower. "Leaving things to fester has never been my style." I was on the floor, sitting in front of the glass coffee table.

"How did you meet Grams, anyway?" he asked, picking up a piece of my cauliflower.

"It's good," I told him. He popped the bite in his mouth, making a disgusted face. "I was stealing a car after..." I hesitated. How much was I telling Logan? I had told Blake too much. I needed to be careful.

He reached out, resting a large hand on the back of my neck, his thumb rubbing circles under my ear. "You can trust me, Olie, if you want to."

Setting down my dinner I turned to face him, meeting his caramel gaze. He didn't remove his hand when I turned, letting his calloused palm rest against my neck.

Was I capable of trusting him?

My mouth decided before my brain could catch up.

"I was running for my life. She was with this guy out on a deserted road and I needed their car," I began, letting the memory swallow me in...

"Four, leave me," Seven grunted softly.

"Fuck you," I replied, keeping my body low in the dense underbrush. I had just blown up everything we had known. If the whiny bitch thought I was losing her as well, she was delusional. "Stay here."

The truck had been parked here for twenty minutes. I didn't know why they were out here, but I was fairly certain I would have to kill them both. Staying crouched, I waited a moment, reaching up to rest my hand on the door handle of the truck. Lord Master was always trying to get me to remember makes, models and years. I never could. I found it useless information.

The sound of crying had me tilting my head, confused. "Please don't kill me," whispered a female voice. My gaze jerked up. I should let the murder happen, it would mean only one person I had to kill, but I didn't. Flinging the door open, I pulled the heavyset man off of her and out onto the ground.

The woman screamed. "What the hell?" the man asked, taking in my bloodied and soot covered exterior. I wasted no time snapping his neck. He was only human, after all.

I turned to the woman, who was pulling her clothing on. She looked at me with wary gray eyes. "What do you want?"

"The truck," I replied calmly.

"He dead?" she asked, calmly finishing dressing.

"Yes," I answered, narrowing my eyes. "Why aren't you upset?"

She laughed, pulling her tangled hair back. "I'm going to guess you ain't from around here."

"I am not."

She nodded. "Look, I need a ride out of here. I can drive you somewhere relatively safe and you can have the car from there."

"I have a friend who is in need of medical attention."

"A hospital?" she asked.

"No, I'd prefer private help."

She nodded. "I know of a guy, but he ain't cheap."

"I can handle the payment. Wait here."

It was a gamble, but what other option did I have? Drag her out of the vehicle and drag Seven back? It was a gamble that paid off. She started the truck and I covered Seven with a thick, dirty blanket.

Shaking my head, I pulled myself back to the present. "Wow," Logan muttered.

"From there I built my empire." I smiled on the last word.

He raised his plastic cup. "To your empire! But why share everything with her?"

"I never dreamed she'd betray me. She was the one stable thing I had going. Besides, if I was ever killed, I didn't want there to be any problems with her taking care of the kids. "

We finished eating in silence after my confession.

Logan stood. "I have to get changed for The Cages."

"Wait, you never told me who you wanted to take over the East as Alpha?"

"Alec." He watched me closely.

"Yeah, I think he's the best replacement for Darren."

"Good. We will announce it soon."

"What are the cages?" I asked.

He stretched. "It's a way for the more violent Supernaturals to blow off steam in a semi-controlled environment. It is, however, very dangerous and I do not want you going in there."

He was spared my retort by the door opening and Grams's laughter following it.

"Twenty minutes," Logan told me before leaving.

I heard Grams greet Logan with surprise before turning the corner and finding me.

"We need to talk," I told her disappointedly.

"What about?" She waved her ensemble away for this conversation.

"Did you know Hash would be here?"

She sighed, taking her scarf and shoes off before turning back to me. "Yes."

I clenched my jaw shut and my hands together, trying to keep my anger under control. "Why did you keep it from me?"

She shrugged, "I knew it would only upset you."

"I have a right to know what you have been up to," I gritted out, not mentioning the tapes I had watched.

She laughed, hauntingly. "I take care of the children, run your businesses, manage the Supernatural Council, and you want to know what I have been up to? That would imply you care about any of the above."

"How fucking dare you," I hissed, standing up. "They are all important to me. I trust you to handle things in my absence, but if you cannot, I will find a replacement."

That pissed her off. She turned, pointing a finger at me, "No one else could possibly put up with your shit and handle all the prissy succubi as well as I do."

"Everyone is replaceable." Then, my eyes narrowing at her, "You would do well to remember that."

I turned away from her, not liking the way this was going at such an important juncture, or the way I kept screwing it up. I just needed her to be honest with me, honest about Hash, about her concerns for her safety. I could—I would forgive all that had happened, if she would just tell me the truth. But I had a meeting to keep, and at this point I might end up in the cages.

Jerry was waiting for me in my room, an outfit laid out. He rested his chin between his thumb and first finger.

"I'm not sure about tonight's outfit," he admitted.

I swallowed my anger; it wasn't with him. "Why?" I asked, coming to stand over his shoulder.

High-waisted white shorts were paired with a navy blue crop top, but my favorites were the knee-high boots.

"These are hot," I admired them, eyeing the flat heels.

I dressed quickly, with Jerry and Mark waiting to escort me to Logan's room. In the extra five minutes we had, Jerry smeared more makeup on me and pinned up my still dark brown locks into an artful mess.

I was admiring my boots and the very neat hiding places they had for my knives when Logan, Hudson and Alec entered, surprising me. I turned my attention to them, smiling.

"How did it go with Grams?" Logan asked me, coming to walk next to me.

I groaned, "Not well." I was closed-lipped, not giving away any more. The walls had ears.

He nodded and we all piled into the elevator together.

"Those shorts are hot, Olivia," Hudson stated, admiring my long legs.

"Jerry picked them. I have zero sense of style."

"That's true," Alec confirmed.

"Although it doesn't have pockets for my phone," I muttered, holding up the object to Logan. He stored it in his pocket with a small smile, his warm fingers brushing my own.

...

The ride went quickly, all of us listening to Hudson and Logan talk about their past exploits. Logan was far older than I had originally thought. Like World War I old.

The noise level surprised me when we arrived. I could hear it from the street as we forced our way between pack bodies into the huge building. I locked my arms around Logan's waist, not wanting to get lost. Finally making it into the main rooms, I was taken aback by the raw needs flooding the space.

"Whoa," I muttered, leaning heavily on Logan.

"You alright?" he asked, turning and resting an arm around my shoulders.

I nodded, stepping back, bracing myself. "I wasn't expecting that."

"What?" Hudson asked. "I figured after your sex tape, open displays of sex wouldn't bother you." He was watching closely the two naked women in the corner.

I shook my head. "It's not what is happening, it's the emotions underneath it all. I've never felt anything as desperate before."

Jerry and Mark surveyed the group. "Where is Alec?" Mark asked.

"Shit," Logan hissed, grabbing my hand and towing me after him. "I fucking told him not to do this."

"Do what?" I yelled at him over the uncomfortably loud music.

We moved into an auditorium and at the bottom was Alec, facing off against two opponents.

"Logan, they're drugged. On the same stuff Bear was," I whispered to him, moving close.

He looked down at me in surprise. "How can you tell?"

I shrugged. "The way they are holding themselves back, the drool, the emotion they are kicking off. All of it is exactly how Bear reacted."

"We are still looking for a companion to fight next to Alec!" the announcer boomed.

"Logan, you have to put someone down there," I hissed at him, desperate to protect Alec.

"What would you have me do, show him favor?" He pulled me closer, whispering in my ear. "I am days away from being challenged here." I felt his anger and his fear in those words as he pressed closer to me.

My shoulders lost some of their resistance at his heat. I pressed my fingers tips against his chest.

"Watch him," I told Mark, darting down the stairs and running to the cage door. My shorts snagged on the jagged metal as I skidded to a stop next to Alec.

"So, any rules I should know about?" I asked, breathless, as the announcer boomed my arrival.

"Don't die," Alec whispered, not looking at me.

"Got it."

The sound of the bell had both shifters across the octagon cage coming at us. The shorter one came at me, fangs extended, mouth open as he aimed for my jugular. Ducking under the attack, I slammed his body into the diamond black metal.

"What is wrong with them?" Alec yelled at me, raking his claws against his opponents back.

"They're drugged. Their beasts are in control and I'm not sure they know what's going on," I yelled back. My contender came back at me with a roar, sporting claws to go with those fangs as I watched him shift into a giant panther.

He was going to die. I almost felt bad about it, almost.

With a shake of his black head, all human thought fled those piercing yellow eyes. He lunged at me with a roar, his mouth closing around the soft flesh of my thigh. I pulled my weight off the injury as he tried to death shake. Pulling the dagger from my other boot I stabbed down into his brain. The teeth in my thigh tightened and I yanked the dagger up before slamming it home again, feeling the teeth relax.

I looked up to see Alec finish, bloody with his own kill. The entire crowd was silent for a breath before their insanity ratcheted up a couple notches. The noise was deafening.

Alec and I turned to the cage door, ignoring the announcer who tried to lift our arms in the air as the victors.

"Come on, let's go out the back." He was sullen. Logan was pissed at us, I had no doubt.

Limping heavily, I couldn't take his offered help. I needed to appear strong. We left the insanity and the noise behind, walking out into the cool, quiet alley.

Alec was slammed against the wall next to me, Logan's caramel eyes darkening as his lion stared back at us.

"You could have gotten yourself killed." His voice was low with restraint.

Alec properly lowered his eyes.

"Why would you do such a thing?" Logan hissed, his mouth crowded with his fangs.

"I wanted to prove I could handle the East territory."

Logan slammed the wall next to Alec's head, releasing him with a spray of concrete.

"We already think you are ready," I told him softly.

Logan turned his attention back to me, his chest heaving.

"I'm okay," I told him, crossing my arms over my stomach, keeping weight off my leg.

"What were you thinking?" he growled at me.

I lifted my chin defiantly. I sure as shit didn't need to explain what I did, even if I did want him to carry me to the car.

"Let's get moving. We have bigger issues than why I decided to help Alec," I grunted, stumbling as my weight hit my leg. Biting down hard on my lip, I took another tense step.

Hudson reached out, swinging my weight easily up into his arms.

Logan's growl had him putting me back down. "Well shit, if you ain't going to—" I wobbled for a moment, reaching out to balance myself against Alec.

"Seriously, we do not have time for this. Someone drugged those shifters Alec and I went against." All eyes riveted to me. "I think—"

Alec flung me to Logan. My arms windmilled and I stomped hard on my injured leg. Logan in turn shoved me behind him with Jerry. Hudson, Alec and Mark formed our first line of defense.

"Dammit," I hissed, pulling my lone dagger from my boot.

Alec was engaged with two shifters. I peeked around Logan's broad shoulder, trying to determine if they were on the same drug as the others. From the control in their movements and the lack of their shifter essences in their eyes, I was hopeful that was a no.

Jerry was chanting softly, his hands building an icy white ball. His hunched shoulder straightened and he looked for an opening. "Mark, down!" he yelled.

Snapping the neck of his current opponent with deft hands, Mark squatted down, kicking at his next adversary.

Jerry straightened, raising the ball over his head before blasting the oncoming shifters, mowing them down with the power ball.

"Wow," I muttered, impressed at the duration of the magic.

It cleaved a path through the oncoming attack but it wasn't enough, as Alec went down to a knee with a groan. Hudson had broken the line formation and was now surrounded.

"Let's go," I told Logan, moving next to him.

He nodded, cracking his knuckles, his dress shirt straining at the seams as he called upon his lion.

Show off.

Without waiting, I moved in between Alec and Mark. Being injured, I needed the extra protection on the sides. Logan stomped past me, helping Hudson clear off the shifters attached to his back.

Blowing out a long breath, I calmed my nerves, blocking out the pain in my leg and focusing all my attention on the task at hand. It wasn't long before a dark haired shifter launched himself at me.

My body hit the ground with a thump, my head bouncing against the concrete. Warm blood spilled on me from where he had jumped onto my blade. I carved it upward at an awkward angle, cleaving him in two.

Rolling up took more energy and time than I was willing to admit, long enough for a shifter to grab me from behind, pinning my arms to my sides, my blade dangling. I wished for heels as I lifted my good leg up, smashing it down in the hope of finding toes to crush.

His chuckle brushed against my ear and I bent at the waist, trying to fling him over me. He didn't budge.

"Scream, bitch," he whispered, before releasing my left hand to dig his fingers into the tender flesh of the bite wound on my thigh.

I hate to admit it, but I gave that asshole exactly what he wanted. The scream tore from my throat as the pain from his digging had my vision completely dissipating. His other arm wrapped around my waist, holding my body up when the pain threatened to be too much for me.

We were both breathing heavily, although for very different reasons. It cost me precious seconds, but I finally regained control enough to braid the pain down and away from my conscious mind, sending it deep so I could fight off the tide of assholes bent on taking Logan's power.

Not on my fucking watch, assholes.

I passed my blade to my hand no longer under his control. With a controlled cut, I removed his hand. Turning, I grabbed a handful of hair, dragging his head back. "Scream for me, bitch," I hissed, slicing deeply against his throat, severing as much as I could as fast as I could.

Hopefully, it would be enough to keep him from regenerating. Pulling my gaze back to the fight around me, I found the boys had done their work and done it well. Logan and Hudson were each taking care of a few stragglers when my eyes cut to the left, catching movement.

A shifter was sulking on her stomach, short red hair caked with blood, a syringe trapped between her razor sharp teeth.

"Logan," I whispered, hobbling to him. Our gazes locked and she sprung up, running at Logan full force. I dropped my blade, pushing my abused leg to propel myself toward him. Pumping my arms to gather momentum.

She could not inject Logan with that beast-making drug. I might have been able to bring Bear back from the brink of insanity, but that was only thanks to Sonny and his magical ring. Well, not to mention my stellar bedroom skills, but I had neither at my disposal while being attacked. I could not lose Logan for the simple fact I would be the one who would have to put him down. I'm sure Darren could forgive a lot, but not killing his brother.

With a final thrust, I lunged for Logan at the same time Red did. He turned, reaching out his arms to catch me. I felt the needle land home in my spine, my eyes widening before she depressed the plunger, flooding my system in raw fire.

I didn't recognize my own scream.

A shifter threw Logan into a chokehold and we all went down heavily, everyone on top of me. Logan used his arms to keep the weight off of me, but it also meant he couldn't break the attack. Raw power sung through my veins. Slapping a hand on the offending arm I pushed, trying to replicate my ability to kill with touch.

It worked, and it also lessened the anger and angst rushing through me.

"More," I whispered, my hand falling away.

Logan looked down at me, confused. My back arched off the pavement as a new wave of rage scoured my insides.

Rolling to my stomach, I army crawled toward the shifter Hudson had on the ground, my leg wound picking up bits of trash and pebbles.

I could hear Logan talking, and I saw Hudson look down at me with a face full of worry and shock before I brushed my fingers against Logan's victim, flooding his system with raw emotions.

Moving to my back, I panted heavily. "More," I whispered again, my vision failing me.

"No!" screamed a voice. "Don't let her touch me. Kill me, but don't let her do it."

I smiled, lifting my head to see Mark and Alec dragging the shifter I hadn't completely beheaded.

"He has her blood on his fingers," Alec growled, looking at Logan.

I reached out and Mark kicked him in the back of his kneecaps, shoving his face into my fingers.

"Die," I whispered, watching the life snap out of his eyes. With a contented sigh, I gave in to the waiting darkness.

Chapter 3

I was fairly certain I hadn't consumed an entire liquor store, but my stomach and head were disagreeing.

"Oww," I whined, reaching up to cradle my head, my eyes firmly shut against the light trying to pour in.

"She's up," Mark said, way too close to my head.

"Shhh!" I scolded, batting him away.

"Olie," Logan said, his hands gently cradling my head. "We need you to wake up and tell us what happened."

"The she bitch with red hair," I started, before my stomach churned.

"Ugh, bathroom," I demanded. Swiftly I was carried, pressing a hand against my mouth. I was lowered just as quickly.

My eyes opened, seeing the toilet bowl before I retched stomach bile aggressively into its depths. As I leaned my forehead on the cool porcelain, Logan cleared his throat.

I groaned in response, wanting to make a smartass comment about not being able to handle a sick female. Turned out I didn't have the energy.

"You done?" he asked, flushing the toilet.

"For now," I slurred, lying down on the cool tiles.

"Olie, this isn't the best place for this conversation," Logan scolded me.

Pulling my knees into my chest, I huffed out an answer.

"Sweetie," Jerry tried, the bathroom quickly becoming crowded, "we need to know what happened to you."

"What about the redhead?" Logan hedged.

"She was going to stick you with the drug," I slurred, nestling my head into my arms.

"The drug that Bear was infected with while patrolling Halfling, the same drug used on my opponents tonight," Alec clarified.

"How the fuck is it here?" Logan asked. Was that the first time I had heard him cuss? He was clearly hanging around me way too often.

"I don't know," Alec stated. "But if it's here, all the shifters are in trouble."

I grunted my agreement.

"We need to figure out who is making and distributing it," Logan growled, leaving the bathroom.

"Sweetie?" Jerry asked, resting a hand against my head.

I grunted.

"Are you okay?"

"I feel like I drank a liquor store."

He laughed softly. "Do you want something to help?"

I gave thought to denying his witchy, or rather mage help, but I was in pain. "Yeah."

"Give me a minute." He moved away and I pulled my legs closer to my body.

Logan walked back in. "How did you get injected with it?"

Hudson answered for me. "The redhead was after you, and Olivia threw herself into the crossfire. You didn't think she was throwing herself into your arms for saving, did you?" he taunted.

"Make me get off this floor, motherfucker," I warned him.

"Damn, you are in a bad way," Hudson stated, giving his professional medical opinion.

"I wouldn't tempt her. She killed three shifters simply by touching them," Mark warned Hudson.

Hudson gave a low whistle. "How the hell you do that, little lady?"

I felt Jerry come back next to me, stroking my hair back. I moved into the touch. "Can you sit up?"

I gave a pathetic groan. "Let me help you," he offered, tipping me up, resting my back against the tub.

I cracked an eye open and everyone sucked in a breath, except Logan.

I looked at him. "My eyes black again?" I asked.

He nodded.

"Shifter magic, it always fucks with me."

"Drink," Jerry instructed me. I pressed my lips to the plastic hotel cup, choking back the thick liquid, keeping my eyes closed.

I finished and he held a hand over my mouth. "Keep it down."

My eyes teared at the effort, my stomach clenching to rid itself of the toxic contents. After long moments I exhaled, resting my head back.

"That is fucking amazing."

"I'm glad you think so. I hate to do this, Olie, but I want to check your power. I know you would rather not explore your magic, but after last night, I don't think we have a choice. People saw you kill with a touch."

"How much time do I have before the first meetings?" I asked, not willing to dwell on or discuss what Jerry had just said, opening my eyes and not receiving any freakout at the color.

"You've got a half hour," Logan said from the doorway. "You have a Q&A session with Garrick."

I smiled before pushing myself up to sit on the edge of the tub, wincing as my thigh muscle protested the movement after being chewed on so recently.

I groaned, pushing again to stand, forcing the pain down. "Everyone out. Sorry, Jerry, but we just don't have the time right now."

I turned, not bothering to see if my command was carried out, stripping out of my shirt.

"OUT!" Bellowed Logan.

...

The hot water pounded on the back of my neck and I rolled it again, trying to work out the knots trapped there.

I was mildly successful. Exiting into the bedroom with a towel wrapped around my hair and one around my body, I dressed quickly.

"How am I doing on time?" I asked Jerry. "Where is everyone else?"

"Impressive, it must be the helpful mage delivering potions to you." He grinned, exposing his perfectly white teeth. "They went to their own meetings."

Grams came around the corner. "We should be leaving now."

I stiffened. I really wanted to throttle her.

"Garrick will be there as well," she offered.

"Wonderful," I muttered. I liked my time with Garrick to be private, naked, and with his expansive selection of toys.

"He sent you over an outfit, Olie," Jerry said, reading the displeasure on my face.

"Why does everyone feel the need to dress me?" I muttered, looking down at my rumpled jeans and t-shirt.

"Because you do it so poorly yourself," Grams called after me.

I took the white gift box with the blood red ribbon into my room, slamming the door behind me. So what if that was childish? I huffed, pulling the silky ribbon off.

"Whoa," I muttered, holding up the navy blue silk pants and matching wrap top.

Exiting my room, I looked for Jerry. "Do I have shoes that match this?"

He looked up and nodded. "Yeah, wow that's impressive."

He handed me matching silk ballerina shoes, my favorite.

"That outfit would do better with heels," Grams criticized.

"And your mouth would do better without critiquing everything I do," I lashed out.

Her jaw snapped up, her eyes meeting mine in surprise. There was only so much shit I was willing to take, and she was dangerously close to hitting my limit. Hard.

"Well," Jerry interrupted awkwardly, "let's be off."

Mercer, Ali and Grant came around the corner and we headed out in silence. This time we went up to the Bellagio Ballroom.

The smaller factions, grouped together by races, sat in front of the raised stage. There were a few vampires, I noted. Their glares warned of interesting questions. I certainly hoped they got to ask them.

This group usually needed a little livening up. In the front row, girls and guys openly gawked at Garrick. I shot him a wink across the stage. He smiled and nodded, acknowledging me before smiling adoringly down on his groupies.

Unlike me, Garrick ruled solely. He thought it a weakness to allow others to have a say, even if that might happen behind closed doors.

I just killed those who thought I was weaker, speaking of which, I wondered where Hash was.

I didn't have to look far. He was seated in the middle and I glared at him with a vengeance.

Carefully, he avoided my gaze, but he did meet Grams's with a self-satisfied smile and nod. I wanted to turn and see if she returned it. But I didn't need to look weak. While there would be no challenges here, that certainly didn't mean they wouldn't come later.

"Olivia," Garrick began, offering me a mic, "would you like to sum up your past year first?"

I stood and crossed the short distance between us, smiling as our fingers brushed over each other.

Turning to the waiting faces, I thought about my year. I got to fight a reanimated shifter, fall in love, and destroy a demigod and his vicious torture rings, all followed by a broken heart and the destruction of the witches. Not to mention my unnerving ability to be a magical conduit and contact my most feared enemy, the Fae.

"It was an uneventful year," I announced, taking my time to survey the crowd in front of me.

Hands shot up all over the room and I sighed. Covering the mouthpiece, I turned to Garrick. "Please tell me I don't have to answer those questions yet."

He gave me a soft smile. "That would be your decision."

"Fuck it," I groaned. I'd rather get this crap out of the way now. "You in the pink, speak," I commanded.

"How are you recovering from the sex video being leaked?"

My eyebrows drew down in surprise. "Fine, thank you," I answered, unsure.

She continued, "Do you plan to seek financial restitution from those who released it?"

I smiled. "Financial, no. I'd like to think I'm more creative than that."

She nodded, giving me a tight smile before sitting down.

"Next, you in the gray." I pointed at a shifter filling out his sweater exceptionally well.

"When do you and your kind plan to come out to the public?" His jaw tightened. He was clearly not a fan of the rest of the Supernatural Community lying in wait while the shifters and vampires took the brunt of the humans' wrath.

"I don't know." I had to handle this cautiously. One, that was a valid question. Two, he was a shifter, so telling him to fuck off was going to piss off Logan. Wait, did I care about pissing Logan off?

"Shifters and vampires are both organized in ways that protect the weaker members of the clans. The Council is a collection of smaller clans. We have to be certain that all of our members are taken care of before launching into the public view."

"You're scared."

"I'm cautious. There is a difference," I all but hissed. "It is my job to protect those who depend on me. I take that job exceptionally seriously. I will not do anything that will put them in any danger."

"Implying that Logan did?" he asked.

"Implying that Logan made the best decision for his packs and his packs are not mine." I stressed each and every word. "Next question, you in the teal."

"What is going on between you and Logan?" the twelve-year-old asked me.

"Fuck, I don't even know how to answer that."

"Are you going to be a permanent fixture helping him?"

I looked at her, really searched her gaze before asking myself the same thing. The sea of people watched me, too damn closely for my liking.

I bit my bottom lip. "I will stand with Logan until he finds a replacement. My position there is not permanent."

Logan didn't need me. I had helped him smooth over the destruction from the whirlwind known as Lorraine, but I was a temporary fix during the transition. Eventually, he'd find a stable, politically correct partner and I would be ... done. I tried to pretend that thought didn't stab me in the gut.

"I'm done, Garrick, you are up." I handed him the mic and went to sit down.

It felt bad admitting that I was replaceable, but I wasn't dwelling on it. Nope, not at all.

Garrick, for the record, was far more eloquent at answering questions.

Fucker.

Chapter 4

I face planted into Logan's bed.

"It wasn't that bad," he assured me, hanging up his jacket.

"Ha! Ha! Ha!" I rolled to my back, scooting up to lean against the headboard.

"I didn't even get to any of the vampires' or Hash's questions. I was so busy fielding questions from the damn shifters!"

Logan grimaced, moving my feet to rest on his lap as he sat on the edge of the bed. He slipped off my shoe, rubbing the arch of my foot.

I heaved a sigh of contentment closing my eyes. "A twelve-year-old asked me if I planned to be a permanent fixture next to you."

His hands stilled.

"Don't worry, I said no."

His rubbing continued, far more aggressively. I pulled my feet off his lap.

"You will find someone to fill my position, Logan. Just give the breakup time to heal." I rested my hand on his knee, pushing comfort into him. I knew all about shitty breakups.

He sighed.

"Do you want to stay on next to me?" he asked, turning to face me.

That question caught me off guard. I narrowed my eyes at him, tilting my head. "I don't mind it, Logan. It has strengthened the relationship between our clans. I like to think it might have helped Darren and Kass. Not to mention getting out some of my very serious anger issues."

I gently hit his shoulder, adding, "Nothing lasts forever."

He nodded. "You ready for dinner?"

"Please tell me it's a buffet."

It was not a buffet, but at least there was dancing entertainment.

...

I chucked my shoes over in the corner of my room, glad this day was over. But while my public performances were done, there were a few calls I needed to make.

Pulling out my smartphone, I dialed Tommy's number.

"Yo," he grunted.

"You sleeping?" I asked, shocked.

"Power napping," he grunted. "What's up?"

"I need help," I confessed.

"You need help? Olie, usually you are a little more specific."

I rubbed my forehead, not enjoying the pressure building there.

"There's a new drug hitting the market that can force a shifter into beast." I probably should have kept that fucking Mae alive or at least asked a few more questions. "Hey, did you find anything from Mae's computer?"

"Um, I'm going to ignore the first part of your scatterbrained sentence in favor of answering the second. I broke down the firewalls but it leads nowhere. The company that paid her was a shell corporation, run by a lady who has been deceased for twenty years."

I grunted. I should have kept her fucking alive.

"So, where do you want me to start on the beast maker serum?"

That was the problem, I didn't even know where to start and because of that I wasn't dealing with it. But they were coming after Logan now, and I needed to figure it out, maybe even come up with an antidote.

I was getting ahead of myself.

"I need to get a sample," I groaned.

"How do you plan on doing that?"

"I don't know, Tommy, but I'll figure it out. When I do, you have the equipment or lab or whoever ready to analyze it."

"That I can do."

"Hey Tommy?"

"Yep, boss."

"Thanks for listening."

"Anytime, boss."

I ended the call, looking wistfully down at my phone. I missed the kid.

I knew I should probably clue Logan in to my idea, but first I was changing, chucking the beautiful garments for yoga pants and a blue fitted t-shirt with flip-flops. Tossing my leather duster over my ensemble, I checked my guns and knives before adding my phone to the mix.

Flopping out of the room I spared a look at Grams, working on her computer. "You going out?" she asked.

I approached her. "What is going on with you?"

She turned her head back to the computer screen. "I'm not going to dignify that with an answer."

I pushed her laptop closed.

"I'm only going to say this once: whatever is going on with you needs to stop or you need to step down. This is my Council and whatever games you are playing will not continue."

"How dare you," she hissed at me. "I have worked just as hard, just as long to create OUR Council."

"Remember who killed to get you there." My voice was deadly low. "Step down or step to my side, make a decision."

I was so livid I stormed out of the door without checking the hall, letting it slam behind me.

Bad idea? Yep, sure was.

I landed hard on the wine carpet, my hands braced under my shoulders from the tackle.

"Perfect, this is just what I needed." I slammed my head back, feeling the satisfying crack of a broken nose. Turning my body to the side, I landed an impressive kick to something soft. The yelp of pain brought a smile to my face.

Rolling away to the other side, I took a quick view of the hallway, seeing three additional goons awaiting disposal.

I pulled a dagger from my duster. Alright, I admit I liked it. There was no way I'd be able to pack all this into my regular jacket. Balancing on my palms, I tucked my legs underneath my body. Shifting my weight onto the balls of my feet, I wrapped my fingers around the ebony dagger handle before I turned. I was still crouched when I slammed my blade into the next attacker's thigh, hard enough to lodge it into her bone.

She went down with a satisfying scream.

Leaving the dagger in the whimpering woman, I inhaled deeply, wondering what the hell they were. I didn't scent shifter and they were going down and staying down.

The next one came at me with blurring speed and I fell back, my hand still in my duster as I attempted to pull another blade.

"You must die, demon whore!" His blue gaze had the same piercing color as Blake's. I took great pleasure slamming my head against his nose before I slammed my knee home between his legs. I smiled as his eyes lost focus with pain.

I'll admit to enjoying that too much. Throwing his light weight off my body, I stood, searching the corridor for the last attacker.

"You cannot lead us!" screamed the woman, standing, leaning heavily against the wall. She wrenched the blade from her leg before throwing herself at me with the dagger.

I ducked, taking the brunt of her attack on my back before rolling her over and down on my other side. She landed on her back and I heard the air rush from her lungs. Pinning her with a knee, I slipped a shorter blade out, slamming it home in her heart. Her eyes widened before her head fell to the side. I looked down at the lack of blood.

"What the fuck?"

This wasn't adding up to—

"Oh, fucking hell." I turned on the two males, still writhing on the floor. The dagger the woman had lodged weakly into my black fell away.

I pulled up the closest one, slamming him against the wall. "Who sent you?" He writhed at my touch. "Siren, why are you fighting me?"

"Demon spawn," he choked. I released my hold slightly. "You will be the death of all of us. War is coming."

I sighed, "I will not be the death of everyone. I will, however, be the death of you."

I had pulled my gun during my short speech, and now put two bullets at close range into his heart. This didn't feel good. I turned to the other siren, who was standing with his hands up before I shot him as well.

My fingers tightened on the gun, hating this. Sirens were not powerful. Seawater ran through their veins, not blood. Why were they coming after me? What was this war?

"Dammit, why didn't I keep one of them alive?" I groaned to myself. I was so concerned with eliminating the present threat. Fucking hell, I really needed to work on my long-term game.

Gathering my weapons, I cleaned them on the dead bodies before turning to walk the short distance to knock on Logan's door.

Mark answered, stepping back when he saw the look on my face.

"Problems?"

"You didn't hear?" I asked, shocked.

Logan exited one of the rooms as I flopped onto their indigo couch. He rolled up his shirtsleeves. I grunted, pulling off the leather duster, fingering the hole in the back with a sigh.

"Sirens attacked me."

"Sirens?" Mark asked, turning me to take a look at my back.

"They said war was coming."

Logan sat on the chair across from me, giving me a knowing look.

"No Logan, I didn't leave anyone alive, and yeah I know that wasn't my best decision." I rubbed the back of my neck, looking at the gold and blue rug.

"This doesn't feel right," I told him, meeting his gaze.

"I know, Olie, we will figure it out." I ignored the comforting look there. Logan was not mine. I was only temporary. It was about fucking time I realized that.

Shaking my head, I let Mark look at my back.

"I'm going to need to cover this so you don't bleed on everything."

I grunted at him.

He took that as a yes and went to gather supplies.

"What brings you to our room?" Logan asked, sitting on a couch

"Oh, right, Tommy hit a dead end on the mage. The payment came from a shell corporation."

Logan steepled his index fingers, pressing them against lips. "I know, I know," I groaned. "I should have kept her alive as well."

He grumbled, shifting his position before opening his big mouth. "Your love of killing is starting to become a problem."

I narrowed my eyes at him.

Mark broke the tension of our staring contest, coming to sit next to me. I shifted, resting my chin against the high armrest, my thoughts pulled back to my fight with Grams.

"Is that all that's bothering you?" Mark asked me quietly.

"That's all I'm willing to talk about tonight."

I turned to see his face. He smiled, nodding understanding before patting my knee.

"If I'm not needed..." Mark looked to Logan, who nodded, dismissing him.

Logan stayed sitting, watching me closely. I pulled on my duster, ignoring him.

Placing my hand on the cool doorknob, I hesitated. I turned my head slightly, seeing Logan in my peripheral view. "I'll try not to kill any more possible informants."

He moved behind me, wrapping his arm around my waist. "Why don't you find another way to work out that anger?"

I turned, shocked by his aggressive come on.

"You're drunk."

"Nope," he answered with a smile, stepping closer. I stepped back, flush against the door.

"I've tried to be patient. I've tried to be subtle, but Olivia..." He ran his thumb over my cheek bone. "I like you. A lot. I'll be honest, I never thought of you as emotionally available until Blake, and now I can't stop thinking of you." His words softened, his lips dipping down to mine, which had a mind of their own, lifting to meet his shapely mouth.

The touch was light between us, tentative on my end. Apparently, my whole "temporary" self-talk was thrown out the window at the first possibility of a boy liking me. The problem was, I was afraid I liked Logan, too, and while I could try lying to myself, my body wasn't listening.

Large, warm palms wrapped around me, pulling my back away from the cold of the door and into Logan's fierce warmth. I groaned and the pressure of his lips increased.

My hands were busy pulling out his dress shirt to feel the finely formed flesh underneath it.

"Hey boss—" Mark called out, coming around the corner, breaking the spell.

Logan moved back, turning to face him. I couldn't see Mark's face, but I could imagine Logan was sporting some pretty fine, hard, thick, evidence of our entanglement.

I had to get out of there.

I slipped out the door before I heard more of their conversation, again not checking the fucking halls.

No one was waiting for me this time and I continued on, belatedly realizing I was breaking my own rule about going out alone. Whatever, they're my rules to break.

I made it back to the safety of my room without incident. Tossing my duster over my suitcase, I landed face first onto the bed. I'd like to say I wasn't thinking about how pleasant Logan's lips felt against my own, but I'd lied to myself enough.

I liked the kiss. I liked his attention and ran away from both, because I'm a chicken shit.

I groaned, pushing my face into the pillow. I needed to make a decision, either I was in or out. I just wished it didn't scare me. I wasn't sure I could handle being hurt again. In some respects I was over and done with Blake. I sure as shit didn't want him back, but being crushed so effortlessly ... I wasn't sure I wanted to give another the opportunity to hurt me like that.

Chapter 5

It was Garrick's and my turn to meet with the European Supernatural Councils.

"I have no use for these fuckers," I told him as we rode the elevators to the meeting.

He adjusted his jacket sleeves, dashingly dressed as always. "You must get better at playing politics, my dear succubus."

He was one of the few people who named my species without disdain.

"Make me," I taunted.

He turned his coffee colored eyes, raking over my black dress pants and gray top. "If only the elevator ride was longer."

I laughed when the ding announced our arrival. "The rest of your group meeting you here?" I asked him.

"Yes, since I was traveling with the highly esteemed executioner, I had no fear for my safety."

I laughed again. "Right, as if I'm any match for the strength of you. Tell the truth, Garrick, it's because I was late." We strolled down the long hallway, scanning diligently ahead of us. I couldn't say a fight wouldn't do me good. I had spent most of the night dreaming of Logan. I was tired and horny.

He smiled as we reached the small conference room. "Do not doubt your abilities, Olivia."

He pushed open the door leading to the meeting room and I smiled at Ali and Grant with Grams. Yes, I was putting on appearances, but a unified front was all anyone was going to be seeing out of us. Well, hopefully. Hash wasn't in the room so my odds were looking up.

"I can't wait to hear this," Garrick muttered, heading toward his own ensemble, knowing full well everyone heard him.

Garrick and I had met one gloriously bloody night. A shifter gone pure beast had clawed a pathway of destruction across two states and three counties, ending up in my territory. Garrick didn't believe I was up for the task.

I don't think I'll ever forget what he looked like, each of us sporting bloody clothing, his wounds far advanced in healing. He smiled at me. "Fancy a drink?"

"From a bottle or my neck?"

I brushed the memory away, focusing back on the present.

We settled in our seats, awaiting the European Council and their antiquated ways. Garrick and I agreed on that wholeheartedly; we had to change with the times in order to survive. It was a lesson they had yet to learn.

True to their roots, the council arrived dressed in matching robes. I could feel Garrick's eyes on me, waiting for me to acknowledge the ridiculousness of that alone, but I kept my eyes trained ahead, allowing the edge of my mouth to curl up slightly.

The European Council had been around forever. They certainly hadn't always gone by the same name, and they gave the underhanded, dirty vampires a run for their money in political mind-bending tricks. I had no use for them. Garrick, who started out in the European circuit, also had no use for them.

"Thank you for attending our meeting. I won't dally, but shall instead dive right into the heart of the matter," Celino stated regally, fluffing his robe before sitting.

I stopped listening, turning to watch Garrick fight a smile as he refused to look at me. Eventually, they got to the good stuff. I was eagerly awaiting another chance to poke fun at their antiquated ways.

"With that said, we have come to an agreement with the Fae..." I couldn't hear anything else, the blood draining from my face as I stared open-mouthed at the idiots in front of me. The Fae? Seriously? The fucking Fae I had just narrowly escaped from in that shit with Destiny?

This was not fucking happening.

Slowly, I turned to Garrick, seeing my own horror mirrored on his face. Good to see we were on the same page.

Shoving myself up, I bellowed at Ali and Grant, "Get out of here NOW!"

"Lock the doors!" called Celino. "They will hear this proposal!" Their guards moved to obey the command, blocking the doors against our fleeing party. Garrick tackled one. They bounced off the thick wood door and onto the ground. I reached to free my dagger, but released the handle. I couldn't kill the European Council's guards without declaring an open war.

At least the guard seemed to think the same, leaving his weapons in favor of hand-to-hand combat.

"I'm going to beat that smile off your face," I hissed, hitting him in the middle. He wrapped his arms around me, lifting me vertically.

"Bring it, little girl," he grunted.

I kicked my feet, seeking to unbalance his hold. He stepped forward. "Go!" I screamed upside down at Grant. He pushed the guard, giving himself room to pull the door open wide enough for Ali, Grams and him to flee. The guard and I fell and I braced my hands in front of my face for his mammoth weight. I felt my nose crack anyway, the air smashed from my lungs.

Seriously, does he not know who I am?"

Balancing on my hands, I drew my body up in a handstand, letting my feet fall behind me. Spinning to face him, I delivered a kick to his midsection. That smug smile flattened as my kick drove him back.

I smiled. "Come on, pretty boy, that the best you got?"

He shook his head, taking a step toward me. "I don't want to hurt you."

I spared a glance to see Garrick having a difficult time subduing his own guard.

"What are you?" I asked, honestly curious.

His smile returned and I almost felt bad about having to ruin his handsome face. "Why, pretty lady, are you trying to distract me?"

I huffed, rolling my eyes as he lunged, taking me down around the middle, "Asshole," I panted out, letting my body go limp. "You fight well, you're humane, and you're fucking intimidating. I'd like to recruit you to my side."

He pulled back, looking down at me, probably thinking he had won this round. "We are not for sale."

I pulled my legs up, hitting him square on the chest. He moved minimally.

I huffed, "I didn't say sale, I said recruit. You know, offer you more money and benefits than what you are currently getting."

That caught his attention. "You pay your slaves?"

That caught me off guard. "I don't keep slaves," I answered.

A resounding crash had all of us looking back to Celino.

"You are fools. The Fae cannot be trusted!" Garrick yelled, untangling from his own guard to stand next to me.

"You are the ones telling us to adapt to the modern world. Now you do not like the route we have taken. There is no pleasing either of you!" Celino yelled back at us, throwing his hands up.

70

The floor rumbled beneath our feet. Garrick and I shared a look before we turned to crash into the door painfully. It didn't move. Wouldn't budge and it wasn't locked.

"Magic," Garrick hissed, stepping back.

I gave the door another tug. Slowly, we turned back around, watching the cloud of gray smoke swirling behind the self-proclaimed leader of the idiots.

"At least they got out," I whispered to Garrick.

"Right, now what about us?" he responded.

I swallowed hard. The Fae were the one race that could enslave me again as Selena had. I had every right to be mortally terrified of them. But terror would dull my senses, not hone them. Exhaling a trapped breath, I pushed my mind away from that nightmare.

The gray smoke grew to an eight-foot shade. Ice blonde hair swirled, purple eyes snapping open.

"It's toying with us," Garrick muttered, shifting his fighting stance.

"Doing a fucking fantastic job, I'd say," I answered, finding myself inching toward the door.

Celino smiled smugly as the smoke behind him bellowed a sound that had the guards moving away from us.

With the speed of a fan, the smoke was sucked from the room, and all eyes were transfixed on the Fae straight out of the movies, complete with ice blonde hair and pale skin.

"I think he's a Tolkien fan," I muttered to Garrick, trying to ease the fear in my chest.

"You don't think that's its natural form?" Garrick whispered back.

"Nope, not a chance," I answered. I squared my shoulders. The Fae were the original shape shifters and they were gods at it.

"You have summoned me," the Fae began, flipping his long hair over a shoulder. I couldn't help the laugh that broke free.

That caught his attention as I shifted awkwardly from foot to foot.

"You have trapped them here," the Fae observed.

"They are difficult to control, at best. They sent their entourages out the door when we told them of our plans," Celino stated.

Purple eyes met my own gaze and I exhaled forcefully, not averting my gaze, not letting the terror-fueled scream in my chest have a voice.

"I cannot include the unwilling," mused the Fae. I didn't believe him for a moment.

Celino waved a hand, dismissing our refusal, "They don't understand, simpletons at best. You see the kind of idiots you have asked me to work with," he demanded, exasperated.

"It was your job to make them understand," the Fae informed Celino coldly.

"We have to get out of here," Garrick whispered to me.

"Agreed," I whispered, turning back to the magically sealed doors.

Months before, I had managed to suck magic inside of me, freeing Logan and Darren's grandfather from the clutches of the puppet master. Maybe it was just that easy again. For our sake, I hoped so.

Garrick pulled uselessly on the doors as I tuned out the yelling behind me, placing my palms against the polished wood.

It burned fucking badly. Sealing my eyes closed, I examined the magic, it roved unlike anything I had yet encountered. A deep purple intertwined with golden sparks danced in my vision. Focusing on the gold, I drew it to me.

If I thought my hands hurt, it was nothing compared to the pain slicing through my veins, but it was enough.

I sagged to the ground against the door, weakened from my pull. The strength of the magic blazed within, draining me of energy. I reached up a flopping arm, latching onto the handle, pulling the latch with everything I had. A powerful tide of purple tried to still my hand. I hung on, panting heavily as I turned the handle, forcing my legs to stand.

I pulled, knowing my hands might be forever ruined by the pain, the fire slicing deep welts as I pulled backward.

Garrick picked this moment to start helping, pushing open the door, wrapping an arm around my waist and hauling me out.

Just as the shield Steven created at the docks had exploded, so did this one, launching us forward. We crashed into the opposite wall, our heads knocking hard against it. Garrick was quicker to respond. My mind felt muddy, murky, unable to focus as he dragged me away from the open door.

"Jerry, get me to Jerry," I whispered as we escaped at vamp speed.

Blackness stole my vision and it felt like ages before I awoke, my eyes crusted shut and mouth parched.

...

"You would do something as stupid as reveal you can work magic in front of the Fae at a fucking Council meeting?!" Garrick yelled at me, pacing.

"Oh I'm sorry, did you want to end up the pet of the Fae? I'm sure they would be glad to accept you," I tried to yell back, but it came out croaked. I rolled over to my side, looking around with a haze over my eyes.

Garrick continued to storm, pacing my room.

"You're fucking welcome, asshole," I told him as he threw up his hands and left.

Turning, I watched Jerry quietly crushing herbs into a paste.

I could hear his agreement and lecture coming. "Don't start, Jerry," I warned.

He shook his head sadly, memories of a past before me playing before his eyes. "I understand, Olie."

With a huff I passed back out.

...

Logan was at my bedside.

I groaned, sitting up and rubbing my head. "Did you move me?" I asked.

"I did."

"Thanks," I offered, squinting at him as I pulled myself into a seated position.

I could feel his annoyance at our earlier parting. I sighed, rubbing the back of my head, swinging my legs off the bed.

He was silent, watching me closely.

"Why did you run?"

Alright, I could appreciate meeting this head on.

I opened my mouth to brush it off as raging hormones, but something in the intensity of his gaze stopped me. I dropped my own to the floor, trying to organize my thoughts.

"I need time, Logan," I stated, forcing myself to look at him with a shrug. "It's your choice if you want to give me that. As much as I am shocked to say it, I like you too, but I'm not good at relationships. I'm not good at letting my guards down. I'm really bad at trusting."

He nodded. "I'm relieved, I thought it had to do with the baby."

I shook my head. "No, I love kids."

"But Lorraine—"

"Will always be a pain in my ass and yours. I can accept that easily enough."

He smiled at that. "I can wait, Olie."

I nodded with a tentative smile. When did we get so mushy? Didn't we dislike each other? Somewhere between The Oracle and her prediction of our emotional attachment and him having my back dealing with getting Blake's niece back, our relationship had changed. I was glad we weren't sending hidden decoder messages about it. There was a certain maturity in being honest and open that I didn't think I was capable of.

Knocking at the door broke up our tender moment. I scowled, turning to Jerry's voice calling out, "Hey, don't forget you have that brothel thing tonight!"

"I was out that long?" I groaned.

Logan nodded. "The European Council has disappeared and I rescheduled with Gretchen when we missed last night."

I threw up my hands. "Will no one believe me about the fucking Fae? Serves them right."

Logan stood, making his way to the door. I adjusted my top, grabbing a hair tie and securing my hair into a high pony tail.

"Let's go see the brothel!" I only staggered slightly.

Chapter 6

Gretchen was outside, nervously pacing the length of the ... hotel? Brothel? Establishment? Hell, what was the right word?

Logan pulled up to the front, handing the keys to a valet.

"You made it," Gretchen announced.

"Yep," I agreed.

"I didn't think you'd come," she confessed.

I shrugged. "This is a great idea, if properly managed. I see a lot of money in your future."

She nodded, regarding me starstruck.

"Can we get a tour?" Logan asked as we stood there waiting for her to recover.

"Yes, of course. Please come in." She took a deep breath. "Welcome to The Lovely Lust."

The front of the building reminded me of a prestigious high-rise apartment complex in downtown New York. A doorman opened the glass doors for us under a red circular awning with a discreet nod and no smile.

The front desk had a well-groomed woman behind it who greeted us with a warm, non-judgmental smile.

Gretchen blathered on about it and I tuned in to listen to her again. We loaded into a gold trimmed elevator as Gretchen pushed the number four.

"Each floor is themed. We have four right now, but I own the entire building. Floor four is Victorian themed," she beamed as the doors opened. Modern light fixtures had been replaced by electric candles, giving the hallway a haunted feel.

Gretchen's phone rang and she looked down at it in dismay. "If you will excuse me, please take a look around. Room four is open."

"Shall we?" Logan asked, ushering me out of the elevator. We strolled down the hallway lined with floral wallpaper. Random tables with skinny legs offered guests lube, handcuffs, and other playful items.

"She has thought of it all," I admired.

Logan grunted, placing a large paw on the vintage brass circular doorknob, pushing open the cream paneled door.

"Logan, we are not going in there together," I reprimanded him.

"Why not?" he asked with a raised eyebrow.

"Did you miss the part where the rooms are enchanted for the guests' pleasure?"

"We're not doing anything pleasurable. How do the maids clean the rooms if one cannot simply be in the room without succumbing to the effects? Unless you have plans to take advantage of me that you would like to share."

I scoffed.

"Besides, you are a succubus. I doubt anything here could actually affect you."

I peeked inside at what I could see. I had to admit he was making some solid points. Besides, what's the worst that would happen? I slept with Logan. I could think of crappier ways to spend my time.

I went in first, turning around, admiring Gretchen's attention to detail.

Turning to Logan, I drew a breath to comment on how pretty the rose wallpaper was. My air caught in my throat as desire shot directly into my belly.

"Logan," I whispered, digging my fingers into my arms, "it's affecting me, we have to leave." I finished in a hiss, trying to control my breathing.

He never had a chance. The spells seeped into him immediately and his eyes began morphing before my own. Slowly he stalked me, removing his jacket in the process, the fabric falling in a heap as he moved closer to my trembling body.

I forced myself back a step on the plush rose carpet, my body wanting to give in to the heat inside of me, a heat I knew Logan could smother. Pulling another jagged breath, I pushed a hand out as Logan followed me back. It connected solidly with firm muscles, a sensation quickly followed by the absence of all rational thought.

"Logan," I tried again, unable to move. "We have to get out of here," I whispered, panting the least of my worries. His energy was unleashed and calling me, his fire and desire my own, doubled and dumped back into me.

Smiling, Logan pulled me into his chest with one strong, long arm, pulling us face to face.

"Logan." It was the last warning I could give him, as his lips slowly descended upon my own, brushing gently, sending scorching heat through my body. Groaning, I leaned into him, forcing my tongue past his lips to swipe a taste of him, just a taste, I told my nagging awareness.

Threading his fingers through my shoulder length hair, gently cupping my head, he growled low before fisting his hand, forcing my lips away from his own as he trailed hot, wet kisses down my neck.

His saliva left cooling circles on my body. My knees weakened, supported by his arm around my waist as he pushed me back to the flowery bed behind me. The back of my knees felt the soft brush from the Egyptian cotton bedspread. As I leaned away, Logan released me in anticipation of my overheated body falling into the promise of sweet softness.

With my one remaining lucid brain cell I rolled off the bed and dashed toward the door, my body despising me with every painful step. Logan's body slammed into the door before I could even touch the handle, a carnal smile on his tempting lips. Growling, he moved quickly, pressing my back against the wall, my body held there under his rugged chest.

"You are mine," he growled, pinning me with his hips to keep me immobile while gently placing both my hands above my head, grinding his massive erection against me.

Feeling his swollen member, I let out a heavy breath, all rational thought fleeing me. I arched my back, pressing myself against his iron chest.

Logan growled low, pulling back to meet my eyes with his own golden gaze. I was disappointed to think he might be regaining his senses. My own muddled brain never had a chance to glean his reason for the pause, as he pressed our lips back together.

The pain in my body disappeared, the nagging sting in my hands gone.

Moaning low, I felt his calloused hands shove my black pants down, tearing the adorable delicate panties I had worn.

My leg snuck up to his hip without my conscious knowledge, kicking out of my pants. My hands fell around his neck he pulled my other leg up, balancing me against the wall with shocking gentleness. Pressing my heels into his back, I forced him closer to my naked depths.

The hard wall disappeared as Logan flipped me. I landed on all fours on the bed, one massive hand landing on my back as his other hand unfastened his pants.

Pressing just the tip against my wet entrance, he paused for a moment, driving me insane with the waiting. I pushed back, working his large erection inside of me. His hands locked onto my hips, his fingertips pressing painfully into my sides. Back and forth, my slick body coated him, allowing him easier passage into me. My back arched when his control finally broke and he slammed into me, his balls bouncing against my ass.

Crying out, I braced against the bedframe under Logan's animal aggression, before he pushed me back to my forearms. My overheated body clenched onto him, sweat beading down my forehead. Logan bent his body over mine. "Kiss me," he demanded.

Turning, I met his greedy lips, sloppy, warm and needing. I pushed back into him, nibbling on his bottom lip.

"You are so beautiful," he whispered, nuzzling my ear. "And you are mine." He growled, moving back to work my heated body, reaching under to pinch my clit. Yelping, I pushed back forcefully against him.

Hissing his pleasure, he repeated the process, picking up the speed. My world narrowed to Logan and what his thick length was building inside of me. Pleasure pushed down on me from every angle as he worked the delicate nub between my legs. Arching beneath his body, I clenched the comforter in my hands, meeting his thrusts and pushing into them.

The pleasure Logan was blissfully bringing to my body threatened to overload my senses and I squeaked his name out. The impossibly fast pace quickened and I slammed my fists against the bed, screaming my release, stars blinding my vision as I felt his equally powerfully release slam into my body.

His weight shifted, pinning me under him, pressing me against the mattress, his white button down shirt pressing against my jacket. My neck throbbed painfully. "Logan," I whispered as he nuzzled my ear, "what happened to my neck?"

Quickly, he pulled out of me and my body missed the contact as he pressed around the wound. Tilting on my side, I looked down at the horror on his face.

"I marked you," he said, meeting my eyes. I read the fear and worry in his own.

Running my fingers absentmindedly though his caramel locks, I asked, "Is that bad?"

"I gave you a mate mark," he clarified, meeting my gaze.

"I thought those were just legends," I answered, terror stealing my earlier warmth.

"They are very real and I have just bound us together," he answered, stroking my side, the room beginning to influence him again.

"We need to get out of this room, Logan," I told him forcefully, unable to actually move.

He shrugged, pulling his tie open. "I'm having a hard time finding a reason to."

Pulling my pants on, I started for the door. Remembering Logan's state of undress, I stood him up and zipped his pants.

He stroked my face absentmindedly as I led him out into the hallway. The pain in my neck increased and I watched the disbelief seep into his eyes. "What have we done?"

I took a step toward him only to have him step back.

"There you are!" Gretchen cried out.

Shit.

I smiled, turning around, pulling my shirt over the bite mark on my shoulder.

"Let me finish the tour!"

Logan gave me a searching look and I glared back at him. This conversation would have to be tabled.

Gretchen flicked a gaze at each of us before she chanced a glance at the room.

"Oh, my."

"Your rooms are excellent." I turned the wattage up full blast on my smile. "I certainly hope you don't mind that Logan and I gave it a trial."

"No, no, not at all!"

"How does your cleaning staff manage?" Logan asked, tightening his tie.

The question caught Gretchen off guard. "We use enchanted talismans they have to have on their person at all times."

I gave Logan a pointed look, which he ignored.

...

"You've done an excellent job, Gretchen. Please keep me posted on when you can get away to look at properties in St Ann."

She beamed, her smile threatening to crack her face.

I smiled back, knowing it didn't reach my eyes.

Slipping into the SUV, I waited a moment before diving right into the heart of the issue.

"Are we going to talk about it?" I asked softly, staring ahead. The throbbing in my neck was starting to wear on me. I reached up, flipping down the visor to inspect the wound in the mirror.

"Does it hurt?" he asked, just as quietly.

"Yes, it throbs."

He nodded. "Do you feel any different?" he asked, casting a fleeting glance my way.

"No, should I?"

He shook his head. "Honestly, I don't know. This isn't a custom done much anymore."

"Why?" I asked, turning to look at him, trying really hard not to have flashbacks to the mind-blowing sex.

"It's forever. If either of us were killed the other could never find another partner. In most cases the surviving partner doesn't last more than a year."

"Why? What killed them, the mark?"

"No," Logan said, stopping at a red light and looking at me, "a broken heart."

I gave him a disbelieving look. "Do you feel differently about me? I know we had the conversation of liking each other..."

I let the question trail off. He gave me a smug grin. "You admit to liking me?"

I huffed, "After that mind-blowing example of your bedroom skills, I really like you."

Logan laughed, moving ahead with traffic, and I loved the sound of it. I shook my head, where had that come from?

"Mind blowing?" Logan repeated, smug.

"Don't let it go to your head. That room was magically enhanced, which may have been the only reason I used that term."

Logan turned a serious gaze to me. "I'm happy to pull this car over for a demonstration without magical enhancements."

"Pay attention to the road, Logan." I was pretending very hard that his offer hadn't sent warmth to where he had just been.

"Maybe the bite won't affect you? Other shifter bites haven't before?" Logan debated out loud.

I nodded, turning to stare out the windshield, numb and uncertain.

"Maybe," I agreed. Fuck, hopefully? If a mate bond was as forever as Logan was making it sound, I was fucking terrified.

...

"So you aren't feeling any different?" Logan asked for the fifth time.

I slammed the SUV door. "Annoyed, I feel annoyed."

He wanted to say something else, I could see it etched into the lines of his face. Whatever it was, he wasn't sharing. He continued to keep his thoughts to himself.

"Let me walk you to your room." Logan positioned himself in front of me on the elevator to hit our floor.

I turned, looking at him as the elevator dinged and the doors closed. "Are you feeling different?" I asked, crossing my arms and leaning against the elevator wall.

He shrugged, taking out his phone and playing with it, not looking at me.

The elevator announced our arrival to our floor and Logan ushered me out with a hand on the small of my back. He stayed close and in my personal bubble until I pressed my fingerprint to the room door.

I opened the door, looking at him. "Do you want to come in?"

Shit, why had I asked that?

He instantly moved closer and I tilted my head up at him, thinking very seriously about a repeat performance, when Mark yelled for Logan.

I groaned, of course they would be keeping an eye out for him walking the hallway alone.

He shook his head and I nodded, closing the door softly behind me.

I went to my room with no interaction with my roommates. Maybe that was the problem with Grams, we were just shoved too closely together. I sighed. That still didn't excuse her betrayal, as much as I wanted to. I didn't want things to crumble between us, but I wasn't blind.

Stripping out of my clothing, I shut my phone on silent and headed to the shower.

I doubted Logan would call. Shit, why would he? I really wanted him to. That desire didn't feel like my own, didn't settle right inside of me. Absently,

I rubbed my breastbone. Maybe this thing just had to run its course. I'd really like to weather the side effects in bed or on any flat surface with Logan's tanned body.

Fucking hell that sex was good. I shook my head, willing myself to pay attention to showering.

The hot water glided over my skin, easing the pain his bite had inflicted on me. How did I not know mate marks were real? I supposed I'd have to shove it in the same category with the witches gaining power by stealing it from other witches. Secrets of the clans.

Heat seared from the bite on my neck, dropping me to my knees. I gasped as my sight was taken from me, my own panting breath dulled from my ears.

Voices whispered to me. Thoughts, feelings that weren't my own bombarded my senses. The hard surface of the tub disappeared and I felt like I was falling, plummeting through golden cords, following the connections as I touched each one with my essence. I received shock and disbelief through the bonds as I traveled faster and faster. Faces blurred together, emotions ripping into me, anger beginning to greet me, followed by hatred and finally envy. I tried braiding the emotions down, but they weren't my own and I couldn't control them.

The falling sensation stopped, but I was still trapped in the intricate web of golden veins. I did what I do best, I threw my guards up, blocking my emotions. Well, I thought it would work that way. Thoughts still pinged around me and I caught the briefest flash before they disappeared. It seemed we were all waiting for something.

I huffed, this had to be from Logan. This was the shifter magic that had allowed Darren and Logan to find Mark when the insane witch Destiny had kidnapped us.

The question was, how the hell did I get out?

I focused on Logan, trusting my instincts to guide me. He blossomed in my sight, blinding me from his powerful radiant glow. I felt his confusion as I merged our essences together.

What the hell, Logan? I screamed at him.

We are not having this conversation here. His voice was level. I threw guards up around us both.

Better? We are going to have to do this here, because I can't get back to my BODY!

I – how did you do that?

Logan, focus! I could be drowning and not know it!

You are in danger? I felt his protectiveness and heard his lion's chant of 'mine.'

I don't know, I was in the shower when this happened.

I'm coming.

That was so not helpful. I bounded around trying not to experiment with the veins surrounding me, these were people's feelings and lives. I honestly had no right to be here.

Finally, warm hands cupped my cheeks and I sucked in a fresh breath, my back arching off the bed. My eyes opened to Logan, slightly bloodied, in front of me.

"What happened?" I asked, instantly regretting opening my eyes. I closed them again, feeling my heart pound painfully loudly in my ears. With a groan I swallowed down the bile creeping up my throat.

"What have you done?" Garrick asked softly.

"Garrick, what the hell are you doing in my room?" I asked, rolling onto my side, wrapping the blankets tighter around my freezing body.

"Logan was attacked on his way to see you. He yelled for me to open your door, that you were in danger."

I grunted.

"You were passed out under freezing water," Garrick informed me. Logan was holding me close, stroking the side of my face.

I didn't even have the strength to grunt.

"I didn't realize you had decided to mate the Alpha of the United States," his voice was deceptively quiet.

"What does it matter, Garrick—and did you know about mate bonds?" I squinted at him.

"Yes, I did. It matters, Olivia. Not only have you demonstrated the ability to use magic against the Fae, now you have a controlling interest in the Shifters and The Council. You are amassing quite a powerbase."

I sat up, pushing Logan down so I could look at Garrick through squinted eyes. "Garrick, I wasn't given a choice. We were touring the new Lovely Lust establishment and—things just happened. I in no way, shape or form am trying to grow my power."

Garrick nodded, watching Logan and me closely. Something flickered into his gaze, but I couldn't catch it between the heat of Logan's hands and the fact I was naked with him in bed.

The asshole had the nerve to laugh. "My dear girl, you are in quite the pickle."

I threw a pillow at him. "This is not funny! I have no idea what the fuck is happening!"

Garrick continued to laugh, shaking his head. "Oh Olivia, my darling girl." He took a step forward but Logan's deep growl stopped his movement.

"Yes, I suppose you are off limits now, unless I want to fight your mate to the death for you."

It was my turn to growl. I squawked when I realized what I had done, covering my mouth. It only fueled Garrick's laughter.

"Well then, I suppose I shall leave you to..." He waggled his eyebrows before heading out.

I heaved a monumental sigh, falling back into bed, hearing the door close behind Garrick.

"What the ever loving FUCK, Logan?" I screamed at him through the pillow I had buried my face in, it muffled the effect.

I could feel Logan's uncertainty about how to approach the situation, his raw need to bed me again flaring alive in my bed with my scent heavy on the air. Damn if my body didn't warm to that thought.

"Argh!" I flung myself out of the bed. "You are not getting in my pants until you explain this shit!"

He smiled. "So, I get in your pants after I explain?" His eyes roved over my naked body.

"Dammit," I hissed, roughly pulling on clothing.

"Better?" I yelled at him, freaked the hell out, my arms crossed over my midsection.

"Olie," he tried to begin.

"Don't you fucking Olie me!" I was freaking out. "I need something to kill." I groaned, raking my hands through my hair.

"Olivia." Logan put force behind my name.

"Logan," I countered, looking at him.

He was smiling. The fucking fool was smiling. I tried hard not to return the smile.

He stood up, closing the distance between us. I head butted his chest. "Logan," I whispered, "what is going on?"

"We are mated, Olivia, bound together through pack magic. You are part of the packs now." His voice was soft and I wrapped my arms around his waist, needing comfort.

"That's what all the golden threads are, pack members?"

"They look like golden threads?" he asked.

I nodded. "What do they look like to you?"

"I feel them, Olie. I've never seen them before."

I grunted, feeling his contentment at this situation.

I felt guilty asking, given how he had confessed that he actually liked me, a lot, "Is this reversible?"

His muscles tightened, rage and anger flooding my brain. I hobbled back, clutching my head before stumbling against the nightstand. I sagged down, focusing on breathing.

"You want it reversed?" Logan hissed.

I checked my internal blocks, finding they had slipped down. Forcing them back up, I imagined solid thick metal protecting me. The throbbing in my head eased and I dropped my hands.

I was pissed. "How fucking dare you be mad at me? I didn't bind our futures together without even asking!" I pushed myself off the floor and into his face.

Guilt and shame hit my shields before he managed to pull back.

"Drop your guards." His voice was low with the command.

"Make me," I hissed back, still too pissed to be rational.

Logan kissed me and all the tension dissipated from my body. I was hungry for him. I needed him. He was mine.

Raw, base instincts had me writhing against him. I was so preoccupied with his hands kneading my ass that I missed the probing of his mind against mine.

Logan broke the kiss, panting heavily. I whined, pulling him back down for more.

"Olie, we need to talk about this," he whispered, not fighting my pull.

"After," I whispered against his lips.

Logan's weight pressed me into the bed.

"You owe me," I whispered, letting his lips work along my jaw line.

He grunted a noncommittal response, his warm fingers pulling up my shirt. I tipped my head and shoulders up, discarding the garment. Logan's stubble tickled against my stomach as I tilted my hips up so he could remove the rest of my clothing.

My lids were heavy with desire. I reached up, slowly releasing the buttons on his shirt. His chest heaved and the muscles of his arms tensed from my slow movements.

I smiled; he deserved every ounce of torture I was about to lay onto him.

Pressing my hands against the coiled muscles of his stomach, I ran the pads of my fingers up to his shoulders and under the shirt, forcing the garment off.

"What are you feeling so smug about?"

"You're going to beg me, Logan." My words radiated confidence, right next to his ear. His startled look was quickly replaced by a disbelieving one.

"Bring it, little girl," he whispered close to my lips.

I tilted my head, taking the corner of his bottom lip between my teeth and biting down hard, his body jerking before I sucked the sting away.

He panted, "You'll have to do better than that."

"Oh sweetie, I'm just getting started," I whispered into his ear, with a whisper of a kiss floating over the lobe. He groaned, pressing the bulge between his legs into my soft flesh.

"No powers," he groaned.

My hands roved down his back, toying with the belt at his waist.

"I don't need them," I breathed against his skin, enjoying his muscles clenching under my soft assault.

"But you if you want me to use them," I said, dipping my fingers into his waistband, "just ask."

He groaned, grinding his length against me. I searched for the band of his underwear and found myself coming up with only more warm skin. Shit, that was hot.

As I worked my fingers to the clasp of his belt, he lifted his hips while his lips continued to trail a path of fire along my neck, dipping down to my breasts.

"Two can play this game," he whispered against my nipple.

I laughed, a sultry sound.

"You can try, love, you can try."

I leisurely pulled the tail of his belt through the clasp, taking my time, being sure my knuckles brushed his tense stomach muscles. Bringing my hands together, I carefully undid the button before sliding the zipper down his engorged length.

A long groan sounded from Logan's throat, his eyes closing.

I smiled, careful not to touch what I wanted to. I slid the fabric over his glorious butt and down his thighs. Logan's body shuttered and he kicked off his pants vigorously.

I gave a low, throaty chuckle. "Just say 'please,' Logan, and all this stops."

He growled, turning his gaze back on me, his caramel eyes darkening with flecks of espresso as his lion roused.

"Here, Kitty, Kitty," I taunted him, my lips closing over his shoulder blade. I let Logan keep his position. I didn't need to be on top to make him plead for his pleasure. Besides, the shaking in his arms was a perfect gauge for me.

I snaked a leg up his, trailing my toes lightly over his calf before moving up, rubbing the inside of my thigh against his hip.

"Olie," he whispered, finding my lips again. I let him kiss me deeply, feeling his desire and need through our bond and our bodies.

"Say it, Logan," I taunted him, lifting my hips to align with the searing heat between his legs.

"You win," he said, smiling against my lips, shoving his hips forward.

I tilted back down, his attempt at piercing me leaving a fiery path against my stomach.

"Uh-uh, you know what I want to hear." Needed to hear. I needed to know I had retained some part of myself in this "bonding."

"Please let me make love to you, Olivia," Logan whispered, drawing back and cupping my face with his large palm. His eyes were earnest, his beast clawing to be let lose.

"I'd love that," I whispered. Somewhere in the back of my mind, my defunct emotions screamed I wasn't ready, couldn't cope and wouldn't be able to care for him as he was on his way to caring for me. I pushed them away. I could handle our bodies at this moment and that was it.

His hips pulled back again, but instead of the throbbing member, his fingers slid inside of me.

"Fuck," he groaned, testing my readiness. "You are so goddamn wet," he whispered, pulling his fingers from me as I whimpered. He brought the digits to his lips, his tongue taking the glistening liquid into his mouth.

"That was hot."

He chuckled, nuzzling my neck, "I'm glad you think so." I tilted my head, wanting his lips back, wanting to taste myself on him. He obliged me, the tip of himself pressed to my wet entrance. I shifted my hips. Lifting my legs to lock around his waist, I pushed against his mounded ass.

He smiled against my lips, ramming into me.

I squealed, part pleasure part pain. Panting, Logan drew back before pushing into me again.

I clutched to him, feeling him filling my body. It felt right on several levels I didn't know I had inside of me.

"Mine," I whispered as I felt his impossibly hardened length grow firmer.

"Forever," Logan whispered, setting off warning bells. His next thrust drowned them out.

"Harder," I demanded, my hands needing to feel all of him, every inch of flesh I needed to memorize.

He pulled back, watching me closely, his beast riding him hard. He was struggling to keep it at bay.

"All of you Logan, I want all of you."

Relief danced across his features, his hips shifting slightly before the next thrust.

I yelped, not prepared for the assault of pleasure. His grin was feral with teeth and I bucked my hips against him, demanding more. He readily supplied what I was craving. There was no doubt I'd be sporting bruises tomorrow.

I just didn't give a shit.

Logan moved within me as though he had done this thousands of times before. He read my slightest sigh of pleasure, knew when to shift positions. He drove me to lengths I'd never experienced.

And that is saying a LOT!

My back arched off the bed as Logan drove forcefully into me, pleasure built to impossible heights. Winding around his thick cock, I clenched my thighs and cried out as pleasure swamped me. I didn't hear his own release, so wrapped up was I in the layers of pleasure wrapping around my own body.

Logan pulled my muscleless head to face him. I stretched under him contentedly.

"I love you, Olivia," he whispered, before kissing away my protest.

...

After a second and equally mind-blowing bedroom romp, I was lying nestled on Logan's shoulder.

His breathing was even, but he was waiting for me.

"How do you control all the voices?" I asked, still safely tucked away in my metal ball.

"You hear voices?" he asked softly, and in any other situation, I'd think he was teasing.

Instead I nodded, shifting so I could look at him. "Yes, you don't?"

He shook his head, shifting the arm it was resting on. "Emotions are what I can feel."

I nodded. "Am I hearing thoughts or speech?"

He shrugged, not worried about either. "We can use Mark and Alec to test it out tomorrow if you want."

I nodded, worrying my bottom lip. "We will figure it out," Logan reassured me, his hand slipping under the sheet to land on my ass.

I didn't have a choice. We were bound together, and I needed to make the best of it or I'd drive myself insane.

"How are we going to handle the packs and my Council?"

"I don't know, Olie, and I'm almost insulted that you can think after all the sex."

I laughed, looking over to his closed-eyed, peaceful expression. My mood instantly fell. "I don't sleep well, Logan."

He cracked an eye to watch me. "Do I have to sleep badly with you?"

I shook my head.

"Do what you need to, Olie. I'm not going anywhere."

I tried to hide the freakout building inside of me at the sincerity of those words. Unlike Blake, Logan had seen me at my worst, had witnessed firsthand the drunken train wreck I was after Blake, and he was still here. I think that freaked me out the most.

Chapter 7

Logan slept peacefully and deeply. I stared at him for a while before I decided to order room service.

Not wanting to wake him, I slipped from the bed, throwing on my discarded clothing before heading into the main room. I found the forest green binder on the end table by my door. Heading into the living area, I stopped in my tracks at the sleeping forms piled onto the couches.

"What the hell?" I whispered.

No one stirred, except Jerry. He roused from his uncomfortable position to glare at me.

"Explain to me first why you didn't do the dirty in Logan's room, and second, why the hell Mark knew before me?"

Mark stirred, trying to pull Jerry into a more comfortable position. Jerry shoved his face, standing and pulling down his rumpled gray nightshirt.

"What the fuck are you all doing here?" I screeched in a whisper.

He narrowed his eyes at me and I could feel my heart rate accelerating as more voices pinged in my head. I shook my head, my breathing labored.

"Olie!" Jerry yelled at full force.

The entire room exploded into movement, shifters standing on coffee tables, fangs and claws at the ready. From behind me, Logan burst out of my room in all his naked glory, stalking toward me.

"What's wrong?" he asked, pulling me against him as I clutched my head.

I nuzzled into his chest, breathing in his scent to calm my erratic heart rate.

"Everyone calm down. Olie is far more sensitive to our bonds then we are," Logan commanded.

Jerry scoffed, "Or she's freaking out being forced and borderline raped to become your mate."

I inhaled quickly, turning to look at Jerry. I lost my footing but Logan steadied me, his low growl warning in the background.

"That's what you think happened?" I asked, shocked.

Jerry's mouth settled into a grim line and he nodded, his eyes flicking back to Logan. "I know how he felt about you, Olie. Mark himself said you'd be a perfect mate. It's all a little coincidental."

"Please don't let him be right," Mark said. I turned my face to him.

"We need her. Logan would never force himself. Damn witch's establishment," Hudson growled. I shifted quickly to look at him.

"The packs have never felt more complete," Alec whispered, and I turned to look at him. No one's mouth was moving.

"Oh shit. I can hear your thoughts," I announced to the room.

Awkward glances were exchanged.

I turned back to Logan. I wanted to ask him to be certain there was no hidden deceit in him, but my instincts warned me not to in front of his pack. Our pack? Fuck.

I need her, Logan thought. I checked, finding my guards firmly between us again. I let them down and was rewarded by his smile.

Was any of this intentional? I thought to him, curious to see how this bond worked.

His eyes widened at hearing me in his head. No, Olie, I would never force you into this. But I want it now that it's here.

I nodded, turning to Jerry. "This wasn't prearranged, nor was it rape. I know the latter well. I'll allow it's weird and suffocating when I'm not feeling all mushy." I rubbed my forehead, feeling a headache coming on.

I sighed, holding up the food menu. "I'm hungry. Let's move this party back to your rooms and we can order food and figure this out."

"We're packing your things," Jerry stated.

I turned. "Why the fuck do my things need to be packed?"

"Because I'm not going to be spending another night on the sofa," Jerry groaned.

I rubbed my forehead again, the vise-like pressure building.

"We will spend the night wherever Olivia needs us," Hudson growled.

My vision was getting annoyingly spotty. "Jerry, load up what I need for tonight. Hudson, stay out of my underwear. Logan, you are going to have to carry me, things are getting blurry."

"Up, Princess," he murmured. I huffed, uncertain if I liked the endearment or not.

"Why does my head hurt?" I moaned.

"Let's get some food in you and we can figure it out," Logan whispered as I wrapped my legs around his waist, resting my heavy head against his shoulder.

My head throbbed in time with Logan's steps.

"Don't forget my weapons!" I growled.

God this was pathetic. I was being carried during the Conferences.

Logan settled me down onto his sofa. I sat heavily, feeling my stomach making an appearance at the party.

"What do you want to eat?" Mark asked me, the phone already to his ear.

"Mac and cheese, grilled cheese, cake—lots of cake, and cookies. Actually, just order the entire dessert menu," I grumbled.

Logan sat next to me, drawing me down.

"Relax, Olie, the blocks must be wearing you down. Can you try lowering them?"

I groaned, sitting back up. "Yeah, there is no way I could kick someone's ass like this."

Logan laughed, "Is fighting all you think about?"

I smiled, leaning forward for a kiss. "Nope."

Logan smiled against my lips. "Point taken."

That mushy moment was brought to you by a powerful fucking mate mark.

I shifted, turning toward him and pulling my legs up, resting my back against the sofa arm. Taking a deep breath, I dropped the blocks. Silence met me, and I smiled at Logan.

Right before I passed out I thought, no one better touch my grilled cheese.

...

"No one better touch my grilled cheese!" I slurred, coming back around.

"Fucking hell, Olivia, do not do that again," Hudson growled.

I sat up, blinking as my sight came back and heaving massive sigh. "How long was I out?"

"Not long. I think your natural block came back online," Jerry observed.

I nodded as a plate was settled into my lap.

"We can feel you, Olie, but can't access you," Mark supplied.

I took several bites, thinking.

"I need to merge the two shields." I looked up at Logan. "That's the only way I won't expend so much energy to manage both of them."

Letting my sight go out of focus, I focused on my shields. My succubus shield wrapped around me, protecting others from my emotions. At least that's how I'd always thought about it. Letting that one fall, I focused on the packs. Golden threads surrounded me, voices echoing everywhere.

Tilting my internal head, I asked, "Why doesn't Kass have a mate mark?"

"Darren was worried about hurting the baby," Logan answered.

I suppose that made sense. I couldn't wait to tell her what was in store for her.

Carefully, I constructed my shield again, wrapping my emotions inside of it along with my own essence, keeping it apart from the packs. Logan's mate bond was the thickest rope I saw and I was unable to block it entirely.

"I'd prefer you didn't block it at all," he murmured.

I nodded, carving out a hole in my shields for him.

I cracked an eye open wearily. "So, how does that feel?"

"Better," Hudson and Mark agreed.

"Wonderful. Hand me my dessert."

...

I woke up in a pile of limbs to an annoying tingling of bells.

"Who the ever loving fuck set an alarm?" I groaned, pushing off a leg from my midsection.

"Make it stop," I groaned, pushing up to all fours, lying across Logan's broad and very sexy bare back to paw at the nightstand. I managed to find the phone and knock it off to the floor.

I rested my head against Logan's warm back. "I don't wanna get up."

"What time is it?" Logan asked, rolling and shifting me onto the ground.

"Mother fucking shit!" I yelled, standing up and stomping my feet. "Get up!" I screamed. "Everyone up. If I am awake, the rest of your alarm-setting asses are also!"

"Eight a.m.," Jerry informed me, fully dressed in the doorway.

"You set the alarm?" I growled, stalking toward him.

"Coffee?" he asked.

I lunged for him, taking him down around the waist.

"HOT!" I screamed, rolling over on the carpet to rub the burn away.

Everyone started rising and walking over to me.

Jerry looked down at me. "Go get dressed," he commanded.

I swatted at his legs before Logan picked me up.

"Shower," he groaned, nestling his lips against my neck. I kicked my feet at being carried like a baby, my mind not properly functioning to blare my usual warning.

I tilted my head, checking my guards and finding them holding. Maybe things would be okay.

...

Showered and dressed in jeans, a Star Wars t-shirt (Tommy's gift to me), and my leather jacket, I sat in the back of the limo talking to Tommy.

"That shirt is HOT Olivia! Everyone is going to adore it," Tommy preened.

I laughed, "Tommy, I haven't seen Star Wars."

"Shh! Do not tell anyone that!" he scolded me.

"Alright kid, give me your wish list."

"Oh Olie, the tech conference is so beautiful. How did I not get an invite?"

I laughed and Logan's hand tightened around my arm as he peered inside my mind. I saw his contentment but he saw my concern.

I pushed both feelings away, focusing on Tommy's list instead. "Alright Olie, look at table four for the new..." Tommy droned on and I checked out, not hearing his extensive list. He was throwing around words I couldn't spell.

"Tommy, you are going to need to text me that, I didn't understand anything."

Tommy sighed, "Logan?"

"Yeah Tommy, I got it," Logan stated, patting my leg.

I looked over at him. "You're a techie?" I asked.

He smiled and nodded.

"Interesting," I noted.

Alec handed me a bottle of water. "Vodka?" I asked hopefully.

He shook his head, opening the door. The swarm of people outside overwhelmed me, hitting my shields full force. I opened the bottle of water, taking a swig, my fingers clenching around the plastic.

I took a deep breath. "I'll call you if I have questions, Tommy."

"Don't forget the—" I handed Logan the phone.

Fuck, was I too dependent on him already? Ugh. I am no good at this shit! I shook my head, peering out the open door as I listened to Logan and Tommy talking. I liked that he played video games with Tommy and I liked that he spoke the same language.

94

I rested my head against the seat, watching the people outside laughing and talking. If I unfocused my sight, I could see who were the shifters and sense their intents. As I dropped my guards further, voices whispered at me.

Interest and curiosity met my hesitant brush. I called on my succubus power, seeping confidence and contentment. Easy relaxation met my touches.

Logan's warm hand wrapped around my forearm. I wasn't looking too closely at how I knew it was him.

"Open your eyes, Olie," he whispered into my ear.

I blinked, bringing the sight before me into focus.

"Oh, oops," I muttered. The shifters at the tech conference had stilled, drawn towards me and my prying.

I pushed out of the limo to the curious stares. "You are the Mate we have been feeling?" a tall man asked me.

Logan's hand came to rest on my shoulder. "Yes," I said softly, suddenly nervous.

Heads nodded and I fortified my shields around me, uncertain how to proceed.

"Your touch is calming," a woman in a pink shirt said.

"Nice shirt!" someone in the back yelled.

I smiled.

"Let's us all get in before all the good tech is taken." Nods met Logan's command.

A few stares met mine, stony and determined. I would be facing more challenges. I wish being mated came with a few added benefits, like you know, claws or fangs.

Nope, now I heard voices. Wonderful.

"You got Tommy's list?" I asked as we moved through the crowd inside.

"Yes, he's texted and emailed it to me." I could hear Logan's smile.

Everything was sunshine and puppy dogs. This shit couldn't last long.

...

Checked in with my tote bag for purchases secured, we waited for Grams, Mercer, Ali and Grant.

I twirled the badge around my neck, my irritation with Grams riding me hard.

She stepped into the scene, surrounded by fierce looking shifters.

"Wow. Is that your doing?" I asked, looking at Logan.

He nodded. I pursed my lips, not exactly sure I liked the fact that Logan viewed my security as not enough.

Ali saw us and relayed our position to the group. They moved through the crowd, parting the seas of people like a freight train. I was so jealous.

Pushing off the wall I was leaning against, I crossed my arms, watching Grams closely. She didn't meet my gaze.

"Did Tommy send the list to you as well? Are we really buying all this stuff?" Grant asked, looking at his phone. "What is this R5 tracking device?"

"Humor him and buy a few items," Grams pronounced, dismissing the rest of Tommy's list as my hackles rose. "We are primarily here to attend the seminar on the detrimental effects of technology on the social setting."

"Gah, well, take notes for me. Also, don't worry about Tommy's list, I got it. Have fun and stay safe; I'm certain to be challenged. Hopefully not around anything expensive."

I smiled and Grams bristled.

"Hey Olie, can we come with you?" Ali asked.

I smiled, "I'd love that."

The Compass Alphas came to join the party, and we were a big fucking party. We pushed into the first rows of electronic contraptions. I moved slowly, my eyes roving over the tables and the people around me.

I felt fairly safe, realizing I had forgotten the humans also came to this event, being that it did dominate the entire Convention Center. I saw them ogling the different contraptions. I probably should have paid closer attention the guide map; maybe there was a Supernaturals only section.

"How are you feeling?" Sage asked me, picking up night vision goggles. No way she would actually need those.

I shrugged, looking at a concealed carry purse for sale. "Fine, it's an adjustment."

She nodded, careful not to keep my gaze long. "It must be a big adjustment."

"Yeah." I was careful not to mention that I could now hear thoughts. If I wanted to.

"How's Logan handling it?" she asked me, leaning closer, trying to force a sense of intimacy between us.

My guards were up and I didn't like her questions. So I met them with a winning, full teeth smile. "Wonderful, he couldn't—I mean we couldn't be happier."

She took the hint and shut up, giving me the cold shoulder.

A ping hit my shields and I looked up to see Logan watching me closely. Shit, I checked my internal guards and found I was locking him out as well.

I rolled my eyes and adjusted the feed of our bond.

"Happy?" I asked him, coming to stand next to him at the booth.

"Overjoyed," he deadpanned. "What do you think of these tracking devices?"

I looked at the table before looking up at Logan. "That's the tracker?" I asked, impressed, looking at the salesman behind the counter.

"Yep, it's our smallest and thinnest model yet," he beamed.

"What's the radius? How reliable?" I peppered him with questions.

He smiled. "We have a 98% tracking rate and have yet to have a unit go down."

"How long does it work?" Logan asked.

The tech paused. "Only for a half hour."

I sighed. "It's so pretty, but so fleeting," I lamented before moving on.

Logan stayed by my side as we moved farther down the rows.

We managed to sort through the first two rows, collecting an impressive stash.

"Tommy is going to freak over those ear buds," I told Logan, excited.

"Do you think I should find something for Lorraine?" Logan asked me while looking at a laptop bag.

I shrugged. "It would be a nice gesture, and considering you may have to tell her about us, it wouldn't be a bad idea."

His eyes shot to mine, like he hadn't even considered he'd have to tell Lorraine, and he might not have. It wasn't like we were soliciting her advice or needed her to like us. She was a pregnant pain the ass.

I squirmed under his gaze, moving on to look at a tablet with impressive capabilities.

We made our way to the far wall with an imposing-looking doorman.

"So this is where they keep the good stuff," I smiled. A girl could never have too many weapons.

Logan smiled. "So, you weren't paying attention when we checked in?"

"Nope." I wanted to add a smartass reply, but as a Mate and an Alpha's partner—real partner, no longer temporary—I had to keep my mouth shut in public. I doubted I'd be able to keep up that pretense for long.

The guard scanned our wristbands before nodding his bald Asian head and letting us pass. The double doors parted and I was greeted by the smell of oil and wood. I twirled, taking in the glittering silver and the empty pop of guns being tested.

Logan looked at me with a smirk. "We're going to need a bigger bag."

...

Six hours, an impressive stash of new toys, and one terrible lunch later we were loading up all our goodies into the limo.

"I can't believe you purchased a cross bow," Sage commented.

"It's actually really practical, and the draw back on that beauty was so smooth. Not to mention the duel firing action."

She looked at me with a raised brow. I went on, "You ever try taking down any Indian demigod? You have to hit the heart with blessed rosewood. Such a pain."

"So, think you will gain some of Logan's immortality?" she asked, closing the trunk.

I shrugged. "Whose to say I'm not already immortal?"

She looked at me, interested. "Are you? Have you experienced anything to indicate you are?"

"Yeah. I'm still alive," I answered evasively.

She laughed, trying really hard with me. "You are so funny!" Turning to the Compass beta, she signaled she was ready. "See you later!" she called chipperly.

"Later," I grunted. I had quite a few questions for Logan regarding her.

I turned from her, ready to call Tommy and relay the success of my purchases.

Apparently, both items on my to do list would have to wait. I exhaled and walked to Logan's side as he faced off against a small nest of vampires.

Logan snarled as I approached.

"Hey, darling. You guys interested in dying today?" I asked, cracking my neck.

Mark, Jerry, Logan, Hudson, Ali and Grant were all primed for action. While the vamps outnumbered us two to one, I had no doubt we'd hold our own.

I stood next to Logan, opening my jacket to showcase my very pretty guns. The vampires were wired, tense and coiled for action. I was about to ask what the holdup was when the lights went out.

"Wonderful," I groaned. The shifters and vampires would have perfect sight. I was affected by the lack of light, and Ali and Grant might be as well.

"Protect the Mate," Alec growled.

"Protect Ali and Grant, too!" I added hopefully. They were shoved into me.

A cell phone flashed on.

"Turn it off!" Logan bellowed.

Ali shut it off quickly. "This sucks," she grumbled.

"Agreed, I'd love to kick some vampire ass," I lamented.

Claws dug into my shoulders and with a grunt I was airborne. Not being able to see the ground rushing at me was disorienting at best.

"Olie!" Grant yelled.

I hit on my hip, letting out a yelp of pain as the cold concrete tried to crack my bones.

I rolled to my knees, deciding to stay low instead of being mobile.

"Light, Ali!" I cried out. It ended in an oomph as I took a hit to my chin.

My head snapped back, pain lacing through my jaw. I flew, landing flat on my back, my skull bouncing on the concrete.

"Ow," I groaned, sucking down air and rolling to my non-injured hip.

Light trickled to my left and I rolled the opposite way quickly, avoiding a boot aimed for my head.

"Get back here, whore," hissed the vampire. Pulling my legs under me, I drew my guns. In one fluid motion, I stood and put two bullets into each heart.

"Asshole," I groaned. "Who kicked me?!" I demanded, turning, my guns still outstretched.

A mouth at my ear whispered, "I did," before clamping down on my neck. I'll admit I screamed. I dropped my guns, my hands scrambling for the dagger at the small of my back. The asshole wrenched my arm behind me.

I stopped my attempt to pull myself off of his fangs, reversing my momentum into him. Caught off guard, he stumbled a step back, the grip on my arm loosening.

My arm freed, I pulled my blade, spinning and driving the recently sharpened point into his chest before drawing it down to cut across both hearts.

He sputtered, fear flashing in his eyes before he turned to dust.

Keeping my center of gravity low, I spun toward the light, seeing the phone on the ground as Ali grabbed a vampire, her hair flying wildly around her. Words left her lips and the bloodsucker collapsed into dust.

I really need to learn that trick.

I surveyed the area, finding only piles of dust to irritate my sinuses. Standing, I watched Logan rip the head off the last vampire, his eyes wild when they landed on me. His breathing was harsh as he stalked to me, his eyes roving over my body, examining my injuries. He cradled my head and I winced, pulling away.

"Disagreement with the concrete," I conceded.

He crushed me to his chest, his breathing slowly evening out. I probed the mate bond, opening the connection. His relief flooded me; his fear at seeing the vampire throw me had almost sent him into pure beast. I smiled, nuzzling closer to him. He loved that there wasn't any doubt of his commitment, but whether it was from the mate mark or from him I wasn't sure.

Chapter 8

Finally loaded into the limo, I settled against Logan before asking, "Alright Ali, you gotta fill me on how that works."

She smiled at me wearily. "It's a pretty light show, but it drains."

"She also has to have the offending party stay still and make eye contact while she is saying the incantation," Grant added.

Ali nodded, her head lolling. I patted her knee. "Good job guys, get some rest."

"Rest?" Hudson asked from my other side. "I'm starving."

I smiled, "Me, too."

"Just drop us off at the hotel, we'll get room service," Grant whispered, stroking Ali's hair.

Logan nodded, relaying the change to the driver.

My head dipped swiftly and I caught myself blinking rapidly.

Logan's fingers reached down to rest against the back of my neck, rubbing small circles.

"Please tell me we are getting pizza," I groaned, checking if my neck had stopped bleeding.

"Just rest. I'll wake you when we get there," he whispered.

...

Logan shook me gently. "Food, Olivia."

"FoodI'mup," I slurred, pushing off his chest to fall off the seat.

"We might need to monitor her for a concussion," Mark said thoughtfully. "I'll check if Jerry has a potion for it."

I nodded, rubbing sleep from my eyes before lumbering out of the limo. We didn't have to wait for a table, and someone had apparently had the good sense to call ahead and order. Appetizers were coming out as we sat down. I snagged a piece of garlic bread, stuffing my face in bliss.

"I don't like Sage," I confessed as I swallowed my bread.

Logan raised his head, giving me a curious look.

Hudson and Alec chuckled. Hudson probed, "Are you certain it doesn't have anything to do with her being female?"

It was my turn to tilt my head. "No, she was just asking lots of questions today."

"And no one is allowed to ask you questions?" Hudson asked.

I narrowed my eyes. "What are you getting at?"

I trusted my instincts, they kept me alive. Too bad they hadn't warned me what would happen with Logan. They thought the worst situation would be sleeping with him, ha. Now I was bound to him forever.

Alec cleared his throat, drawing my intent, domineering gaze away from Hudson. "What Hudson is trying to say is that you probably don't like her because she is an alpha female around Logan."

I tipped my head to the side. "So your rationale is that I don't like her because she's too close to my mate?" I asked, my irritation spiking.

I let it seep out into both of them. They fidgeted uneasily. Fun, I could now influence shifters without touching them.

"Listen and listen fucking well. My survival instincts have kept me alive. I do not like the questions Sage was asking me. If she suddenly grew a pair of useless balls and a dick, I'd have the same motherfucking opinion. You will not dismiss me because you think I'm jealous." I spat the last word, my irritation moving up to full-fledged pissed the fuck off.

"If I wasn't mated to Logan and I said that I didn't trust Sage, would you have treated it differently?" I asked.

The entire table squirmed and I could feel Logan riding our bond hard, wanting to shut me down. Good luck, motherfucker. This bitch wasn't about to be shut up.

Alec and Hudson didn't have an answer. Jerry came to their rescue.

"It is an interesting thought. Since you don't in fact have an animal riding you and influencing you with its own instincts, are you in fact behaving similar to the shifters?" Jerry thought out loud.

Hudson grunted, not meeting my gaze directly as he opened his mouth. "I wonder how you would feel knowing Logan and Sage slept together?"

He looked at me then and rage filled my chest, irrational rage.

"Now that, fucker, makes me jealous. Congrats." I slammed myself way from the table, blocking Logan from my head as well.

I stormed out the back door, leaning heavily against the brick wall, trying to get my emotions in check. As previously discovered, my control had to be perfect, otherwise I risked influencing the other shifters around me. I hadn't tested how far my reach went, however. I shook my head, it didn't matter.

It also didn't matter that Logan and Sage had fucked. I turned, slamming my fist against the brick wall, scraping my knuckles. Then why was it riding me so hard? I had fucked plenty of people. I didn't see Logan getting up in arms.

"That is a sweet smell," a voice in the shadows whispered.

I turned, having a momentary panic when four vampires stepped out.

The front one smiled, his fangs prominently on display.

"Olivia, Head Executioner for The Eastern Supernatural Council and Mate to the Alpha of the US, you are a prize, indeed." He drew out the last word and I thought about using my bond to call for help.

Instead I smiled, flexing my hands at my side.

"You going to stand there all day talking, pretty boy, or we going to throw down?"

He laughed, his shoulder length hair shifting around his high and defined cheekbones. "No, my dear girl, I would not throw away the lives of my clan knowing the odds are not in my favor."

I scowled, "Well that sucks." I crossed my arms over my stomach. "What do you want?"

"A private audience."

I waved my hand around. "Doesn't get more private than this."

He nodded. "I suppose you are correct."

He took a step forward, extending his hand. "My name is Raphael."

I extended my hand with the bloody knuckles, okay so I was testing his control and looking for a reason to dust him. Instead, he turned our hands, kissing away the blood and healing the flesh with his saliva.

"Thanks," I grunted, my anger diffusing.

He nodded, almost giving me a small bow. "We would like to seek an alliance."

I'm pretty sure my face gave away my shock and disbelief. "Why? I'm not currently a favorite of the vampires."

Raphael nodded, searching my face, debating about how much he could trust me, no doubt. Whatever he found there had him looking away, shaking his head.

"The djinn was only the beginning. You are targeted and I believe you will come out the victor. I do not agree with what is happening in the Clans. It has made me and mine vulnerable."

"I can't offer you protection. Clan law overrides my Council when it comes to vampires."

He nodded. "We understand that. It is a delicate line we walk, but know that when the dividing lines are drawn, we are on your side."

It was my turn to search his face. What I saw there worried me. I took a step forward unconsciously.

"You are betting your life on this," I whispered, moving on to search the other grim faces in the alley way.

They all bore the look of those who have accepted their thread ending soon.

"We have made our peace with history repeating itself," Raphael said stoically.

"I don't want your deaths on my conscious."

Fuck, I might have been willing to kill them just moments earlier, but that was before all the cryptic shit.

"What is repeating itself?" I asked.

"For that you would do well to look at my history."

"As in the ninja turtles?" I asked.

He laughed, his face softening. "Thank you, Olivia, it has been some time since I have found humor in anything. No, the archangel."

I nodded, "I'll look into it."

He peered at me and I could tell he wanted to say more, but instead he just smiled.

"Be safe, all of you. Just stay alive." I liked these guys, which seriously, after the last bout of shit with vampires, that was saying something.

"You as well," Raphael whispered.

The back door slamming open had me jumping as Logan jumped down the concrete stairs to stand in front of me.

"What is going on?" he asked, not turning to look at me, instead inhaling the air where the vampires had just been.

"Nothing," I replied, moving to go back into the restaurant. I was still hungry.

Logan spun and caught my forearm. "Do not lie to me," he hissed.

I pulled out of his grasp. "I don't know what's going on, Logan! All I know is that four vampires just pledged themselves to my side. What the fuck is my side? And who am I going against?" My voice hitched up and I clamped down hard on my emotions.

"It was a foolish risk to come out here by yourself and not call for help."

I took a step closer to him. "I have been taking care of myself long before you came into the picture. I am not weak. You would do well to remember that."

"You are angry about Sage," he stated.

I growled, "That is the least of our worries, and no, I haven't figured out how I feel about that."

Our anger rode our conversation hard. I let the mate bond flare into its full glory just so he could feel how fucking annoyed I was at being treated differently.

The back door flung open again. "The food has arrived," Hudson announced, the door closing behind him. "I wanted to apologize, Olivia."

"Never apologize for speaking the truth, Hudson," I told him, moving up the stairs quickly, offering forgiveness to no one, haunted by Raphael's words.

As I sat back down at the table, Jerry leaned closer to me. "Are you okay?"

I picked up my phone, opening the browser as Tommy had taught me. "Fine."

I typed in "Raphael angel" and clicked on the first link, skimming the contents quickly. The angel Raphael was considered a healing source in human legend, defeating demons and protecting the small bands of humans he was traveling with.

I chewed the inside of my lip, thinking. Human history was steeped in encounters with the Supernatural. So let's say that Raphael really was—

Logan hit the mate bond hard.

I sighed. Relenting and opening the connection back up, I quickly summarized our conversation.

You think he is the angel Raphael mentioned in various religious documents? Logan asked me.

I have no reason to doubt him.

What do you think he meant by history repeating itself? Logan questioned.

I rubbed my forehead, a heavy feeling settling on my chest.

Selena used to talk about the days of old when vampires, shifters and everything else treated humans and weaker supes like cattle. That was her goal, to bring about the downfall of humanity and the rise of her leadership as Queen, with her perfect and powerful soldiers. Sadness laced my words and Logan took my hand.

You were her solider?

Yes. My answer was clipped, even in my mind.

Shaking my head, I continued, I know it's a jump but let's call Raphael a protector of humans. If history is repeating itself, then he would resume that title.

Logan leaned back, crossing his arms over his massive chest, straining the fabric of his sleeves. God that was hot.

He smiled; apparently that thought had made it through as well. I smiled back, my irritation and anger receding.

I'd like that not to be true, or perhaps him to be overdramatic. I nodded and he squeezed my hand. But I trust your instincts and if you find him genuine and believable, then I do as well.

Thank you. It felt good to be respected and validated.

"Anyone else think we are missing something?" Mark asked around a piece of pizza.

"Who ate all my cheese pizza?!" I demanded.

They all gave me sly smiles.

...

Lugging all our packages, we headed up to our rooms. The elevator was crowded and my feet hurt.

"Is there anything else for tonight?" I asked, dragging myself down the hallway to Logan's room.

"No, the tech conference was scheduled for the entire day," Jerry answered.

"Wonderful. I need to check on Ali," I groaned.

"I've been texting with Grant. She's sleeping peacefully," Mark informed me.

I grunted, my hip twinging and my feet dragging.

Logan opened the door to his room and I dropped my bags, face planting into the soft pillows.

...

I woke up after only a few hours of rest, rolling onto my back, careful not to displace Logan. He was snoring, lying on his back. Scooting into a sitting position, I checked my phone, finding it was far too early to expect Logan or anyone else to be up.

I rubbed my eyes, wishing I could sleep more. I looked over at Logan, debating waking him up. Was this what every night was going to be? How was he going to handle it when I was gone for weeks at a time? Shit, how was I going to handle it? My chest tightened at the thought of being separated from him.

I exhaled loudly. This shit complicated everything.

I toyed with my phone, deciding I wasn't going to bother Kass, who was hopefully sleeping, but I was going to see her first thing when we got back. I needed some perspective.

Logan rolled over, squinting as the light of my phone flashed.

"Go back to bed," he growled.

"Make me," I growled back.

He scooted closer. I watched him curiously, feeling his irritation with the mate bond. Reaching over the comforter I turned toward him, liking where this was going. He snaked an arm around my waist and yanked me down flat.

I huffed, my own irritation spiking. He settled his tree trunk limb over my stomach, bending the limb to rest his hand on my shoulder.

"Now," he grunted.

"It doesn't work that way Logan," I informed him. "Do you need me here to sleep?"

"I'd prefer it. Do you have somewhere else you'd rather be?"

"Killing something sounds appealing, or figuring out what the fuck is going on with the vampires and the djinn, and let's not forget finding out who is making the serum for forcing shifters into full beast."

"And you think by not sleeping you will suddenly figure all that out?" Logan asked wearily.

"No." I was being grumpy.

"Give it an hour. If you still want to prowl the halls looking for trouble, I'll go with you."

"Deal," I conceded. "At least we get to leave tomorrow."

Chapter 9

Showered, dressed, and with a few more hours of sleep, the horde of shifters I called my own and me waited outside my former room, leaning against the hallway walls.

I felt a tap on my shoulder and turned with a raised eyebrow, not sensing a threat. I mean, if you were going to announce your presence with my current horde, you were either not spoiling for a fight or suicidal.

"Your lips are the red rubies sought after by countless others," began the siren in front of me. "Your skin the smoothest pearl to behold."

"What are you doing?" I asked, confused.

"Your eyes the sea herself is jealous of."

I still didn't sense a threat.

I turned, seeing Mark laughing. "I fail to see the humor in this situation," I informed him.

"Your breasts, the subtle swell of perfectly formed mountains." The siren was adding dramatic dance to his blathering.

"Please tell me this is going to stop soon," I grunted, crossing my arms over my stomach.

"I can't wait for Logan to see this." Mark rubbed his hands together excitedly, casting a look behind him at Logan, who was on his cell phone, watching everything.

The siren reached out for my hand, cradling it in his own very soft and weak hands.

"You are aware I have shit to do?" I asked the siren.

He reached out to touch my hair. "The softest strands of lovely locks."

Alec came up beside us. "If you value your life, you will leave the Alpha's Mate alone."

"What is he doing?" I asked Alec again, since the siren had never bothered to answer.

"The lady does not deny my affections," the siren preened.

"Affections?" I repeated, seriously confused.

A low growl behind us had me trying to turn, but the siren tugged me closer to him, under his arm.

"Seriously, what are you doing?" I huffed, irritated at losing my footing thanks to ridiculous shoes.

Logan's eyes were changing, flecks of espresso spreading around the raw sienna.

"Release. My. Mate," he commanded. I'm not going to lie, just that commanding voice alone was dampening my panties.

I pushed the siren off easily. "So, are you going to explain what's going on?" Down raging hormones, down.

Logan looked at me and I felt him nudge the mate bond I had been keeping on lock down. Having another with that level of access was unnerving. Blowing out a breath, I let him in. His face relaxed with the connection, arms coming to circle my waist. He bent to my ear and explained, "He was trying to seduce you."

I jerked back, needing to see his face to determine how serious he was. A small smile played over his lips and I wasn't sure if that was from the mate bond being reconnected or his amusement at the situation.

"Mate bond," he answered, pulling me in for a bruising kiss. "There is no humor in another touching you."

He broke the contact and I smiled, ready to haul him in the room for more.

"Where did he go?" Logan asked. I could feel the need to eliminate the threat that dared attempt to steal his mate away.

I couldn't help but laugh. He looked down at me, not seeing the humor in the situation.

"Oh, come on, it's a little funny," I teased him, taking his hand as we walked as a group to the elevators. Ali, Grant, Mercer and Grams joined the party.

Logan growled.

"The siren was doing his best to seduce me and I had no idea what was going on."

Logan pushed the call button harder than necessary and I checked for cracks. The doors opened at my back and he stalked me into the enclosed space.

"You guys should probably take another elevator," I warned over Logan's shoulder. None of them had even taken a step into the small space.

...

Logan helped me pull down my skirt and adjust my underwear, copping a feel of where he had just been. I batted his hands away before the elevator doors opened and a room full of Supernaturals got a whiff as to what was going on in there. Can't say I even gave a damn.

Actually, I was hoping there were cameras in there and it got leaked, 'cause that was some of my better work. Shame me now, motherfuckers, shame me now.

"What are you feeling smug about?" Logan whispered, nuzzling his mark on my neck.

I let the mate bond slip again, not realizing I had locked it up. I watched my train of thought play over his face before he laughed. He leaned close and I felt his words in my mind. That was a lot to get used to.

If that video of us becomes public, I will kill everyone who sees it.

Aww, my big, protective Kitty.

He growled even in my head.

Grams approached me, anger tightening her eyes. "Were you ever going to tell me? Or do I have to find out through third party gossip?"

I took a step back, feeling the pack around me stepping closer.

"You would do well to mind your tone," Jerry warned, eyeing the shifters cautiously.

"Give me a minute," I whispered to Logan, taking Grams arm, pushing her backwards.

"No!" she yelled, throwing me off. "I will not be shoved around. This conversation will keep until later."

With that she stormed off, without protection. Ali and Grant gave me long looks and I inclined my chin, giving them permission to go after her. Mercer watched the exchange before turning and following them.

I blew out a breath, adjusting my white blouse over my pencil skirt. "This should be fun," I grunted, following behind them.

I rubbed the back of my neck. "What's on the agenda for today?" I groaned, looking over at Logan.

"A seminar on How to Manage Talent." I'll give Logan credit, he delivered it with a straight face. The group around me chuckled and coughed.

"There better fucking be food," I groaned.

...

I rubbed my forehead as I sat next to Logan and Ali at the farewell dinner. We had pushed two tables together to accommodate our now larger numbers.

"Fucking finally, did you hear that speaker on sexual harassment?" I groaned. Logan had fibbed: Managing Talent was the first of a long-ass day of seminars.

Ali laughed next to me, imitating the speaker. "Now Olivia, perhaps you can explain to us how you keep everyone's hands to themselves with a highly sexual species."

Grant laughed on the other side of Ali. "His face, Olie, his face was shocked!"

I cracked a smile.

"I can't believe you have been having group orgies and not telling us about them," Hudson teased.

"You're not invited," I shot back.

He held his heart, pretending to be wounded.

The same announcer who began The Conferences smiled his same fake smile at center stage. "Welcome everyone and thank you for being with us."

I drummed my fingers on the table, inaction making me cranky as I tuned him out.

He extended his hand to welcome Hash to the elevated platform and I sat up, paying close attention.

Hash had a shit-eating grin up on the stage. "I'm happy to announce that Grams with the Supernatural Council has agreed to do what I am hoping everyone will. She has released to me, and to the government, all the names, address, and types of Supernaturals under her protection."

I roared, clearing the table, sending food splattering to the ground and dishes crashing. I landed with my forearm against her throat, rage pouring from my body, slipping past my guards.

"Tell me he is lying!" I screamed at her. "TELL ME!" I begged her.

She coughed, and I eased back slightly. "I did."

I screamed, a noise of pure frustration and outrage, leaning my forearm heavily against her throat, planning on ending her life.

The djinn chose that moment to bombard the Conferences, hundreds of them swarming through the doors and attacking everyone without bias. Still I kept the pressure against her neck, a tear slipping down her cheek as she silently begged for her life. The wetness was mirrored on my own face. I screamed again, pain cutting a clear path through my chest at her deception.

Searing pain in my side forced me off of her. Hash ripped her from my grasp, a gun dangling from his hand. I reached down, touching the seeping wound in my side in disbelief.

"The fucker shot me," I grunted, pulling myself up. Mercer's expression was torn: did he stay and try to fight off the Supernatural monsters that weren't his responsibility? He owed me for saving Mindy, but his loyalties were being tested after I had just tried to kill his girlfriend.

"Go Mercer, get out of here. Go back to Mindy."

I didn't see if he took my advice, having instead to block a meaty arm from slamming against my temple. The pain in my side only fueled my insane anger. A hatred and fury born of rage flooded my body and I destroyed any of the djinn who were foolish enough to cross my path.

"Olivia!" Mark cried.

I turned, trying to find him in the crowd, too much going on for me to focus on the mate or pack bonds closely.

Instead, I threw myself into the fight, slicing with my dagger, rounding and stabbing. They weren't killing blows, but it was about survival at that point.

A shifter bellowed and I felt the energy he pulled as he changed forms. My head spun as I was pulled into his change, seeing the world through Alec's wolf's eyes. Shaking my head, I took a blow to the stomach, doubling over and crashing to the ground, slashing out at my attacker's shins.

The blow earned me a moment to suck down air.

A rust colored wolf lunged at my attacker. "Thanks, Alec," I wheezed

Fucking hell, we needed to find the actual djinn. Only by killing him or her would we eliminate the clones. With this many, the fucker would be weakened and hopefully easy prey. The problem was I had no idea where he or she was.

Why were they attacking everyone? This made no sense.

I sighed, taking my frustration out on the throat of my next opponent. We were winning, slowly.

An anguished cry went up from a shifter and I felt her pain as the drug exploded inside of her—no, no, no. Was all of this just a distraction?

"Alec, cover me!" I yelled, going down on a knee. Closing my eyes, I threw down my guards, sifting quickly to find her golden thread turning black. I latched on to it, sucking all the toxins I could. The cord grayed. I fisted my hands, my nails digging into my palms, before pulling again. Her cord turned yellow and I opened my eyes, finding Alec overwhelmed. I lifted my blade, finding it pointless.

I closed my eyes, found Logan's thread and tugged. I sure as fuck wasn't about to beg for help, but after saving her ass, I needed some.

His lion answered, bowling over djinn and slicing their heads off in one fell swoop. I stood unsteadily, opening my senses to the other shifters. Someone get a sample of that crap so I we can make an antidote.

Another anguished cry and I sucked myself back into the golden pond, slipping, tumbling, my cheek coming to rest on the cool tile as I finished.

Shit, this took a lot out of me. A third and fourth cry rent the air, and I lost the ability to hear as I was busy pulling out black crap.

A warm nose nudged my side. "Didyougetit?" I slurred.

"Not sure that was English, Olie," Grant informed me.

"The sample," I tried again.

Logan stoked my hair back. "We did."

"Good, call Tommy and let's get the hell out of here."

Apparently, we were already out of there. Like a computer doing too much at once, I had been overloaded by the four almost simultaneous pulls, causing me to slow down. While I was successful at saving all the parties, it was with a huge personal toll.

"I hate flying," I groaned, flopping over on the couch.

"We know," the cabin chorused.

Logan's phone on speaker reverberated with the sound of ringing across from me. I plunked an arm over my face.

"Yo, boss man," came the voice at the other end.

"We have the sample, Tommy, and we are on our way," Logan informed him briskly.

"Check and check. We will be ready when you arrive. Olie there?"

"Yeah, I'm here," I groaned.

"I need to, I mean, I need your approval." He sighed and tried again, "I think Grams is up to something."

Ali scoffed, "Yeah, she released our names, address and species to Hash."

Tommy grunted, "Was she supposed to?"

"No, she betrayed us," I whispered softly, the sting overriding my currently exhausted state. Grams had betrayed me and everything we had worked for.

"Good, because I corrupted the file. Hash got nothing."

"What?" I breathed the word, not daring to hope, sitting so quickly my head spun.

"I monitor our computers tightly here, and the email sent up several red flags." I could see him shrugging.

I closed my eyes, pressing against the stupid fucking tears that wanted to fall. "Hey Tommy, you know how I said you couldn't have a dog?"

"Yeah?" he asked, excited.

"We're going to adopt one when I get back."

"WHAT? Are you serious? Olivia, you cannot tease about this," he screamed at me.

"I'm not teasing, Tommy. I need you to get with Becky and cut Grams off from everything. She isn't to be allowed in the house. Have the locks changed. I'm hoping we beat her back to St. Ann, but if not, remember she's a traitor. Treat her as such."

"Are you going to kill her?" Tommy's voice was soft. Grams had been a part of his life for the last five years. Hell, she had helped raised all the children I rescued. Could I take her away from them?

"Yes, Tommy," I answered honestly. I hated that I was hurting him. "She betrayed us, all of us, to the human government. She put us all in danger. If I don't kill her, I'm making myself look weak."

Silence met my confession.

"I'm so sorry, Tommy."

...

There was too much on my mind to even give the plane ride more than a few minutes of irritation as we glided over the skies.

I looked over to Ali and Grant, who had been silent since my conversation with Tommy.

Tapping my fingers against the leather of the sofa, I met Logan's gaze. He inclined his head to them and I nodded, the unspoken message received.

I moved to sit across from Grant and Ali. It wasn't lost on me that Grant was looking out the window blinking rapidly or that Ali's eyes were dripping with silent tears. The leather dipped as Logan took a seat next to me. I checked the mate bond, finding I wasn't blocking it, waves of reassurance washing over me. At least one person understood the situation I was in.

"I never," Ali started, drawing a breath, meeting my gaze. "I never dreamed it would come to this. That she would betray her own kind."

"We're not her kind though, are we?" Grant asked me, anger replacing his sorrow.

"No, Grams is human. I've made no attempt to hide that fact," I answered softly.

"But, but I thought she was like you, a succubus?" Ali asked, her tears forgotten for a moment.

I shook my head, clenching my hands together.

"Why would you put a human in charge of the Council?" Grant demanded.

I leveled a look at him, debating if I needed to put him in his place or let his anger run its course. "I am the one who put her there, and I am the one who kept her there. I am also the one who has put you both there and will keep you there."

His eyes widened slightly as he looked over at Ali, taking her hand. Their silent exchange had me shifting in my seat. I hoped they were up for the challenge; they had been hand selected by Grams.

Grant turned, meeting my gaze. "Did you mean what you said to Tommy?"

I sighed. I could understand their need for confirmation, but my decision could not be swayed. "Yes."

Grant looked back out the window, his jaw tense.

I drew a breath. "Neither of you are bound to this position yet. You can refuse it and me."

Both of their eyes ricocheted to me, widened in shock, before they looked at each other.

"No, Olie, we want this. We want to protect our kinds by your side. We trust you to keep us safe," Ali said, reaching out a hand to my own.

I smiled and Grant choked out, "I agree," his throat thick with emotion.

...

We touched down in St Ann five hours later. I was checking my cell phone, mentally gearing up for what I had to do.

Logan stopped abruptly from exiting the plane. "Olivia," he called, not turning around.

I stopped gathering my luggage, coming to stand by his side in the cramped space.

"Everyone stay here." My voice had steel undertones. I took the steps rapidly, Logan hot on my heels.

"I'm assuming I wasn't included in that comment," he muttered.

"You weren't," I whispered back, my lips hardly moving.

Grams stood next to Hash in front of a black town car with a smirk.

"You can't kill me, Olivia," she began. "I'm a 50/50 shareholder in everything and I've named Hash my beneficiary if anything were to happen to me." She threw the paperwork at me. I caught it, crumpling it up.

Bitch was smug. "I'm okay with killing you both," I answered with a shrug.

"Try it, see what happens," she threatened, taking a step forward.

"I made you," I hissed, narrowing my eyes, "I took you from the gutter and made you a Queen."

She scoffed, placing her hands on her hips. "You do not get credit for what I am. I made myself who I am today."

I shook my head. "You betrayed us. You are unwelcome at the manor and Kitten."

She crossed her arms over her chest. "Try and keep me out, Olivia. My name is on the deed."

I was done. They were both dead.

I lunged, intent on the throat I had left bruises on earlier. Logan's arm around my waist dug painfully and I screamed in frustration. If anyone was watching and/or recording us, I was not doing myself any favors.

"You will be permitted to take your belongings from the manor in one hour," Logan warned, not even struggling with my weight, asshole. "So I suggest you make arrangements."

Grams leveled him a long look. "This isn't over. I will take what is mine."

That only renewed my attempt to kill her. She looked at me, disgust etched onto her downturned mouth. If I wasn't so pissed, I'd have been hurt.

I fought to keep my turbulent and poignant emotions from spreading to the pack. I wanted them both dead, heads on a fucking silver platter. While I'd prefer to do it myself, I wasn't above putting a price on her head.

Logan led me to the car Jerry had pulled up and I got into the back seat, fury flooding my veins.

"Get to the manor," Logan relayed to Jerry.

Grant and Ali watched Grams walk away, sadness lining their features.

I clenched and unclenched my fists, imagining all the twisted things I'd do to the bitch.

...

Tommy was waiting on the steps for me when we drove up.

He stayed sitting but lifted his head, following the progress of the SUV.

I stepped out of the vehicle, making my way over to him.

"I don't want a puppy, Olie. Promise me you won't kill Grams." His eyes were red from crying as he pleaded with me.

I wrapped my arms around him, only to have him push me away.

"Promise, Olie!" he yelled at me. "This is all I want," he added, his voice cracking.

I cringed. "Let's go inside and talk about it."

He relented, stomping up the stairs.

I turned to meet Logan's gaze.

What do I do?

He shook his head.

All the children were gathered in the foyer, sitting on the steps and spilling into the living room. They watched our return closely, some with angry eyes, others with sadness. They were anxiously awaiting something deep and meaningful I couldn't give them. What I could provide them with was the truth.

"I'm sorry, guys. Grams betrayed us. She tried to give Hash a list of every Supernatural under the Council's protection." Muttering met my announcement, heads shaking in disbelief.

"Tommy said you are going to kill her?" a small voice squeaked.

I nodded. "Yes, I have to. To protect my standing and everyone here." Tommy whined. "But I can't. She is a 50/50 partner in everything and she has named Hash her beneficiary. If I kill her I'll be dealing with Hash, and if I kill them both, the humans will have my head."

"So she lives?" Tommy asked hopefully.

"For now," I confirmed.

Logan cleared this throat, stepping next to me. "Grams will undoubtedly be hiring an attorney to negotiate how much money she will want to leave us alone."

"Money?" a small voice asked. I turned to Mindy. I'd forgotten she was here while we were in Vegas.

"Mindy, hasn't Mercer come for you yet?" I asked, surprised.

She shook her head. "You mean that Grams is going to abandon us all for money?"

"Yes," was my answer, not as strong as I'd have liked. "She chose her side and it wasn't with us."

Mindy watched me closely. "You are always welcome here, Mindy."

"But she's human. Grams is human and she betrayed us," one of my teenagers supplied hotly.

"We don't judge based on species, Connie. We judge on loyalty, and Mindy has been loyal. I've been betrayed by Supernaturals more often than by humans."

"You also don't interact with humans," Connie interjected. The kid was making sense.

"Look, Mindy is one of us. She has suffered as the castoff of a society that doesn't want to get its hands dirty. Our protection is hers until she decides she doesn't want it," I stressed.

Connie glared at me and I broke. "I know, guys. I miss her too." The entire room sprang into motion, rushing into me, hugging me, sobbing, grieving for the surrogate mother they had lost. It wasn't fair. Every single kid in my care had suffered, some worse than others, and here I was taking away their rock.

I fucking hated being put in this situation. This is exactly why I could have forgiven so much from her, but the public betrayal of every Supernatural we were created to protect crossed lines not even I could ignore.

My heart broke and I met Logan's gaze, even though he appeared blurry. A few of the kids had wrapped around him as well, needing comfort. He rubbed small circles on their backs, comforting as best he could. I let comfort and peace seep from me, willing it into each and every precious soul.

Ali and Grant moved in as well, bending down to hold and reassure everyone they could. I had saved these kids from their own private nightmares. I'd given them safety, and now I was stripping them of it.

"Who is going to replace her?" Connie asked, leaning against me. I kissed her hair.

"Ali and Grant will be moving in and taking over," I answered. We hadn't clarified if they were moving in, so maybe I shouldn't have said that.

I peered over Connie's head at them. Ali met my gaze and smiled warmly, nodding.

...

The kids settled down, going back to their usual routines. Ali and Grant went to pack Grams's things. Logan and I sat on the steps outside. I had tried to help Ali and Grant, but raving hadn't been helpful for anyone.

"Do you have things you need to do?" I asked him.

"We have things to do," he corrected me.

I slanted a look him. "Hey, we may be sleeping together, but I'm still charging you for taking down beast shifters."

Logan laughed, "I expect nothing less."

I sighed, "We need a plan."

"You need a lawyer."

"You know of any?"

"Several, but only one is ruthless enough for this situation. Do you want me to call her?"

I nodded. "Set it up. I can't imagine it will take Grams long to give me a dollar amount."

Logan fidgeted and I felt his uncertainty about his next question. "It's okay, Logan, you can ask."

"How much can you afford to pay her?"

"A lot. I'm a hoarder."

"Really?"

"Yeah Logan, don't worry, I won't run you into bankruptcy," I teased him. "Like Lorraine and her generous spending habits."

I smiled and he wrapped an arm around my shoulder.

"We will get through this, Olie."

"There is no other way but through," I murmured.

I patted his knee, "Come on, Ali and Grant can handle this. Let's go see Kass and Darren."

The door opened behind us and we turned. "I think you need to see these," Ali said, handing me a manila folder thick with paper.

I opened the file, my fingers running over the glossy photos. Grams walking across the street downtown. Mindy at her side as they laughed at something at the park. Mercer and Grams on a date night, leaning closer to each other over their wine glasses. The pictures kept going and I turned to Ali.

"Turn them over," she rasped.

I flipped the thick stack over.

"Where did these come from?" Logan asked, peering over my shoulder.

"I don't know. I found them in her top drawer," Ali stated, coming to sit next to us.

"I'll skin her alive and make you watch," I read aloud in a whisper, flipping the photo over. It was the one of her and Mindy.

"Why didn't she bring these to me?" I asked no one in particular.

Logan leaned closer, lending me his warmth.

"Does it matter?" Ali asked.

I shook my head. "Honestly, I could forgive a lot for her. I would have forgiven the other issue with Hash and the secrets she was keeping, but trying to give our information to the humans is a line I cannot bring her back from. So no, Ali, while it does clarify why she did it, these don't change anything."

I handed her back the file, but before I released it, I turned to her. "I will protect you and Grant, only death can keep me from that promise."

She squeezed my shoulder, holding the vile stack of photos to her chest. "We know, Olie."

Logan rubbed my shoulders. "Do you still want to see Darren and Kass?"

"Yeah, I could use a little kiddo love."

...

We stopped off at a toy store first since neither of us had gotten the kids anything.

I laughed as we knocked lightly on the door, careful not to wake up Harris.

"It's a good toy," Logan defended.

"A nerf gun is a little old for him, but Hannah will love it," I informed him.

A dark-eyed Kass answered the door, her face lighting up when she saw us. "You're back!"

I moved in to hug her. "We have arrived."

"Thank all the gods, can you watch the kids while I shower? I can smell myself and it isn't pretty."

I nodded, giving her a shove. "Go, we got this."

"OLIE!" Hannah yelled, rushing into our arms. Kass cringed on her way to the shower as Harris let out a cry.

She turned partially to get him. "Go, we got this," I encouraged her.

She hustled away. Logan picked up Harris from his bassinet, cooing and rocking.

"What did you bring me?" Hannah continued in an outside voice. Logan gave me a glare.

"Outside, monster child, outside."

An hour later I had chased, hid from, and surprised Hannah in every corner of the yard. The kid was still raring to go.

I poked my head in to check on Logan. He had Harris sleeping on his chest as he watched a home improvement show.

I grunted, closing the door quietly.

...

Kass showered and managed to snag a nap, and Logan caught up on his DIY show.

"You look good, Olie," Kass commented, pulling down plates for dinner.

"Holy hell, Kass. I have so much to tell you."

"Wait until Darren gets here. I only want to tell the story and answer the questions once," Logan grunted as Harris woke up.

Kass smiled, taking the squirming baby. "You hungry little man?" she cooed. "Logan, don't let Olie cook anything."

"Hey," I called out after her, "I can make mac and cheese!"

"No you can't," Hannah offered.

...

Darren literally dropped his fork, the food in his mouth on display.

"You mated Olivia on accident?" he asked, shocked. He had scented the change as soon as he entered.

"Why haven't you heard of this?" Kass looked over at Darren.

Logan and I shared a look as we continued on our story. It turned out being mated to Logan was actually the highlight of our trip to Vegas. The irony of us being mated in Vegas was not lost on me.

...

"Wow," Kass said, walking us out.

"I can't believe it," Darren echoed, holding Harris.

I sighed, hating that I had to relive Grams's betrayal yet again. Logan's hand was solid on my shoulder.

"Hey Olie," Kass offered, turning me from the door, "if you need anything, I'm here."

I gave her a weak smile. "Thanks," I sighed, embracing her. "Just take care of yourself and the kids."

Logan and Darren exchanged their own goodbyes and we were off.

"Where do you want to sleep tonight?" Logan asked.

"With the kids, do you want to stay with me?" I asked, not sure how he'd feel about that.

He nodded, but the unease in the mate bond wasn't so agreeable.

Chapter 10

"Cheater!" Tommy cried as I tickled him.

I laughed. "It's the only way I win!" I answered as Mindy worked my controller.

I leaned back on the floor, laughing, releasing Tommy to try and gain back the lead Mindy had taken.

Slowly, I felt the mate bond awaken as Logan woke up. I could almost see him reaching over and checking how warm the bed was before rolling out.

I focused my attention back on Tommy pulling off a near win.

"Victory is mine!" Mindy cried out, jumping up and down.

"I demand a rematch," Tommy complained, flopping back into his gaming chair.

"After breakfast," Logan commented from the doorway. I turned and heat flooded my body. The white undershirt was pulled tight across his chest, skimming his flat stomach. I bit my bottom lip, pursing my lips, giving thought to whether I wanted to eat food or lick the delicious skin above his navel.

Logan moved away from the doorframe, stalking me as the predator he was. I tilted my head up, a smile playing over my lips.

"I'm hungry, so the feast currently playing in your mind will have to wait," he whispered, pressing a kiss against my cheek.

I pouted. "EWW!" Mindy and Tommy yelled in unison.

I turned to them, standing up and rolling my eyes. Logan moved to glide down the stairs and I ushered the kids out to the kitchen.

Somber faces met me around the large kitchen table and breakfast counter.

I drummed my fingers against the counter. Spoons dipped into cereal and toast was crunched with sorrow.

I took in all of their faces and was annoyed no one was pissed off like me.

"They need time to grieve, Olie, they've lost a mother figure," Logan whispered under their hearing.

I grunted. "Hey, any chance you cook?" I asked hopefully.

Logan smiled. "Sit and be amazed."

I rested my chin on Cindy's shoulder and she leaned into me while we shared a bar stool. Shifters weren't the only ones who found comfort in touching.

An hour later we were out of flour and Logan was finally getting to eat.

Logan slid next to me. "I had no idea succubi ate so much."

"We need our calories, too," I answered, shoveling another forkful of sugary goodness into my mouth.

He grunted and nodded, starting in on his own plate.

I was avoiding asking what we were doing today. I was certain it had something to do with Grams and her massive backstabbing.

I slowed down eating, the food turning sour in my mouth.

Logan nudged my elbow.

I relented to my gut's demands, setting down my fork. "I need to find an attorney."

"Let me set up an appointment with the ruthless bastard I was telling you about," Logan offered.

I rubbed the back of my neck, nodding. "I need a shower first."

Logan stood, tossing his uneaten food into the trash. "Let's go."

...

"I hope she lives up to your expectations," I told Logan, riding shotgun to the attorney's office. She had gotten us in quickly and I was trying really hard not to question if she also had slept with Logan.

Sophie Wilson currently had all my eggs in her basket.

Her office was located downtown, on the thirteenth floor of a massive high rise. Parking was a bitch.

"If you will follow me," her secretary chirped, meeting us at the elevator and ushering us into Sophie's office.

I flicked a gaze over the opulent space before I landed on Sophie's own shrewd gaze. She leaned forward in her cobalt suit, which matched her eyes perfectly, her blonde hair pulled up into a smooth bun.

"Olivia, The Executioner, you are in quite a mess," she began the conversation.

"Yeah, I'm aware."

"I'm perfectly shocked Grams hasn't made her passing yet," she commented. "Releasing a list of Supernaturals to the government." She hissed the last word, her eyes narrowing as she leaned forward.

Right, she was on that list.

"I'd like to have fulfilled your expectations, but the file Hash received was corrupted, and Grams has named Hash her beneficiary if anything were to happen to her."

Sophie nodded, her full lips drawn down.

"We will put out a press release stating that. I have full confidence there is a bounty on her head."

I cringed. "I hadn't even thought of that."

Sophie cracked a small smile. "That's why you have me."

I nodded.

"And what do you expect me to do for you?" she asked, meeting my gaze steadily.

"I expect you to slam everyone who dares threaten me and mine—legally speaking," I added.

Sophie smiled. "We will get along well." She pulled her laptop over to her. "Now, let's start from the beginning. What assets do you hold with Grams?"

I rubbed my forehead. "Everything. Kitten, the manor, various bank accounts, and the shell company that receives payments for jobs the executioners complete."

Sophie typed furiously. "What are you willing to give up?"

"Nothing," I hissed, sitting back in the overstuffed chair. I thought about it and added, "She just wants money. I've let her get accustomed to a certain lifestyle."

"Would you be okay making payments to her for the rest of her life?"

"However short that might be," Logan growled.

I smiled at him. "I find that acceptable."

Sophie nodded. "Now, how much does Hash know? He was at The Conferences."

"I don't know. I certainly haven't given him any information, but Grams is a different story and I wasn't with her the entire time."

Sophie nodded. "He's going to be a wildcard. I'm hopeful he will stay out of this, but rumor has it he is running for the Senate and using this as his platform."

I groaned.

"Now—" She was interrupted by my cell phone ringing.

"Crap, sorry, I thought I had it on silent." Grant's two missed calls popped up and I answered, worried.

"What's wrong?"

"Are you at the attorney's?" he questioned rapidly.

"Yes," I answered. "What's wrong?" I repeated.

"Put me on speaker phone," he demanded.

I did as he said, holding the phone. "Grant, what is wrong?" I was losing my patience.

"All the bills are behind at the manor, not to mention Blue hasn't been paid in over a month." I could hear him typing in the background.

"What? I saw the accounting report, that money was debited."

"The money is also missing from the bank, but it hasn't been used to pay for what she claimed it was," Grant answered.

I sat there dumbfounded. "She was stealing from me?" I whispered. Her betrayal stung deeply, but I had assumed it was recent and Hash-inspired. "She has been planning this."

"Are you able to pay the bills now?" Sophie asked.

Grant paused. "No, Grams went to all the banks and froze the accounts for impending legal action."

A pit of despair opened in my stomach. She had not only frozen me out, but all the children. Cold steel hardened my growing hatred.

"Is Logan there?" Grant asked. I heard a door open and footsteps falling.

Grant hesitated. "Can we take a loan from Logan?" Ali asked.

"NO!" I responded.

"Of course," Logan answered, looking at me.

"I will not be a kept woman!" I told him, furious.

"Olie," Ali started softly, "we don't have much of a choice. The power was shut off about twenty minutes ago."

My jaw was in danger of snapping off from how hard I was clenching it. Logan reached out and massaged my neck lightly.

aniels boy," I answered, coming to sit next to him on the couch in
oom.
"
d on my thumbnail. "I didn't even ask the circumstances. What if
was a logical reason why the Council shouldn't be involved?"
licked the laptop closed.
." I didn't need the mate bond to feel his disbelief of Blake. "You take
children all the time. Blake knows this. He knew you would help
d trying to attach strings is his way of screwing with you."
you are right," I sighed. "Did you find anything good?" I asked,
bject change.
let's take a look together to see if we can't narrow down our options.
tomorrow and look at some of these."
led next to him. He opened the computer back up, settling next to
entment seeping through our link at our physical contact.
m not living that far away."
grunted, his contentment fading into annoyance.
I demanded.

...

a horrendous amount of time to sift through all the potential
eyes burned and I was exhausted from debating the pros and cons.
p with thirty houses.
ed. "You expect to see all of those houses tomorrow?" I questioned.
shrugged, his massive hands deftly manipulating the keyboard. "I
realtor, some are occupied. We will see what we can get into on
."
ed, rolling up from the couch. "Let's go find a fight to join," I
etching.
?" Logan questioned.
need a work out."
rubbed his jaw, thinking. He stilled, looking up at me with a gleam.
dea."

...

sly, Logan, I said I wanted to fight, not kill someone and bury the

"Call my office and ask for Francisca. I'll text her now and tell her to get
you anything you need. This isn't a loan. Olie is part of the shifters now, the
funds are hers."

I grunted, feeling my independence being stripped from me.

"I'll keep track, Olie, and try and keep expenses minimal," Ali offered.

I sighed, releasing my jaw. "Do what you need to, Ali, to ensure the kids are
taken care of. And pay Blue, no wonder he's been so pissy."

Logan laughed, finishing his text to Francisca. "Well, that and other
things," I amended.

"I hate to ask this, Olie, but you don't have a stash of cash somewhere as a
getaway fast fund?" Grant questioned me.

I huffed an amused snort. "No Grant, I do not. I do not tuck tail and run
when shit gets difficult."

"No offense meant," he muttered.

"Do you have anything else to tell me?" I asked, feeling the stress wearing
on me. I'd love to get attacked leaving here, I thought.

"Yes, we have the name of Grams's attorney."

Grant relayed the information to Sophie and I thought about killing the
attorney, just to send a bloody message. It was too public, though, too showy.

"Good," Sophie declared. "I have what I need to get started. I'll be in
touch." With that, we were dismissed.

...

"I can't believe this," I muttered to Logan over an early dinner. We had
missed lunch running around with the meetings and we both were hungry.

Logan leaned against the black wooden chair, stressing the joints. He put
an arm over the empty chair next to him, watching me.

"Do we need to revisit the kept woman issue?"

"No, I took the money, didn't I?"

"You are planning on paying it back." he tapped his temple.

"Bah, blasted mate bond," I grunted.

Our server arrived with another waitress in tow, swiftly filling the table with
all our orders.

"Everything look okay?" The server asked. We nodded with our mouths
full. "Alright, dessert will be out in about thirty minutes, and you wanted two
of everything on the menu?" he asked again for clarification.

I nodded around a mouthful of garlic knots.

Logan and I were eating in peaceful silence, the bond between us taking care of the fight we were having.

A throat cleared behind me and Logan's eyes flicked over my shoulder, his raw sienna gaze darkening at being interrupted or because of who was there, I wasn't sure.

"I'm sorry to interrupt your meal," Blake began.

"Oh, fuck no," I hissed, turning around, ready to lay hands on him.

"Olivia," Logan's sharp tone had me stilling my movements, which had to look foolish as I dropped my hands back down, easing into the seat again.

I pulled my attention off the asshole known as Blake and noticed the terrified little boy and his parents.

"What?" I growled.

"I was hoping you could spare a few moments to meet my friends, the Daniels family," Blake recovered smoothly.

"Why?" I asked, peering intently at the little boy. My shields were up at one hundred percent to keep the packs and those around me from my volatile emotions. It was unnerving, this extra responsibility.

I smashed the mate bond into a metal ball inside my head, and then I felt it. Looking back at the little boy, his terror and wonder washed over me.

Blake made a self-satisfied grunt and I turned my laser-focused attention back to him, trying to control the look of disgust that expressed my wish to rip his fucking throat.

"You found a baby succubus?" I asked Blake. "Do you want an award?"

He shifted slightly as he stood.

Blake leaned down and I felt Logan pushing at the mate bond, unhappy with my treatment of it.

"I need you to help them without involving the rest of your Council," he whispered.

"No," I told him, easy and fast. I felt the little boy's hope dim. "I'll help them, but I'm not playing your games, Blake, and I will not allow them to be caught up in the games you are playing. Now, if you are finished."

He sneered. The handsome man I had fallen in love with was gone, replaced by a vampire with ambering eyes who didn't like the fact I was over him.

That thought surprised the hell out of me and
up to a rush of anger. Trampling it back down, I ga
eased back in his threat of bodily harm, slightly.

"You can't have them if I can't be a part of the
Pushing my chair back I closed the short dista

He must have been eight. He stood with his h
though that would keep his emotions from floodi

I knelt in front of him.

"My name is Olivia. I am the Head Exec
Council and a powerful succubus." His wonder
slightly parting. "You are an incubus. Our powe
only be used for good."

I was pretty sure I heard Logan laugh behin
later, at least he wasn't still throwing anger around

I slipped my card into his hand. "Call me if yo

He nodded before his parents hustled him aw

"You're dismissed," I informed Blake before si

He seethed, his eyes glowing. "You will regret
a mouth of fang.

"Not nearly as much as I do you." I met his ga
I was done with him and he needed to learn that.

He left and I exhaled a long, deep breath, turr

"Do not block your mate bond from me agai

I opened my mouth to tell him to back the
keeping me safe washed over me. His base desire t
the protest on my lips.

I nodded, not trusting my voice, as his love w

...

The conversation with Blake annoyed me and

"I'm not sure I handled that situation well,"
manor.

He stopped looking at new homes on his lapt

"With Blake?" He said the name with
possessiveness.

He slid out of the SUV, giving me a pointed look before closing the door.

"Can't take a joke," I muttered, slipping down onto the soft pine needles.

I had running shoes strapped to my feet, thick leggings, and a moisture wicking top under my long sleeved jacket.

Logan breathed deeply the crisp night air.

He reached back, taking my hand before moving deeper into the clearing, leading us to a small animal path I would have missed if he hadn't pointed it out.

"You run here, I'll run next to you," Logan commanded, lost in his joy at being able to run.

I grunted an affirmative as he began stripping out of his clothes, hanging them over a tree.

"Aren't you worried about vandals?" I asked, admiring the dimples in his ass.

"The packs own everything within thirty miles and we patrol our territory well. I am comfortable with the safety of my clothing and my mate."

I dragged my gaze north, blinking, hoping I wasn't drooling. "What?"

Logan laughed, "Just try to keep up."

With that, he was gone into the undergrowth, a blur of magic and snapping bones.

Heaving a sigh I started off, wishing for some action aside from organized running.

Even if the moon was really pretty. I almost tripped twice staring at how full and low it was.

Logan cuffed, Pay attention.

"Oh, great, I can't ignore you while in lion form now," I droned out sarcastically.

He lunged, bumping his flank against my legs. I danced away, tangling my legs in vines before I pushed through, picking up my pace. I didn't have any delusions about who was the faster of the two of us.

...

My chest heaved for air as I sprawled on my back on the pine needles, my moisture wicking shirt pushed to the limits as sweat dripped down my temples. I flexed my feet, watching the moon sink lower.

A cold nose nudged my side, followed by a blast of warm breath on my cheek.

I grunted, physically exhausted and mentally refreshed after the intense run. Not that I'd admit it had helped.

Logan shifted back, draping his warm body across my middle, resting his head on my shoulder. I ran my fingers through his hair in contentment.

"Call my office and ask for Francisca. I'll text her now and tell her to get you anything you need. This isn't a loan. Olie is part of the shifters now, the funds are hers."

I grunted, feeling my independence being stripped from me.

"I'll keep track, Olie, and try and keep expenses minimal," Ali offered.

I sighed, releasing my jaw. "Do what you need to, Ali, to ensure the kids are taken care of. And pay Blue, no wonder he's been so pissy."

Logan laughed, finishing his text to Francisca. "Well, that and other things," I amended.

"I hate to ask this, Olie, but you don't have a stash of cash somewhere as a getaway fast fund?" Grant questioned me.

I huffed an amused snort. "No Grant, I do not. I do not tuck tail and run when shit gets difficult."

"No offense meant," he muttered.

"Do you have anything else to tell me?" I asked, feeling the stress wearing on me. I'd love to get attacked leaving here, I thought.

"Yes, we have the name of Grams's attorney."

Grant relayed the information to Sophie and I thought about killing the attorney, just to send a bloody message. It was too public, though, too showy.

"Good," Sophie declared. "I have what I need to get started. I'll be in touch." With that, we were dismissed.

...

"I can't believe this," I muttered to Logan over an early dinner. We had missed lunch running around with the meetings and we both were hungry.

Logan leaned against the black wooden chair, stressing the joints. He put an arm over the empty chair next to him, watching me.

"Do we need to revisit the kept woman issue?"

"No, I took the money, didn't I?"

"You are planning on paying it back." he tapped his temple.

"Bah, blasted mate bond," I grunted.

Our server arrived with another waitress in tow, swiftly filling the table with all our orders.

"Everything look okay?" The server asked. We nodded with our mouths full. "Alright, dessert will be out in about thirty minutes, and you wanted two of everything on the menu?" he asked again for clarification.

I nodded around a mouthful of garlic knots.

Logan and I were eating in peaceful silence, the bond between us taking care of the fight we were having.

A throat cleared behind me and Logan's eyes flicked over my shoulder, his raw sienna gaze darkening at being interrupted or because of who was there, I wasn't sure.

"I'm sorry to interrupt your meal," Blake began.

"Oh, fuck no," I hissed, turning around, ready to lay hands on him.

"Olivia," Logan's sharp tone had me stilling my movements, which had to look foolish as I dropped my hands back down, easing into the seat again.

I pulled my attention off the asshole known as Blake and noticed the terrified little boy and his parents.

"What?" I growled.

"I was hoping you could spare a few moments to meet my friends, the Daniels family," Blake recovered smoothly.

"Why?" I asked, peering intently at the little boy. My shields were up at one hundred percent to keep the packs and those around me from my volatile emotions. It was unnerving, this extra responsibility.

I smashed the mate bond into a metal ball inside my head, and then I felt it. Looking back at the little boy, his terror and wonder washed over me.

Blake made a self-satisfied grunt and I turned my laser-focused attention back to him, trying to control the look of disgust that expressed my wish to rip his fucking throat.

"You found a baby succubus?" I asked Blake. "Do you want an award?"

He shifted slightly as he stood.

Blake leaned down and I felt Logan pushing at the mate bond, unhappy with my treatment of it.

"I need you to help them without involving the rest of your Council," he whispered.

"No," I told him, easy and fast. I felt the little boy's hope dim. "I'll help them, but I'm not playing your games, Blake, and I will not allow them to be caught up in the games you are playing. Now, if you are finished."

He sneered. The handsome man I had fallen in love with was gone, replaced by a vampire with ambering eyes who didn't like the fact I was over him.

That thought surprised the hell out of me and I opened the mate bond back up to a rush of anger. Trampling it back down, I gave Logan a pointed glare. He eased back in his threat of bodily harm, slightly.

"You can't have them if I can't be a part of the process," Blake hissed to me.

Pushing my chair back I closed the short distance between the boy and me.

He must have been eight. He stood with his hands held tightly together, as though that would keep his emotions from flooding the room.

I knelt in front of him.

"My name is Olivia. I am the Head Executioner of the Supernatural Council and a powerful succubus." His wonder washed over me, his mouth slightly parting. "You are an incubus. Our powers are strong, but they must only be used for good."

I was pretty sure I heard Logan laugh behind me. I would deal with him later, at least he wasn't still throwing anger around.

I slipped my card into his hand. "Call me if you need help."

He nodded before his parents hustled him away.

"You're dismissed," I informed Blake before sitting back down.

He seethed, his eyes glowing. "You will regret this," he informed me around a mouth of fang.

"Not nearly as much as I do you." I met his gaze, letting my features harden. I was done with him and he needed to learn that.

He left and I exhaled a long, deep breath, turning to Logan.

"Do not block your mate bond from me again. Promise," he demanded.

I opened my mouth to tell him to back the fuck off, but his worry about keeping me safe washed over me. His base desire to protect and love me silenced the protest on my lips.

I nodded, not trusting my voice, as his love warmed me from the inside.

...

The conversation with Blake annoyed me and kept eating at my conscience.

"I'm not sure I handled that situation well," I admitted to Logan at the manor.

He stopped looking at new homes on his laptop to look at me.

"With Blake?" He said the name with disdain and I felt his lion's possessiveness.

"The Daniels boy," I answered, coming to sit next to him on the couch in the living room.

"Why?"

I chewed on my thumbnail. "I didn't even ask the circumstances. What if there really was a logical reason why the Council shouldn't be involved?"

Logan clicked the laptop closed.

"Olivia." I didn't need the mate bond to feel his disbelief of Blake. "You take in wayward children all the time. Blake knows this. He knew you would help that boy, and trying to attach strings is his way of screwing with you."

"I hope you are right," I sighed. "Did you find anything good?" I asked, needing a subject change.

"A few, let's take a look together to see if we can't narrow down our options. I'd like to go tomorrow and look at some of these."

I snuggled next to him. He opened the computer back up, settling next to me, his contentment seeping through our link at our physical contact.

"No, I am not living that far away."

Logan grunted, his contentment fading into annoyance.

"Next," I demanded.

...

It took a horrendous amount of time to sift through all the potential homes. My eyes burned and I was exhausted from debating the pros and cons. We ended up with thirty houses.

I groaned. "You expect to see all of those houses tomorrow?" I questioned.

Logan shrugged, his massive hands deftly manipulating the keyboard. "I emailed the realtor, some are occupied. We will see what we can get into on short notice."

I grunted, rolling up from the couch. "Let's go find a fight to join," I groaned, stretching.

"A fight?" Logan questioned.

"Yeah, I need a work out."

Logan rubbed his jaw, thinking. He stilled, looking up at me with a gleam. "I have an idea."

...

"Seriously, Logan, I said I wanted to fight, not kill someone and bury the body."

He slid out of the SUV, giving me a pointed look before closing the door.

"Can't take a joke," I muttered, slipping down onto the soft pine needles.

I had running shoes strapped to my feet, thick leggings, and a moisture wicking top under my long sleeved jacket.

Logan breathed deeply the crisp night air.

He reached back, taking my hand before moving deeper into the clearing, leading us to a small animal path I would have missed if he hadn't pointed it out.

"You run here, I'll run next to you," Logan commanded, lost in his joy at being able to run.

I grunted an affirmative as he began stripping out of his clothes, hanging them over a tree.

"Aren't you worried about vandals?" I asked, admiring the dimples in his ass.

"The packs own everything within thirty miles and we patrol our territory well. I am comfortable with the safety of my clothing and my mate."

I dragged my gaze north, blinking, hoping I wasn't drooling. "What?"

Logan laughed, "Just try to keep up."

With that, he was gone into the undergrowth, a blur of magic and snapping bones.

Heaving a sigh I started off, wishing for some action aside from organized running.

Even if the moon was really pretty. I almost tripped twice staring at how full and low it was.

Logan cuffed, Pay attention.

"Oh, great, I can't ignore you while in lion form now," I droned out sarcastically.

He lunged, bumping his flank against my legs. I danced away, tangling my legs in vines before I pushed through, picking up my pace. I didn't have any delusions about who was the faster of the two of us.

...

My chest heaved for air as I sprawled on my back on the pine needles, my moisture wicking shirt pushed to the limits as sweat dripped down my temples. I flexed my feet, watching the moon sink lower.

A cold nose nudged my side, followed by a blast of warm breath on my cheek.

I grunted, physically exhausted and mentally refreshed after the intense run. Not that I'd admit it had helped.

Logan shifted back, draping his warm body across my middle, resting his head on my shoulder. I ran my fingers through his hair in contentment.

Chapter 11

"Olie, wake up!" Tommy yelled, barreling into our room at the manor.

His urgent tone had us flipping out of bed, Logan's claws extended and my hand reaching for the blade under my pillow.

"What's wrong?" I rushed him, pushing him to Logan who moved him behind us as I surveyed the hallway.

"You guys are NAKED!" he screeched.

I turned, having found nothing worthy of my blade. "Speak," I commanded.

"I – I – got the chemical compound back from the labs," he squeaked, covering his eyes.

Logan grunted, pulling on a gray pair of sweats. I moved to dress quickly as well.

"What's in it?" Logan asked.

Tommy flailed the arm not being used to cover his eyes. "It's in my room."

"We are dressed, Tommy, let's go," I dictated to him.

He nodded, uncovering his eyes cautiously and marching out of the room.

In his own accommodations, he sat at the multiple computer screens, furiously typing. "The lab was able to identify everything, which is unexpected at best."

Logan leaned over the back of Tommy's chair. "I'll be damned," he muttered, reading the long-ass words I couldn't pronounce.

"That would explain why they haven't attacked more shifters," Logan continued.

I waited a moment, watching Logan's eyes skim over the ingredients to make insta-beast.

"What is it?" I asked, done waiting. Patience, not a virtue of mine.

"The main ingredient is nesiota elliptica, also known as Saint Helen Olive, which is extinct," Logan mused.

"It doesn't sound extinct."

Logan nodded. "I wonder where they are finding it."

I chewed my bottom lip. "That's a break. We find out where it's being grown, and we can stop it."

Tommy sighed. "That's going to take a while—researching the plant's habitats, finding greenhouses that can accommodate said habitats, and, barring that, surveying satellite photos of the plant."

I kissed Tommy's cheek. "I have full confidence in you. Besides, if you need help, just call Becky."

He nodded and Logan and I excused ourselves while he was lost in thought.

"At least he learned his lesson on knocking," Logan muttered, stretching.

"Too true," I agreed, smacking his ass.

"Keep it up and I'll test how sore your legs are after that run," he threatened.

"Promise?" I asked, jumping onto his back.

He growled and I giggled.

...

"Where are all the kids?" Logan asked, dishing out scrambled eggs.

"School. The humans' schooling starts at 8:30 a.m."

"I'm surprised you don't home school them," Logan commented.

I shook my head. "It's important for them to be around humans to learn to gauge their control."

"Not to learn how to manipulate?" Logan asked with a smile.

I laughed. "No, control is the essence of their survival," I explained. "Once their control is excellent, we start their training on how to influence others."

"What about self-defense?" Logan asked.

"Monday night is boxing, Tuesday is karate, Thursday is strength training and Friday, weapons," I detailed.

Logan stopped eating with a forkful of eggs, gaping at me. "And they do their school work?" he asked, shocked.

"Yeah."

"But they are kids, Olie," he said, dropping his fork on his plate.

"They are succubi and incubi who don't have packs to protect them. They have to learn to do it themselves. They have to learn to be strong. As proven by Grams's betrayal, I won't always be in a position of power to keep them safe."

Logan bristled at that. "You will always be my mate."

"And what happens if you want to retire?" I asked.

His eyes narrowed and his lion pushed against his control. "Only death could take my title."

I let my mind walk down that path and found myself shutting down that train of thought rapidly. Logan could not, would not die. That, I was betting my life on.

I rubbed my chest, uncomfortable with the sudden intensity of emotions.

Thankfully, the ringing of my phone saved me from further introspection.

"Garrick," I answered.

"Olivia," he uttered on an unnecessary exhale, "do you have everything under control there?"

I shifted uncomfortably. I debated telling him to fuck off and mind his own business. Instead I answered honestly. Garrick had always been an ally to me and I was betting he would continue to be.

"I think so, I hired an attorney today. Logan and I are staying at the manor and Ali and Grant are now running The Council."

Garrick was silent for a moment. "And the finances?" he asked.

I huffed, "Fuck, that just happened yesterday." I groaned, looking over at Logan.

"Grams called me, stating that you would be having financial issues and warning me this legal battle would be lengthy."

"She WHAT?" I hissed, slamming the counter with a fist and standing up.

"She was very adamant that I would be funding you and your expensive children for a long time. That she wanted me to understand the commitment I would be locked into."

I paced, looking for something to break.

"She stole from me, she's been planning this. The power was shut off to the manor yesterday," I hissed.

"Do you need money, Olivia? I know you. I can't imagine you will be without funds for long. Your pride won't allow it and your jobs pay well," he stated matter-of-factly, as if my entire world wasn't falling apart.

I leaned against the counter, rubbing my forehead, holding back my tears with sheer willpower.

"I have it covered," I answered, turning to look at Logan.

He was watching me, his face unreadable.

"Power has been restored?" Garrick asked.

"Yeah, we're okay, Garrick. I have it under control."

Logan got up and put his bowl in the sink. "Good, I am glad to hear it," Garrick said. "Tell me, how are things with your lion?"

Complicated. I was on a teeter-totter between blissful happiness and freaked the fuck out about my life being tied to him forever.

"It's good. New, but good," I decided on.

Logan broke a bowl in the sink and I looked up at him mouthing, "What the fuck?" Oh crap, he had heard the teeter-totter comment.

He stormed out of the room and up the stairs. I sighed watching him go, wishing I wasn't so conflicted. He deserved someone more stable than me. Sorrow dragged me down. I was a burden, emotionally and financially.

"Did you hear me?" Garrick asked.

I turned away from the stairway. "No, what did you say?"

"I have a very lucrative, very dangerous job if you are interested in it."

I fought the urge to get Logan's opinion on the matter. I needed something to kill, hopefully several somethings.

"You have my attention."

...

The details hammered out, I leaned back on the barstool, toying with my phone.

I recognized Logan's steps coming down the stairs and I turned to see him put his bag by the front door.

"I don't understand why this is so hard for you," he began, his tone clipped.

I took a step toward him, wanting to explain, wanting to ease his pain.

He held his hand up to stop me and I felt his resolve form his own shield between us. It broke my confused heart.

"I'll be here for you, anything you need, you only have to call. But I'm not going to keep pushing you somewhere you don't want to go." His pain sliced through me.

"Logan, I just need time," I whispered, searching for right words.

He reached out to cup my face, leaning down to place the briefest kiss against my lips.

"I love you, Olivia, and I trust this bond, even if it was forged—" He stopped, and here was our problem.

I closed my eyes, leaning into his hand. "Without my knowledge," I finished for him.

He leaned down, resting his forehead against my own. "I am sorry, Olivia. I'm willing to spend the rest of my life making it right."

I turned away from him. "I have a job to do for Garrick. I'll be gone for about a week."

Logan's irritation spiked, his nostrils flaring and lion speckling his eyes. He huffed once and turned his back on me, slamming the door behind him for good measure. Yeah, I can't say I'd love him taking a job from his ex-lover, either.

Ugh, how were we going to make this work?

I slunk back into the chair. I felt terrible hurting him, but distance was exactly what I needed.

I wasn't built for this, I wasn't relationship material. Blake proved that.

I sighed, stashing my bowl in the sink before heading upstairs to pack.

...

I checked my clips for a second time before I flipped open my bag, stowing them next to the throwing knives, daggers, and my pretty new crossbow.

"Are you certain I can't convince you to take backup?" Grant asked from the doorway.

"I don't need any, but thanks for the concern." I turned to him, my bag over my shoulder, seeing him leaning on the doorframe.

"Where's Logan?" he asked.

I sighed, "We're fighting ... I think. Honestly I have no idea."

Grant moved aside as I lumbered out.

"I'll check in once I'm done."

"Be careful, Olivia, you are our protection now."

I turned and smiled at him, reaching out to pat his arm. "Don't worry, Grant. I'm hard to kill."

Chapter 12

I looked out over the burnt landscape in front of me, pulling out the map of the White River National Forest from my pack.

Garrick was right, this burn wasn't natural. I bent down, picking up a charred piece of wood. My fingers came away oily. I brushed my hands on my jeans after dropping it. The sun was starting to set in the distance, casting brilliant oranges and pink across the sky.

I turned away from the fire and hiked back to my hotel room. I had selected a room above my usual crap grade because it had a door that led directly to the scene of the unusual activity, including the random fire circles. But of course random fire circles weren't the only thing screwy.

I'd made the fifteen-hour drive with only a few stops and as the sun set behind me, my exhaustion weighed heavily. So did the fact I hadn't heard from Logan. Granted, I also hadn't reached out. The mate bond was limited this far away. I wasn't sure if I liked that or not.

I stomped the snow out of my boots before removing them to enter my warm hotel room. I slid the door closed behind me, pulling off my knit cap.

The files from Garrick were lying scattered on the queen bed. He had lost two executioners on this gig, and had only given it to me with my promise I would deliver my own special brand of justice.

Tossing my jacket on the couch, I sat down cross-legged to go through the files again, hoping some nugget would jump out at me.

I rubbed my eyes, finding my brain going back to Logan and not the information in front of me. With a groan I hopped off the bed. I needed a shower and a few hours of sleep before I went back out. The fun things always came out at night.

Showers were pretty boring without Logan, not to mention quick. I dried off, dressing in warm, dark clothing before I cleared off the bed.

Freshly cleaned, I toyed with my phone as I sat on the bed.

I decided to text Logan. Even though we hadn't clarified the level of communication I needed to provide him, I still felt obligated to let him know I was alright.

Arrived in Aspen, going to catch a few hours of rest before I start hunting.

I'd like to pretend I didn't sit there and wait for a reply, but I'm a big believer in honesty.

It didn't come. I felt crushed. Brushing a tear away, I stretched out, willing myself to get some rest. The last thing I needed was to add another dead executioner at this thing's feet.

I was lying curled up on my side, the curtains pulled back from the windows, snow falling leisurely. Burrowing under the covers, I gave serious thought to waiting until morning to check things out. I hate the snow.

...

I dreamed of Logan. Standing on a hillside, his back to me. I exhaled, leaning against his warm strength.

"What are we going to do, Olivia?" he whispered.

"Survive," my answer came quickly.

"I don't want survival, Olie. I need you to love me."

I backed away. Apparently, even in my dreams I was having to deal with this conversation.

I was being watched. Logan tried to say something else to me, but I didn't hear it as I regained consciousness.

I didn't open my eyes right away, straining my ears for any clues as to what was stalking me.

I heard a tapping, which could have been the trees outside, and I probably would have attributed it to that, except for the small hairs on the back of my neck standing up.

Well, lying there playing dead wasn't doing any good. I opened my eyes.

"Holy fuck," I whispered. "That's impressive."

Long claws tapped against the class, fading into a dark robe, with twin fires where eyes should have been. It moved closer to the glass, the hood hiding any additional features. Tossing the comforter off, I walked to the glass door.

The claws reached for the handle and I unlocked it, stepping back. "Come on in. We have business to settle."

The hand stilled, and the fire eyes stared deeply into my own.

"You are not afraid?" it hissed.

"I am afraid of a good many things. You, however, are not on that list. Now, are you ready to die?" I asked, placing my hand on the door handle.

It hissed again, spraying fire out its mouth, igniting the glass.

"Whoa, neat trick," I muttered, stepping back. When the cold air put the flames out I relocked the door and went to get dressed.

If that wasn't a fucking calling card, I didn't know what was.

My leather was out in this frigid climate. I opted for layers, lots of fucking layers. The silk long underwear wasn't cheap and it had taken a chunk out of my ego to ask Logan for the funds. It was followed by the lightweight flannel and topped off with snow pants, shoes, jacket, gloves and a hat. I huffed. The only good thing about the damn snow was that I now had lots of hiding places for knives.

Unlocking the door, I slipped out into the cold night air, wishing this little visit could have come during daylight hours, when the sun was beating overhead and my nose didn't feel like an ice bunny was gnawing it off.

I looked down at the ground as I hefted my backpack on, and was rewarded with tracks.

It was such a trap. I hoped they were well prepared.

I bent down, running a hand over the tracks that looked very human. It couldn't be, though, since humans didn't have red eyes or breathe fire. I honestly wasn't sure what we were dealing with—what I was dealing with. But the silver strapped to my back was my best bet at eliminating it. Not much can survive without a head.

I pulled my jacket closer around my throat. Logan wouldn't need this gear.

Fuck, I was not thinking about him. I had enough worries with Grams and the lack of our—my funding.

The tracks stopped abruptly. I turned around, checking if I had missed something in my musings. Turning back around, I grunted in frustration, scanning the area ahead.

I shifted, turning and surveying the area again. What was I missing?

A bird flapped its wings above me in the tall pine tree. I twirled my dagger, annoyed, debating my next move. The smart decision would be to go back to my room and wait for daylight to hunt.

I've never been accused of being terribly bright.

I moved through the snow, watching for more tracks while scanning the area in front of me.

"Come on, asshole," I taunted under my breath, "come out and play."

...

I stayed out until the sun began cresting the sky. The last thing I needed was to run into a human, curious as to why I had a small arsenal of weapons strapped to me.

I found nothing but a cramp in my neck and a cold that was engraved into my bones. Turning on the water to warm up, I called Garrick.

"Olivia, done so soon?" he questioned.

"Do you know what has claws, human feet and breaths fire?" I asked.

"No, why do you ask?"

I sighed, sitting down to unlace my boots. "I had a visitor last night, who I believe was trying to warn me off. Breathed fire over my hotel room window."

"Are you changing hotels?" he asked, a note of worry edging his voice.

"No, whatever it was disappeared after the little trick and I couldn't track it down."

"What does Logan think?"

At the sound of his name, pain laced my heart and I made a primitive noise of agony. Clearing my throat, I managed, "He's not here."

"Olivia," Garrick reprimanded. "Please tell me you are not going after an unknown Supernatural killer with no backup."

"Okay." I wouldn't tell him.

"Dammit to hell, call Logan and get backup. This thing killed two of my best executioners."

My fingers clenched around the phone as I debated how nasty my retort was going to be.

"Why isn't Logan there with you? I was under the impression mates did not like to be separated."

I groaned at his question. "We are fighting. I'm having a hard time with this whole thing."

Garrick scoffed, "By the Gods, Olivia, you having a hard time giving up control?"

I narrowed my eyes. "That's not it."

"You certain about that? You trust no one, rely on no one and refuse to be a burden to anyone. Logan is a powerful Alpha, obviously. If you two were getting along I'd be shocked."

"He keeps telling me he loves me," I whispered softly. "You know me, Garrick, I'm no good to him. I never would have agreed to this."

"Why are you no good?" His question was rapid fire.

I rubbed my forehead. Fighting back the tears there, I exhaled a shaky breath. "I'm not dependable, polished, politically savvy or fuck even mentally stable. He runs the entire US! What do I do? I run around the fucking country killing things because my own mind is so fucked up I can't deal with it. Did you know he can feel my emotions, borderline read my fucking mind? There is some fucked up shit there and he is feeling and seeing all of it!" I ended my rant on a high-pitched note.

"You fear his rejection," Garrick succinctly stated.

"He's stuck with me, Garrick, forever and ever. What if he doesn't like what he sees?" The words left me in a harsh whisper, giving voice to my darkest fear.

"Perhaps he won't, but isn't that his choice to make? The distance you are forcing will work, it will keep you miserable, but why? You have a chance to be happy, Olivia. I know the circumstances are not ideal, but trust in the chaos. Trust in your mate that he already knows you and loves you for it."

I smiled, a few rebellious tears slipping down my checks. "When did you get so wise?" I asked, too softly for a human to hear, but his vampire hearing didn't miss it.

"I've had lifetimes, Olivia. Take my advice, call Logan."

"Alright, alright, thanks, Garrick."

I hung up, scrolling to call Logan before I lost my nerve. His voicemail picked up.

"Hey, I need backup on this case." I heaved a sigh. "I probably shouldn't have left like I did. I – I – I don't know what to say, Logan. Except this whole situation terrifies me. No one should see inside of me the way you do. You deserve better than what I have to offer. Fuck, this isn't going—I'm in Aspen, Colorado if you can spare someone. If not, I understand."

I hung up before I could blather even more. The shower helped chase away the lingering cold and I closed the blinds before trying to get more sleep.

I fell into the soft sheets, pulling the comforter under my chin, visions of red eyes dancing in my mind.

Chapter 13

...s later I rolled over, staring at the ceiling, debating if I needed to ch... my phone or not. I was a light sleeper; my phone would have woken me up.

I sighed, rolling onto my stomach, looking at the closed curtains.

"Fuck it," I huffed. I illuminated the screen. My heart sank with the sight of no notifications and I sucked in a breath. I needed backup, I could admit it.

I dialed Mark. "Olie," he picked up in a hush.

"Hey, I'm sorry, is this a bad time?" I asked.

"Give me a minute."

I heard doors closing when Mark finally came back on. "What's up?"

"I need backup on this case I'm running. You available?"

"Yeah, I gotta clear it with Logan first."

I rubbed my forehead. "He's not answering my calls," I confessed.

"Of course not, he's a little busy right now," Mark chided me.

"Yeah, I guess."

"Olie you can't be jealous of Lorraine."

"What?" Anger blasted through my veins.

"Oh shit, no one told you."

"Told me what, Mark?" I asked.

"Lorraine went into labor, the baby was too early." His voice contained sorrow.

"What?" I whispered. "Is she okay? The baby?"

Mark sighed. "She's in the NICU. Logan won't leave her side. I'm having a hard time getting Lorraine to pump for her. The doctor said breast milk would be the best for her."

"Give the phone to Lorraine," I demanded. "Mark, now." I infused my voice with the power of an alpha.

I heard his steps, rapidly followed by the opening of a door.

"Get out, Mark, I am not putting that leech on my boob," Lorraine yelled.

"Calm down," I heard Blue's voice.

"You are on speakerphone, Olie," Mark informed me.

"Listen, Lorraine, and listen well. You will pump as often as needed for your child. If you don't, I will find every living member of your family and force you to watch as I slaughter them. It won't be quick. I will take my time, until their screams haunt your dreams and their voices are hoarse from begging for death."

"She has a sister in New York," Blue offered.

I smiled. "Do I need to find her?" I asked softly.

"No, you psychotic bitch. I'll pump." Her voice trembled and I took great pleasure in it.

"Excellent. Blue, you want to come give me a hand in Colorado?"

"Bloody hell, woman, I'd love it."

I smiled. "Let's go. Mark, tell Logan I'll get back as soon as I can."

...

I hung up with Mark and Blue, debating if I should wait for Blue or go ahead. I felt shitty, but I actually felt better about Logan's silence. I wanted to be there with him to take turns comforting the poor little girl who entered the world too soon and to a worthless mother. At least she had Logan. I wonder what he named her?

I dressed, my mind made up. Any intel I could gather would help speed this process along and get me back where I belonged.

I just hoped Logan still wanted to give this a try.

I dressed similarly to the previous night, opting to go with my hidden silver, leaving my pretty crossbow and swords. Twisting my dark locks up into a bun, I headed out, stowing my phone and room key in my jacket pocket.

I went down to the restaurant, ordering enough food for two people.

Two college-aged kids watched me closely and I pointedly ignored them as I stuffed my face with French toast.

Charging my meal to my room, I headed outside to walk the path I'd followed in my attempt to chase down my fire breathing warning system.

Fresh powder covered the tracks and I was just as lost as before. I huffed, deciding to head over to the scene where the last executioner was killed.

...

The cab dropped me off at a trailhead and I shifted my backpack, wondering if only bringing water and food was my smartest decision. But the last thing I needed was to get noticed by the police for brandishing my silver collection.

The hike had me breathing hard as I crested up the mountainside. The trail wasn't more than an animal path and it made me think of Logan. I sat down hard on a smooth rock, betting I wasn't the only one who had used it for a break.

The sky stretched out before me, the blue dotted with fluffy clouds. I thought about Logan, alone and dealing with his fragile little infant, and an idea formed.

Checking my phone, I found it had two bars. Hopefully that would be enough.

I dialed Mal's number.

"Olie?" she asked groggily.

"Hey Mal, I'm sorry to wake you, but I have a proposition for you." I woke Mallory up at a lot, poor thing. I honestly did feel bad for her. She ran security at the Centennial compound and occasionally helped out at Kitten. Our last conversation had not ended well; she wanted to keep me on the good side of the vampires, but too many others were working against her.

She groaned, "I'm not into chicks."

"Logan's daughter was born early."

"How early?"

"She's only thirty weeks." I refused to let my voice crack.

"I'm listening, Olie. You have my attention."

"Do you remember our last conversation about being on the wrong sides?" I was being intentionally vague in case others were listening.

"I do." Her voice had lost the tensing.

"I'm willing to take you to the side you desire if you can help Logan."

"Are you certain of this?" Mal asked, her voice low.

"Yes, I guarantee it."

"What hospital are they at?"

...

I gave Mal the details and texted Mark to let him know what would be happening. Easing my eyes closed, I relaxed the shields in my mind. Golden threads sprung into my vision and I searched for Logan, finding his thread, thicker than the rest. I followed it back, nudging it against his consciousness.

I tried to give him my confidence and hope about the situation. He relaxed against my touch and his joy overflowed into me.

She's beautiful.

I smiled, letting my emotions wrap around him, hoping he took comfort in it.

"Breathe deep, bitch," a voice said. My eyes snapped open. I was staring into the eyes of the college kid from earlier today.

I slipped a dagger free, slicing out at his forearm as he held the wet rag to my mouth. My slice wasn't nearly forceful enough, but it caused the kid to hiss, wincing in pain.

I stood, lunging my body weight at him. I toppled instantly, hitting my knees hard as the kid backed up.

"Careful Aaron, don't let her get way!" another voice called out. Aaron pressed the cloth back, covering my mouth and nose. I attempted to get my limbs under me and kick his human ass, but the incoming darkness had different ideas.

The fog surrounding my brain wasn't as deep as my captors thought, but it had effectively blocked my mate bond. Awesome, so glad that I actually might need to be rescued and the pack magic tracking system wasn't available to me.

At least I wasn't being thrown into a sweat-inducing nightmare.

How the feeble humans got me down the mountain and into the windowless van I didn't know, but it was clearly a struggle based on the bruise forming on my hip. I rolled to my stomach, lifting my head up to take a quick glance at my surroundings.

My hands and legs weren't bound. Idiots. I lunged for the driver, Aaron. My arm around his throat, I leaned back, closing off his airway. Sputtering met my efforts while the vehicle swerved.

"What the fuck is wrong with you two?" I demanded, leaning back, applying more pressure.

"Tsss," Aaron hissed.

I leaned back, my bicep flexing uncomfortably.

Aaron batted at my arm, gurgling. The human next to him was searching for something, bent down. I'd deal with him in a minute. The van careened over a sidewalk and I was ready for this fucker to die.

My normal rule of not killing humans was voided when they tried to kill me first. Fair is fair.

The passenger pushed a black, hissing taser into my neck. I seized up.

"Fucking bitch," Aaron coughed. "Give her more," he hissed, rubbing his neck.

I'd never been tased and it wasn't an experience I cared to repeat. My muscles locked up, my head rolling back while asshole number two shoved another gag over my mouth. I tried landing a kick on him, but the shaking reduced it to a harmless shutter before I was forced back into the darkness.

...

I was chained. The weight against my wrist and ankles was familiar, along with the smell of unkempt cells.

Could I go back to the basement chains? At least they smelled better.

"She's pretty. They'll pay good money for her."

In another cell, chains shifted, and sobbing began. I inhaled, scenting human, only human.

Motherfuckers. I had been kidnapped by humans? The executioners were killed by humans?

Fuck, this was embarrassing.

"Don't touch her, the boss wants first crack at her."

Wonderful. I'd like first crack at the boss also.

I kept still on the floor until I heard the door close again. My eyes flicked open, rapidly adjusting to the low light. The door cracked again and I closed my eyes, not to appear still knocked out, but to save my night vision by not blinding myself on a sliver of the sun.

Chains directly in front of me rattled.

"No," a soft voice chanted. My eyes focused through the gloom on the speaker, a dark haired beauty. Even the dirty smudges and dried blood couldn't hide her high cheekbones and full lips.

She backpedaled in her cage, trying to wrap her stained and torn short sun dress closer around her.

I sat up, seeing her attacker's legs and torso blocking out her frail form.

"Come on, pretty, Daddy wants a ride."

"No James, please," she whispered.

My chains rattled and he looked back at me as he unlocked her cell door.

"Oh good, you're up. The boss will be having his fun with you after that little stunt in the car," James taunted.

"You should run," I warned him, my voice deadly low.

He stopped unbuttoning his pants, his belt flapping open. "What you gonna do about it?"

He kicked the cage and I didn't back up or flinch. That unnerved him.

"Stupid bitch, you ain't the first copper we've taken out."

My lips turned up in a small grin. "I'm no cop."

He huffed, "Yeah right, how else you explain the gear your carrying?"

"This isn't the first cage I've been thrown in."

He kicked the cage again. "Shut up, you're ruining my wood."

"I'm going to skin you alive, James," I taunted in a singsong voice. "I'm going to make you eat your own wood first, though."

His eyes widened when I licked my lips. I do crazy real fucking well.

"Shut up, I'm not going to tell you again."

I rattled my cage and James jumped.

"What is wrong with you?" James hissed.

"So much, James, so very much."

I palmed my hidden silver, which I had brilliantly forgotten about during my kidnapping, and was ready to launch the pointy end at James's little bits, when the door slammed open again.

"God dammit, James, what the fuck have I told you about sampling the merchandise?" boomed a deep voice.

I turned in my cell, seeing the dirty pile of rags next to me also lift her head, watching the large man. He stood in the doorway, blocking out the light, before moving into the space and shutting the door with the same force he'd used opening it.

"Shit, Nolan, I didn't think you were back." James scuffed his boot against the ground, not looking at his boss.

The woman next to me hissed. "Silence!" Nolan bellowed. The woman hissed again, her body sliding around the cage, her shoulder banging against the enclosure.

I took another look at her and my radar went off. She wasn't fully human. I was doubting demigod, but she had a dash of the Supernatural running through her veins.

"I said silence," Nolan repeated more quietly, stalking toward her.

Her beating increased.

Nolan sighed and I turned my attention back to him, inhaling deeply. I scented mint and sweat. I scented human.

A low growl rumbled up my throat. Logan would have been proud.

Nolan's attention shifted. "What do we have here?"

He squatted down in front of me and I flicked my eyes over his strong jaw, dimpled cheeks and thick black eyebrows. He'd be attractive, you know, if one could overlook the whole sex trafficking.

"You know who I am," I said softly, smiling.

Nolan's gaze traveled leisurely over my chest, trailing over my hips and back up to analyze my face.

"You, my dear girl, will fetch quite a price."

I laughed, tilting my head back before wrapping my hands around the iron bars. "Guess who I am," I whispered.

Nolan wasn't fazed by my unique brand of crazy, oh but he should have been.

"I don't actually care." He stood. "Open the cage," he commanded James.

James fumbled with the keys, taking them from his previous rape victim's lock and inserting one into mine.

My gaze never left Nolan's, the self-confident motherfucker was smiling.

I was going to carve that smile off his fucking face.

The door swung open. Nolan reached down, fisting the front of my shirt and yanking me out, knocking my head against the top of the cage. The chains strained as James worked at releasing them.

Freeing my appendages, Nolan leaned down and kissed me hard, biting through the delicate flesh of my bottom lip.

I palmed my hidden silver and stabbed him between the legs. He went down with a wonderful, satisfying scream.

I rounded on James, his gaze flicking between his boss writhing in pain and me. I took out a throwing knife and let it fly. He reached down to cover his wood and the blade pierced both his hands.

I enjoyed his screaming as well.

"Alright ladies, how many more are there? I know of Aaron, but who else?"

The hissing woman next to me regained her composure first. "Three including Aaron, they are rounding up more girls and I expect them back soon."

I groaned, pulling the keys out of my cell.

James freed his hands, holding the bleeding appendages to his chest, rocking back and forth.

I turned on him, picking up the discarded blade.

"Stop, stop, stop, what is wrong with you?" he chanted, crying.

I leaned close to him. "How many times did she beg you to stop?" I demanded. Seeing the truth in his eyes, I slammed my blade between his legs, severing his wood. His eyes rolled back into his head, blood flowing freely from the wound. He passed out.

"I wish I had more time with you," I told him before I rounded on Nolan, still screaming.

With my booted foot I stomped on his face, cartilage snapping, teeth crumbling. I didn't stop until he was unrecognizable.

"Feel better?" the hissing girl asked.

"Mildly," I admitted.

"Are you going to leave us in here until they come back?"

"What's your name?" I asked.

"Nila," she answered.

"Okay, Nila, I'll free you since I'm betting you would like to take a crack at the other three." She nodded eagerly, wrapping her hands around the cage.

The other women started to cry out, begging to be released. I sighed, turning to face them.

"Shut up!" Nila yelled. I tried various keys, finally finding the one that freed her from her cell.

She held out her hands to me and I worked quickly at releasing her from the chains.

"Do you have any more knives?" she asked.

I pulled out two additional silver blades, handing them over to her. She held them, her shoulders relaxing.

"Do we hide the bodies?" she asked.

I looked over the mutilated corpses, chewing on my bottom lip, debating.

"Yeah, let's move them. We need to trap them in here."

We lugged the bodies to the back and I was surprised at how easily she completed the task.

"What are you?" I asked.

Her eyes flicked to me, alarmed.

"I'm Olivia, Head Executioner for the Council."

Nila's eyes narrowed in recognition. "The Council? Why are you here? You work for the Eastern Council, don't you?"

"I do. Garrick sent two Executioners here who didn't return and he hired me to find out why."

Nila nodded slowly. "I've been here for a week, but no one like you has been here."

I chewed on my lip, thoughtfully. "Well that doesn't make any fucking sense," I huffed, taking a hiding place behind the cages.

"Hey, you didn't answer my question," I added. "What are you?"

"A quarter dragon," she answered, letting her eyes grow into red pinpricks of light.

"Nice," I said, impressed, as she went around to the rear of the cages to hide.

"Hey, you don't happen to know a being with human feet and claws for hands that can breathe fire?"

Nila turned to me, coming out from her hiding place, shocked. "That's my father."

"Oh, well he paid me a visit. Actually, talking to him would have been nice. I prefer to come in to kill the bad guys under my own power."

Nila was opening her mouth to say more when the door rattled. We both ducked into our hiding places. The voices were complaining about how heavy the body was that they were lugging in.

I tightened my grip around the handle of my blade, waiting. I needed to block the exit, so I had to wait until they were all inside.

I fucking suck at waiting.

Aaron came in, tossing down the body of a girl with little regard to the way she landed wrong on her neck. I heard the snap but apparently they didn't, Aaron dragging her by her arms, throwing her into a cell.

"Hey, where did the crazy bitch go? I wanted to take a run at her," Aaron asked, locking a dead girl into a cage. What a surprise, the succubus is popular.

"Boss wanted her first," said another, grunting.

"What's taking so long?" said the third asshole as I fist pumped silently before putting myself between them and the door.

"Thanks for the joining the party, gentlemen. We'll be relieving you of your genitalia now." All three turned to me, shocked.

"Fuck," Aaron stated. I let my blade loose, lodging it in his thigh. He went down hard, belting.

Nila turned the corner, slashing thick gashes into one of the men. I kicked Aaron in the head, snapping it back with a satisfying crack. He fell back dead. It was too quick a death for them, but I was a little pissed. Okay more than a little, a lot.

I looked to see if Nila needed help, only to find her panting, her body sprayed with blood like a warrior's.

I smiled at the mess of body parts. "Nice job."

She nodded, her hands shaking as she pulled herself together.

"Let's get everyone out and get you home."

Nila nodded, blinking back the tears that were threatening to fall.

We worked quickly. Many of the girls had to be carried out, a few from fear, others from injury. We set them in the sun, leaned up against the old barn. I used Aaron's cell phone to dial 911, handing the phone off to one of the more vocal women.

I turned to Nila. She nodded and we climbed into the van that had taken me here, driving away from the madness.

...

We dumped the van at one of the burn sites, hoofing it to my hotel room. I opened the sliding glass door to the room, ushering us in.

"Feel free to shower." I waved her into the bathroom. "I have clothing that will fit you."

A pounding at my door had me going for my gun. I peered through the peephole quickly, careful not to keep my body in front of the door for too long.

I breathed a sigh of relief, throwing open the door and letting my gun point at the ground.

"Hallo luv, did you have all the fun without me?" Blue asked, sauntering into my room.

I hugged him in my guts-stained, sweaty, dirty outfit. "I missed you," I whispered.

He held me close, patting my back. "Rough time of it, luv?" he asked in his thick Irish accent.

I groaned, "We got one hell of a mess here."

"Please, fill me in."

I unloaded onto Blue, everything, all the dirty details, while Nila showered. He listened intently, nodding, asking questions to clarify where he needed to.

"Humans?" Blue asked.

I nodded, "Humans."

"Where are the other executioners?" Blue asked.

"Dammed if I know."

"I think I have an idea," Nila said, coming out dressed in my yoga pants and tan top. They were big for her slight frame. "I think my dad has them."

"Why would he have them? I thought he was trying to help," I asked, confused.

Nila shrugged. "He has a unique way of helping. I'm assuming he thought to use the executioners as leverage to get me back from the humans with Garrick's help."

Okay, I couldn't fault that logic, "But why not just go after you himself?"

Nila shook her head. "The cages were iron."

"Oh, right." Everyone knew dragons and half dragons had an iron allergy. Okay, well, I did now.

"Do you know where to find them?" I asked.

She nodded.

I rubbed the back of my neck. "Let me clean up and we will head out."

Thirty minutes later Nila was directing us to her father while I tried calling Logan again. It went straight to voicemail.

"Hey it's me," I sighed heavily. "I hope the baby is okay. I'll be back soon."

I called Mark, it also went to voicemail. I didn't bother leaving a message.

Yeah, no worries guys, I was just kidnapped by some psycho humans running a sex trafficking ring, but I'm fine.

I groaned. Why did I care? I was used to doing shit on my own and I needed to stay that way. I hardened the guards around my heart, leaning my head against the cool window.

I must have zoned out at some point. When we came to a stop I blinked, getting out of the car at the entrance to a tunnel. Abandoned train tracks curled up at the entrance and dead leaves crunched underfoot.

Nila ran into the dark cave. Blue looked at me and I looked back at him. "After you, my dear."

I huffed, following Nila at a much slower pace.

A language I didn't recognize bounced off the rock walls, Nila speaking excitedly, her voice constricting with her tears.

Blue and I came to a stop in a huge cavern littered with gold treasure.

"Touch nothing," I hissed to Blue. "He's half dragon."

Blue's eyes widened before he nodded. "I didn't know dragons still existed."

"Me either."

Nila came out sans her father, with two vampires following her. They looked disgruntled, bound with silver, but unharmed. She stopped a safe distance from us and I was almost insulted. I had just rescued her ass.

"I'll give them back to you if you promise no retribution. He did what he thought he needed to in order to save me."

"Fine, but next time, have him call me."

Nila nodded, smiling as she released the two annoyed vampires. "Thank you, Olivia."

"Anytime."

...

"Hi Garrick, I found your executioners," I announced to him chipperly on the phone, driving said executioners to their vehicles.

"Really?" Garrick asked. "They're alive?"

"Yeah, but you can't seek retribution," I informed him.

"Did you agree to that on my behalf?"

"Yeah."

Garrick groaned. "Olivia," he chided.

"Just hear me out."

I filled Garrick in on the details. Turned out the half dragon father was burning the areas as a warning and he thought the vampires he collected might have something to do with his missing daughter since they were poking around. He had no idea he had bagged himself two powerful executioners. Remind me not to piss off a dragon. However, aside from being hungry, they were unharmed.

"Do you think the humans hurt the dragon girl?" Garrick asked.

"I know they did." My voice was soft.

Garrick grunted, "How did he manage to capture the executioners?"

"Don't ask," they both answered in unison.

...

I gave my SUV to the displaced executioners when we found their vehicles were not where they'd left them, hitching a ride in Blue's SUV.

"So Olivia, are you going to ask me about Logan?"

I grunted.

"The man is beside himself, which you should be able to tell if you allowed your damn wall to crack."

I grunted.

Blue sighed, exasperated. "Tell me, how do you plan on handling this?"

I thought back to Garrick's advice. "I'm going to try, Blue. I don't want to be alone forever."

His head turned abruptly, shocked.

"Not a fucking word," I warned.

Chapter 14

We made it back to St Ann in record time and went straight to the hospital.

"You're a fucking terrible driver," I scolded Blue, getting out of the car.

He smiled. "You just took down an entire ring of bad guys with minimal help and you fear my driving skills?"

"Abso-fucking-lutely."

"Bags?" Blue asked, opening the back of the SUV.

"You going back on guard duty?" I questioned.

"Probably. I'm already attached to the little shit."

I smiled, taking the bag Blue handed to me. "What's her name, anyways?"

"Ginny."

"Ginny," I repeated.

A few nurses gave us strange looks and wide berths. Even though I had washed all the blood off, apparently I hadn't dropped the killer gleam in my eyes or my scowl.

Blue led the way to Lorraine's room, where we put our bags down. The room was empty and we headed down to the NICU.

We turned a corner and I stopped in my tracks, seeing Logan holding Ginny, rocking her gently. His white shirt looked dirty, the bags under his eyes pronounced. I went to the glass, holding my hand against the cool surface, smiling at him.

Slowly, he registered I was there, the relief etched onto his exhausted features.

He indicated the side door with a flick of his head. A nurse went to open the door and I walked into his outstretched arm as his other held Ginny close to him. I nuzzled into him, feeling my shields dropping away of their own accord. Damn traitors.

He kissed the top of my head and I held onto him, watching the small bundle cradled against his chest.

"Can I hold her?" I asked softly.

"Yeah," he said, relieved, handing off the small bundle.

Ginny squawked, probably pissed about losing her comfy warmth. Moving her up, I laid her check against my chest, bouncing and swaying while I cooed to her. She settled pretty quickly, snuggling in.

I looked to Logan, finding his eyes brimming with unshed tears. "She's perfect, Logan."

He leaned, in kissing me hard. "You saved her," he whispered.

I blinked back my own fucking tears, assholes. I shrugged. "Go shower and eat, I got this."

He nodded. "Lorraine has been pumping behind the curtain. What did you say to her?" he asked me softly.

I smiled. "Motivation. Did you know she has a sister in New York?"

Logan laughed, softly kissing Ginny's head. "I won't be long."

I nodded. "Relax, I got this."

...

Ginny was fed, burped, and in a clean diaper before she fell asleep on my chest. I lounged in the recliner, my hands rubbing small circles on her back.

Logan had tried to come back but I sent him away.

"How you doing, sweetie?" the night shift nurse asked me.

"Good, you need to check her vitals again?"

She nodded, taking Ginny's temperature, listening to her heartbeat. "It's the darndest thing how quickly she recovered. I don't think I've ever seen anything like it."

I smiled. All it had taken was giving Mal protection under The Council. I closed my eyes, leaning my head back to rest.

A warm hand landed on my thigh and I kicked out before my eyes opened.

Logan rubbed his stomach. "Sorry," I muttered.

He leaned down to kiss me firmly, his tongue seeking entrance into my mouth. I obliged him, sucking on the heated flesh.

Logan leaned closer, cupping my cheek. Reluctantly, he leaned back, resting his forehead against my own. "I was worried about you."

"Ehh, no need to be. Just a couple of humans."

"That kidnapped you?"

"Fucking Blue, did he rat me out?"

Logan laughed, taking Ginny from me. "Come on, we are being released."

I groaned, standing and rubbing the kink out of my neck, wrapping an arm around his waist.

We went back to the room and I didn't see Lorraine.

"Where is she?" I asked, a pang of jealously hitting me unexpectedly. She was able to bear Logan a child, something I could never do.

Logan looked around, "I don't know. She should be here."

I nodded, shrugging. "Mark and Blue?" I asked.

"Bringing the cars around."

I nodded, picking up my bag and Logan's. "Ready?"

He nodded, strapping Ginny's little form into the car seat before picking her delicately up.

...

Mark and Blue were waiting for us with Logan's SUV and Blue's. I rocked Ginny in her car seat as we waited for Logan to finish the paperwork.

I recognized the click of the heels before turning to see Grams purposefully walking toward me with Lorraine.

My lips flattened into a thin line.

"Where do you think you are going?" Grams asked.

"With my baby," Lorraine hissed, trying to snatch the car seat from me.

I slapped her hand away with a resounding smack.

"You threatened to kill her, you signed off on all your rights to her after she was born. What makes you think you can touch her?"

"I signed that under duress. She is my child and I want to take care of her," Lorraine sobbed.

"Really? Then where is her milk?"

Lorraine blinked rapidly. "She doesn't need it anymore now that she is better."

I scoffed at her, "You are pathetic."

"And I don't suppose you know how Ginny's miraculous rapid healing occurred?" Grams mused.

"Fuck off, Grams, you will not get involved here," I warned her. Was her hatred for me so great that she would even meddle in all this?

She held her head regally high. "I must protect those you steamroll over with your single-minded focus on what is best for you."

"This will not end well for you," I gritted, my voice low with menace.

"Is that a threat?" she asked gleefully.

I smiled. "A prediction. Meddling in business that doesn't concern you never ends up well."

Mark and Blue stepped up next to me. "Problem, luv?" Blue asked.

"Is there?" I asked Grams.

"You will be hearing from my lawyer regarding this gross violation of a mother's rights."

"Do what you need to," Logan said, done with his paperwork. "I'm not afraid of you or your idle threats, Grams. If you want a legal battle, I am happy to accommodate."

...

"Thanks for all your help, Blue," I said.

"Anything for you, my dear." He turned to Logan. "Do us all a favor and don't knock up anymore obnoxious humans."

"He won't," I answered, a little too quickly.

Mark nudged my arm. "Feeling a little possessive?"

I huffed, "Homicidal is more like it."

"Oh dear, and here I thought you got that out of your system earlier," Blue teased.

I shoved him. "Later, Blue."

He tipped an imaginary hat to me. "Later, luv."

"So, where to?" Mark asked, behind the wheel.

I turned to Logan in the backseat with Ginny.

"I guess I need to find a house pretty quickly," Logan commented absently.

"The manor," I said. "The kids will be overjoyed to see her."

Logan nodded, leaning back against the headrest, watching his small daughter.

...

As we pulled into the driveway, I noted my SUV was back. That was quick.

The children couldn't get enough of Ginny, cooing and entertaining her for hours on end, allowing Logan and me to meet with Tommy.

"I have a list," he said, handing me the printout. "I emailed it to you," he told Logan.

I looked over the six possible locations. "This is well clustered."

Tommy nodded. "It has to be. Only those six locations provide enough rainfall, sunlight and humidity for the plant to survive."

I nodded, turning to Logan.

"Do you want to come with me?" I asked him. His gaze shifted out the door to where we could hear the kids playing with Ginny.

"I can take Jerry and Mark," I offered.

He looked back at me with sad eyes. I stepped closer to him, laying a hand on his arm. "It's okay, Logan, take care of our girl. I'll go kick ass."

He laughed, "I am your mate and Alpha. You should be staying here, and I going."

I shook my head. "She needs you, Logan, and I do as well. But I can wait."

His eyes searched my own and I let the mate bond flare into full force. He nodded, feeling the truth of my emotions.

"OLIVIA!" Grant yelled, bursting into Tommy's room. "What in the seven hells did you do for this kind of money?"

I smiled, "Rescued Garrick's executioners."

Grant heaved, panting, "That's it?"

"Also took out a group of human traffickers, but that was a side project."

He stared at me, dumbfounded, and I patted him on the arm. "Does Garrick have any more jobs he wants to throw our way?" he asked eagerly.

I shook my head. "This was a fluke. Apparently, Grams called him, warning that I would be asking for a loan. I took a job instead." I took a loan from my mate, though. Ugh, that still didn't sit well.

"Great," Grant said, shaking his dark locks back. "Also, we sent all the accounting discrepancies to the attorney. She was pretty excited about it."

"Wonderful, let's hope it's enough to bury the bitch."

I took out my phone, calling Mark and Jerry. No time like the present to hunt down an extinct plant.

...

I sent the kids back to homework and weapons practice while Logan laid Ginny down in the bassinet in our room.

I had the baby monitor set up on the island while Logan worked in the kitchen. I took out two wine glasses, pouring myself one and setting one next to Logan at the stove.

"How does it feel to be a dad?" I asked.

"Terrifying. It's insane to me, to think I am entrusted with such a being."

I nodded. "I could see that."

"I want you to contact Sage tomorrow. It's her territory and I want her to help you."

I swallowed back my protest. "If that's what you want."

He nodded. "It is. I know you don't like her, but she is a powerful ally."

I smiled, taking a long sip. "I'll try to get past it."

He nodded and met my gaze. "Thank you."

Chapter 15

Morning arrived with Ginny sleeping on my chest and Logan passed out circled around me as I leaned against the bed frame.

I stretched my toes, running a hand over her soft, bald head.

She stirred, squawking before laying her head back down. Logan picked his head up, reaching out to pat her back.

"Want me to take her?" he asked groggily.

"No, get some rest, I have time before I leave." He nodded, sliding his body around mine once again.

I combed my fingers through his hair, enjoying the silken way the caramel locks felt against my skin. I could get used to this. I could wake up like this every day. That thought had me closing my eyes with a smile.

...

Three hours later, I released my hold on the precious little Ginny, transferring her to the bassinet so Logan could get a few more hours of rest. Silently, I stalked downstairs, slipping my boots on.

I peeked outside and as usual, Jerry was right on time to pick me up at this ungodly early hour. Even the kids weren't awake yet. I slung my bags over my shoulder and was headed to the door when Logan came padding down with Ginny wrapped in his arms.

"Hey, go back to sleep," I said, turning to him. I watched them together, my heart warming. I took a step toward him, tilting my head for a kiss. He met my lips gently.

"Be careful," he warned, his irritation and frustration seeping through in the mate bond.

I should be going with you.

I shrugged, kissing Ginny. "I'm always careful and there are more important things now."

He regarded for a long moment and I could feel he wanted to say more, probably along the lines of "I love you." I just smiled and left as quickly as I could.

Sliding into the back seat, I complained, "I still don't see why we can't take my vehicle. I have all my weapons organized in the back.

Jerry laughed, "Because it stinks."

"It does not," I shot back.

"It does," Mark agreed. "Possibly even worse since the vamps returned it."

"Whatever," I grunted, settling against the clean interior of Jerry's vehicle.

I rubbed my forehead, "Which Compass Alpha's territory are we heading to?"

I knew the answer.

"Sage," Mark said, turning around. "Why?"

I chewed on my fingernail. "Do you have her number?"

"I do, but I thought you didn't like her."

"I don't, but it would be helpful to have another set of eyes so we can split up the list. Call her and see if she has anyone in Iowa we can borrow."

Mark nodded, hitting a few buttons on the touch screen console. Sage's voicemail spoke over the speakers.

"Hey Sage, it's Mark. We are doing some research and we're hoping you might have a few shifters near Humboldt, Iowa. Give me a call back."

...

Eight hours later, we arrived in the small town of Humboldt. I stretched, arching my back, relieving the kinks from being cooped up in the SUV.

"We are losing daylight, Olie, let's move," Mark warned.

I looked over at the setting sun, lighting up the sky a rosy pink color. "Yeah, let's move. I don't have the advantage of shifter sight."

Jerry came around the front of the vehicle, cracking his knuckles with a flourish. "I can help with that."

The wiggling of his fingers, I was pretty certain, was for show and not for function. Six balls of light lifted from his hands, growing in size as they encircled us.

"That is cool," I muttered, impressed.

Jerry brushed imaginary dust from his shoulder. "I know."

Mark pushed ahead through the dense foliage.

"Does anyone know what we are looking for?" I asked, trying to summon the picture from Tommy's computer.

"Here," Mark said, passing me his phone. Green waxy leaves with little red flowers met my gaze.

I grunted, "It's gotta be the flowers that cause it."

163

"Why do you say that?" Jerry asked.

"It would make sense that something so small could be so deadly," I answered. "Did Sage ever call you back?" I asked.

"No," Mark grunted.

I nodded and thought, she must know I'm here.

It didn't matter, I was perfectly capable of handling this with Mark and Jerry. The bitch's help was not needed.

"What is it, Olie?" Mark asked. "I can feel your irritation and resolve."

I huffed, "That is going to take time to get used to. I was just thinking we don't need her help."

Mark nodded and we proceeded on our nature walk.

Five hours later we made it back to the SUV.

"Why didn't we take water, again?" I grunted, opening the door and searching for the bottle I had purchased at the last gas station.

Grunts met my question as they searched for their own refreshments.

Jerry came up for air first. "I feel we can cross this location off our list."

"Agreed," Mark grunted, sitting in the passenger seat.

"We passed a hotel not far back. It looked clean," Jerry said, starting the car.

...

I had my bags slung over my shoulder as we climbed the stairs to our suite.

"Why are we taking the stairs?" Jerry complained. "I have blisters the size of quarters."

I chuckled. "It was faster, and Mark is carrying your luggage."

"But he's not carrying me," Jerry whined.

We exited the stairwell in front of our rooms. I opened my door, tossing my bags onto the bed before I opened the door to the suite.

Jerry had his door open also.

"Hey Olie, just remember if this door's a-rocking, don't come a-knocking," Jerry teased.

I laughed, "What about your blisters?"

He huffed, "Darling, it's all in the hips."

"Goodnight, or actually morning, I guess," I told them, leaving my door cracked and heading for the shower.

The hot water soothed some of my irritation with Sage, but it didn't sit well. Assuming she knew I was here, why would she not call Mark back, knowing

Logan would find out? And if she didn't know I was here, why was she ignoring Mark?

My gut said something was wrong, very wrong.

Dressed in a nightshirt and pants, I sprawled on the bed, texting Logan.

First stop was a bust. How's Ginny?

She's good, feeding right now. Lorraine had us served.

That didn't take long. What does she want?

Full custody, child support, and alimony.

Greedy fucking bitch, I answered. I don't suppose she has bothered to check in on how Ginny is doing? Or send more milk for her?

She's claiming the stress of you threatening her stopped her milk.

I laughed. Good luck proving that.

My phone rang and I picked up.

"She getting ready for bed?" I asked in a hush.

"No, she's downright refusing to do that."

I laughed at that. "Hey, have you heard from Sage?" I asked.

"No, why?" he asked wearily.

"I had Mark call her on our way here and she hasn't responded."

"That's odd. Think you should check on her?"

I sighed, "Are you okay if I kill her? I may need to send a message."

"Yes, her disobeying you is not acceptable, but be sure she knows it was you."

"I will. I want to check out a few more locations before I deal with her."

"I understand." Ginny squawked in the background.

"I'll be back before you know it," I told him, meaning every word.

"I hope so. I'm looking at houses tomorrow. Hopefully I'll find something."

"Something close to the kids," I reminded him.

He laughed, "Yes, I know, close the manor, easily defendable, and close to Kass."

"Glad you've been paying attention."

Ginny squawked again.

"I'm also going to be interviewing sitters. Kass has a few very good recommendations."

"They have to be able to defend her," I answered quickly.

"I am aware, Olivia."

"Guns, knives, hand to hand, explosives, throwing knives, swords—"

"I got it, Olie. She will be well protected."

"Right, you know that, obviously. The recommendations from Kass are solid, I vetted them myself for Hannah."

"Good to know. Get some rest, it's late.

"You too, Logan. I miss you."

I could feel his happiness at that confession after my dashing out at the mere possibility of the L word. "I miss you, too," he said softly.

"Goodnight."

"Night." I hung up before he could utter the L word. I was in no way ready for that. Just because I had accepted that the mate mark had me feeling things I normally wouldn't, that did not mean I was ready for that life-altering step.

Chapter 16

I rolled over, squinting at the red digital display. "Crap, I missed breakfast," I groaned. Tossing the covers off, I threw my hair up into a bun before using the facilities. I dressed hastily, stowing my trusty dagger at the small of my back before putting on my leather duster, needing the extra warmth.

Rubbing my eyes, I peered through the crack in the door, finding Mark and Jerry gone.

I huffed, snatching my phone off the nightstand and calling Jerry.

"Sleeping beauty arises," he greeted me.

I grunted in response.

"We are at a café at the end of the block, do you want us to order you something?"

"Waffles, French toast, scrambled eggs, toast, and lots of hash browns."

Jerry laughed, "As you command."

I hung up, heading downstairs. I turned the corner of the first flight and dived to the side.

"Motherfucker!" I yelled, as the beak of a giant bird tried to take a bite out of my forearm.

I dodged to the side in the cramped space, landing a blow against its feathered head. I kept smashing, not daring to take the time to pull my dagger, hoping to buy some time.

So focused was I on the large beak that would tear me limb from fucking limb, that I missed the tail until its spiked end connected with my shoulder.

I yelled, going down under the beak of destruction, wetness coating my hand as I pulled the pain in deep. My breathing was labored as I used my good arm to pull my blade, holding the dagger hidden beneath me, all the better to hack at and stab, my dear.

"Come on, bitch," I taunted, as it tried to expand its wings in the tight space to help its balance.

Wicked talons slashed at me, slicing through my shirt and cleaving through the soft flesh of my stomach. I took the blow. The head followed, the beak looking for a tasty piece of flesh. I stabbed downward into its feathered head with both my hands wrapped around the hilt. The griffin gave a surprised squawk.

I twisted the blade, my shoulder spilling warm blood over my bicep. The head shuttered before the beast's massive girth fell into a lifeless lump.

I groaned, pushing the beak off of me with a sigh.

"How the hell am I going to clean this up?" I groaned, pressing a hand against my stomach.

I kicked the griffin for good measure.

The serrated beak snapped at my foot before the eyes turned to focus on me.

"Fucker," I groaned. "Any chance you want to hand my blade over?"

It lifted its head, releasing a roar of outrage.

"Wonderful." I ducked, rolling under the beast. I expected to look into feathers and fur, not the slick gray skin of its stomach.

"Djinn?" I questioned, to no one but myself

The beaked asshole looked down between its legs and snapped at me, scratching the dagger against the carpeted floor. Frustrated, it shook its head—well, now that I was under it, let's call it what it was: a boy.

My dagger flung against the wall and I knew my little reprieve was over. Darting under his side, I lunged for the dagger, my hand closing around the hilt as birdie's beak dug into my calf.

I screamed. The asshole pulled back and I twisted, pain from my calf burning up my leg. I pulled my legs under me and threw myself to the left as he crashed down again.

The pain in my calf was far beyond my other wounds, and I knew my time was limited. I'd never seen a griffin with the stomach of a djinn but shit, if the djinn could clone themselves, why not other creatures?

I charged as the griffin's wings fought to extend in the cramped space. He reared back, deadly claws extended, slicing down at my shoulders as I plunged the dagger deeply into the gray area and pulled up at an angle, hoping to sever the heart.

Gritting my teeth as the claws clenched around my shoulders, I hit resistance and kept pushing. I let out a triumphant cry as my blade hit pay dirt and the griffin deconstructed into gray goop all around me.

"Motherfucker," I hissed, spitting a glob out of my mouth.

I turned around and went back up the stairs.

...

I loaded all our bags into the SUV and drove to the diner, carefully surveying the exterior as I walked in to get Jerry and Mark.

They were sitting by a large window and saw me approaching. Mark signaled for the check.

I slid next to Jerry, greedily devouring the needed calories.

"Olivia, what happened?" Mark asked, inhaling deeply.

"I got attacked," I answered around a mouthful of food. "The fucking djinn created a damn griffin."

Mark's gaze flicked to Jerry, whose slight raise of a hand instructed him to wait.

I finished eating and leaned back, careful of my new injuries. A night's sleep would heal them, but I didn't have the time.

Mark was still looking at me, worried and irritated at being put off.

"Let's go, I'll fill you in on the drive."

Mark nodded, sliding out of the booth with stiff movements.

Jerry slid behind the wheel and Mark sat next to me in the backseat.

"What are you doing?" I asked him.

"Let me see your wounds," he commanded, which was brave to say the least.

"Hey guys, any particular destination?" Jerry asked from the front seat.

"The next possible location on the list," I instructed.

I pulled off my leather jacket, already missing the duster destroyed by the djinn, followed by my shirt.

Mark looked over my wounds, his jaw tightening.

"Why didn't you call for help?" he asked.

"I was a little too preoccupied to grab my cell phone."

He tapped his head. "With the pack bonds?"

"Oh, I didn't think of that. Besides, I had it under control," I shrugged.

"Your calf disagrees."

I flexed the muscle in question, biting back a hiss. "Yeah, well—" I had no smartass answer for that.

Mark finished with my shoulders and stomach. I pulled my shirt back on as he pulled up my yoga pant leg from my calf, removing my makeshift bandage.

"You are lucky you heal quickly, or this would need a skin graft," he chided me.

Mark sighed as he finished bandaging my calf. "Olivia, you have to understand that you need to stay alive and in good health for the sake of the shifters and Logan. He would be devastated without you, and I'm not sure Ginny would be enough to keep him among the living. "

"Tomorrow is guaranteed to no one, Mark. I understand your concern; however, I will not stop being who I am in the hope that my life expectancy will be longer."

"That was deep," Jerry commented, trying to break the awkward tension between us.

"Where are we headed today?" I asked, rubbing at my temple, where I could feel Logan's awareness of the situation.

He wasn't happy. While I wasn't blocking him, I certainly wasn't advertising my distress. Apparently, Mark didn't have the same reservations.

"A farm. We called ahead yesterday and they granted us permission to look for foreign plants threatening the native species," Jerry answered.

"That's an impressive cover," I answered.

"I saw it on a show," Jerry laughed.

Mark moved into the front seat and I gratefully stretched out. Logan wasn't leaving things be, though. I focused on our link, finding it present but not as strong. I sent him reassurance, hoping it would be enough, or that maybe taking care of a newborn would distract him. Either way, the pressure lessened and I slept.

...

The lack of motion had me sitting up and taking in the surroundings. I exited the SUV before Mark could make any additional comments. Why I was suddenly not capable of taking care of myself was beyond me.

Jerry had parked on a hill, away from the main house and barn. We were looking down onto both of them. I checked my weapons, running the pads of my fingers over my blades reassuringly.

Jerry took the lead, pulling out a tablet. "Looks to be past these trees."

I followed him, silently brooding, Mark bringing up the rear. The undergrowth was thick and it wrapped around us, impeding our progress. Honestly, it was great to have something to work out my irritation on.

We must have hiked a mile, struggling for every step. I was regretting my decision to wear fleece lined leggings when Jerry's tablet beeped at him.

"Fucking finally," he grunted, also not dressed for this. He pushed through the last of the low hanging branches and into a pot field.

"What the fuck?" he asked over the sound of guns being fired.

"Get down!" I yelled, tackling him from behind.

Mark landed on top of the pile and we rolled a few feet away.

"Guns?" I yelled over the rapid succession of poorly aimed shots.

As suddenly as it began, the shooting stopped.

"Anyone hurt?" I asked, checking Jerry for holes as Mark slid off the dog pile.

I turned to Mark, seeing red blossoming in the center of his shirt. His eyes rounded, his breathing turning into pained pants. He sat down hard on his ass, his pupils heavily dilated.

"Fuck," I hissed, pulling the small throwing dagger from my boot.

"What's wrong?" Jerry questioned, coming to stand beside me as I pushed Mark onto his back. I grabbed Jerry, pulling him lower. Tossing a leg below the wound to straddle Mark, I pushed the dagger into him, my jaw clenching. The bullet was in his heart, lucky fucking shot.

"Olivia, get your silver knife out of him!" Jerry yelled at me, trying to pull me away from Mark.

"The bullet, Jerry. It's silver, too," I informed him calmly. I dropped the dagger. My slippery fingers brushed the tip of the metal burning inside of Mark. He writhed under me, foaming at the mouth. I twisted further, my nail digging into the silver, ripping it out of his body. I flung it away.

Mark clutched his chest, sucking in air greedily. I moved off of him, careful to scan our surroundings and keep Jerry low. I pulled another throwing knife. It was a terrible cliché, bringing a knife to a gun fight.

Who uses guns? Okay, well aside from me.

Humans, oh, fucking humans use guns.

I tilted my head, listening. How would humans know to use silver bullets?

I didn't get to travel that train of thought long before a fresh burst of gunfire shot through the woods, closer than before.

"Shit." I was out of my league here.

Mark took huge, gulping breaths of air, his chest knitting back together.

"We need help," he wheezed.

"Agreed, but we aren't going to last long enough to wait for it," I countered.

"We need to get you and Jerry hidden." Mark shook his head and tried to stand. He faltered and Jerry eased him back down.

"Dang, Jerry, you been hitting the gym?" I questioned.

He gave me a disbelieving look. "Take him, and let me deal with the assholes who shot my man."

I debated for a moment. "Bitch, get over here!" he demanded.

"Jerry, you are the only one who is allowed to call me that and live."

"Noted." Gone was my carefree driver. In his place stood a pissed off mage, rolling up his sleeves.

Jerry muttered a few words and an opaque shield popped into place. He marched forward, bullets harmlessly brushing against his powerful magic.

"I sure hope he knows to kill them all," I muttered.

Mark shifted limply in my arms, his breathing evening out as he started to drift off.

I shook him, easing him into a sitting position. "Hey now, buddie, stay with me."

An explosion rang through the field, deafening me and shaking the ground. I moved in front of Mark, shielding his already tender chest. A body went flying with a high-pitched squeal in the distance.

"That's my boy," Mark muttered, his eyes rolling back into his head.

More screaming and the fields caught fire, the flames licking out to each and every plant. I stood, balancing Mark upright as I searched the field for Jerry.

He passed through the flames unharmed like a badass in his own right. He helped support Mark's weight as we booked it back to the SUV.

"So, see any of the plant we're hunting?" I asked.

"No, although if it was there, I have full confidence it will be destroyed." Jerry smiled, a self-satisfied grin. "Teach those motherfuckers to mess with my man."

"You sure showed them," Mark muttered.

"Hopefully, the whole county isn't stoned," I laughed.

Jerry stopped a moment, looking over at me. "Right, can't say I thought of that."

...

I wiped the dried blood from Mark's chest, impressed at his healing. A thick pink line remained from where my silver had scored him. He was asleep before I finished and I eased him down in the backseat. I closed the door gently before slipping into the front seat with Jerry.

"You okay to drive?" I asked Jerry.

He nodded. "Where to next on the adventures of Olie?"

I rubbed my forehead, seeing signs for Fort Dodge. "Head there," I said, pointing at the sign. "We need a large city to get lost in until we figure out who the fucking mole is."

"Mole?" Jerry repeated.

"How else would a group of pot farmers know about and be able to afford silver bullets?" I asked.

Jerry was silent, his hands clenching around the steering wheel. "I didn't think of that."

"Who else knew where we were going to be?" I asked.

Jerry sighed, "Logan, Ali, Grant, Sage, and Tommy."

I chewed on my fingernail. "Sage, you say?"

Jerry cast a searching look at me. "Yes."

"I really hope Mark knows where she lives."

...

"This is a little fancy," I told Jerry, looking at the stone waterfall in front of the hotel he had picked.

"It's the last place anyone will think to look for us," he informed me. "Besides, after my power play, I'd like a soft, cushy bed with room service."

"Alright," I consented, too tired to fight. "How you feeling, Mark?" I asked.

He pulled on a clean shirt, running a hand though his dark curly hair. "I could use a shower."

I nodded as our muddy boots squeaked against the polished stone floor of the hotel.

Jerry and Mark hung back while I smiled at the girl behind the front desk.

"Welcome, do you have a reservation?" the perky blond asked.

"No, I need two rooms for tonight."

"Names?" she asked.

I opened my mouth, ready to give her my real name, when an idea came to me. "Suzie Parker."

She smiled, clicking away quickly on her computer. I turned to Mark's questioning stare.

"Tell no one where we are," I said softly, not needing to raise my voice for his shifter hearing.

The clerk was easy to slide the extra funds to, along with a touch of succubus magic to make her forget about my ID. She slid our room keys over, her impossibly wide smile straining her cheeks at her additional income.

"Thanks," I muttered, annoyed being in her presence.

Mark waited until after the elevator ride to ask, "Why can't we tell anyone where we are?"

"Because someone is rooting for us to die, and my money is on Sage." I unlocked my room, moving to open the suite door.

Mark met me there with a disapproving look. "I know you don't like Sage for her past with Logan, but she would never try and kill you."

"While I realize any bullets will kill me, silver bullets will kill you, too. Secondly, while I do not like that she slept with Logan, I am capable of putting that aside to make rational decisions." Red hot rage burned in my chest.

The color drained from Mark's face. He rebounded quickly, though. "We could be bugged."

"Possibly," I agreed, "but the pot farmers were well prepared. I suppose someone could have gotten them silver while we hiked in. The simplest way to cross Sage off the list is to visit her tomorrow."

Mark grunted, "She's in Chicago. She has a penthouse downtown."

I raised an eyebrow at that. "For work only?"

He shook his head. "No."

"Where does she run?" I asked, bewildered. Shifters loved their open space.

"I don't know, Olie, it's not something I've ever pried into before. She takes care of her territory. The fact you keep throwing her name around as a traitor is very disturbing. Compass Alphas are charged with taking care of millions of shifters. For one to be as deceitful as you are claiming—it's just not possible. They protect the pack, they always have."

I nodded, pressing my lips together to stop my words. I couldn't see Sage with Mark and Jerry. I'd have to go alone. But leaving my backup raised its own problems. How did I get into the nest of Sage and leave again in one piece?

"Go get cleaned and up and get something to eat," I said. "We can figure out the mole later." Mark nodded, relieved I was letting it rest.

Jerry had ordered room service and I sat in their room eating in silence. Jerry raised an eyebrow at me when Mark excused himself to go the bathroom.

I shook my head, Mark would hear us.

He pulled out his phone. What's going on? he typed.

I debated telling Jerry. I thought he'd understand, but his loyalty was to Mark. I took his phone. We will figure it out tomorrow.

Jerry shook his head. But you know who the mole is.

I think I know. Mark's having a hard time accepting it.

Jerry read the message, locking his phone when the door to the bathroom opened.

After we ate I went back to my room to text Logan. Mark may have accused me of being reckless, but I knew when I was getting in over my head. Well, usually.

I think Sage is trying to kill us.

I opened the mate bond fully, feeling Logan's shock and immediate dismissal. What was the deal with this bitch?

He felt my irritation at the situation, I was sure. Olivia, jealousy is a powerful emotion for shifters.

Seriously? Do you really think I give a fuck who you shoved your dick into? Never mind, I'll deal with it myself.

I locked my phone, my anger spiking when he tried to push the mate bond.

I texted Tommy, Can you find the address of Sage the North Compass Alpha please?

You really pissed off Logan.

I really don't care.

You should be nicer to him. He's struggling with Ginny and keeping the legal battles at bay until you get back.

Well fuck if I didn't feel guilty now.

I went back to the mate bond and let my unspoken apology seep into the golden threads. I felt his emotions unwind, instantly merging with mine.

We good? Logan texted me.

Yeah, I responded. There was more to say, but I let it go. Tommy was right, we each had our own burdens right now. It wasn't fair for me to add to his plate.

Get some rest, I texted him.

You too, I heard about the griffin.

I scoffed, wondering who told on me. Yeah, apparently the djinn isn't done with me yet. Oh, and it ruined the duster.

Dammit, you've only had it for a few weeks.

Such is the life of an executioner.

For now, Logan responded. My ire snapped to the surface and only years of concealing my emotions kept it from reaching the mate bond.

We will see, is what I opted for instead. It was sweet he wanted to protect me, but I was an equal, able to protect myself. That was a point I was going to remind everyone of.

Chapter 17

I awoke after only a few hours of sleep and tested my calf. The skin was pink and new, the muscle beneath reknitted together. My shoulders and stomach bore no reminders of the griffin attack. I dressed quickly in jeans and a black shirt, my leather jacket over the ensemble.

Following the directions on my phone, I went to a 24-hour hardware store to pick up a few items. After lugging my purchases back, I spread them out on the bed and debated. I could continue with this plan of breaking into Sage's by myself, or I could bring Mark and Jerry on board.

My ego demanded I prove them all fucking wrong and show how badass I was.

Common sense had other ideas. The bitch.

I sighed and waited for them to wake up.

...

I had my gun collection spread out around me, oiling and cleaning them, when Jerry stuck his head in. His sleepy eyes took in the collection before landing on my bag of goodies. He woke up quickly after that.

"What's going on?"

"I went shopping," I sighed. "I have a plan. Neither of you are going to like it."

"It's too early for this shit!" Mark yelled at me, and I heard the bathroom door shut.

Once Mark and Jerry were dressed and we had called for room service, I outlined my plan.

"That's a terrible idea! You cannot go to see Sage alone!" Mark yelled, pacing.

"Does Logan know about this?" Jerry asked softy.

I turned my frosty, sea green gaze to him. "No, and he won't, either. He is looking at houses today while Ginny is being watched by the new nanny."

Mark grunted and I countered, "If Sage isn't a threat and isn't the mole, I fail to see the problem.

"You are two females who want the same male," Mark stated, exasperated.

"First off, I have said male. Second, if she tried to kill me, she would be signing her own death warrant." He couldn't fight with that logic.

"She's right," Jerry told Mark after a pause.

Mark glared at him. Jerry continued, turning his attention to me, "How are we going to get on the roof?"

"There is a landing pad there. I called in a favor, you two will be dropped off fifteen minutes after my scheduled appointment," I told them.

"How do you plan on hiding the sound from them? There is no way a helicopter will not be heard," Mark asked, happy to be picking holes in my plan.

"I don't want to hide the sound. It's going to be my distraction if things go badly."

"Go badly?" Jerry questioned. "What if things go fine?"

"Then I'll owe everyone a giant apology for my jealously making me see things that aren't there," I huffed, annoyed.

Jerry barely hid a smile. "I'm in."

I glared at him. "You just want to watch me eat it."

"Yes, very much," he smiled.

"When is your appointment?" Mark asked.

"Tomorrow at midnight." I slid my clip back into my pearl handled gun.

Mark grunted, "We leaving now?"

"No, I want to check out another location on our list. It's an hour from here on our way to Chicago, in Waterloo."

Mark and Jerry both raised their eyebrows in disbelief. "I'm testing my theory," I explained. "If no one attacks us, we have narrowed down who is responsible."

"Or it was just a coincidence," Mark tried.

"I don't believe in coincidences."

...

We drove to Waterloo without incident.

Slipping down from the leather seat, I stretched, taking in the boarded up warehouse.

"Inside or out?" I asked Jerry, who was working on the tablet.

"Outside," he said as he began walking. Mark and I followed.

We walked a full five miles in and around the complex. No one attacked us. We didn't find the plant, either.

"No one was here. It makes sense there was no one to attack us," Mark proclaimed, continuing to deny my logic.

"We will see, we will see."

...

Five hours later, we were pulling into the parking garage for the hotel across the street from Sage. I didn't even want to know how expensive it was.

"Are you guys clear on the pick up?" I asked for the tenth time.

"Yeah, Olie, we got it," Jerry told me yet again.

Mark had been silent and brooding since the uneventful search.

I nodded as we unloaded our packs and headed to check in.

I was overly alert to say the least. In my mind we were in the belly of the beast. Nothing happened, however, and I was wondering if perhaps I was being paranoid.

Once in the room, I called Logan.

"Hey," he greeted me. Warmth instantly spread across my chest.

"Hi, how did house hunting go?"

"I think I found one. We must have looked at twenty."

"Wow." I heard his turn signal click on. "Where are you headed?" I asked.

"I got an emergency call from two new members of the pack. They're having trouble controlling their animals." He sounded tired.

"Ginny doing good with the new sitter?"

He grunted, "I've called every hour and I swear she hasn't cried once."

I laughed, "That's a good sign."

"Yeah, the kids are watching her while she sleeps now."

"They're old enough to watch her sleep," I agreed.

The sound of his seatbelt clicking signaled the end of the call. "Be careful," I told him, wishing I was there to back him up.

He laughed, "Always."

We hung up and I went to shower and change for tonight's festivities. I felt a little bad not telling Logan about Sage, but I didn't want to hear about my jealously anymore. Besides, if I was wrong, I'd be making too many apologies already.

Emerging dressed in jeans and a royal blue shirt, I slipped my gun holsters under my leather jacket, followed by my dagger in the small of my back and throwing knives in my boots.

Overkill? Maybe. Unless I was right, and then I'd feel a little underprepared.

The hustle across the street was chilly. I rushed into the pristine white lobby, grateful for the warmth.

A large shifter stood up behind his small desk, giving me a once-over. "Can I help you?" he rumbled.

I needed an ID to flash in these situations. "Olivia, here to see Sage."

His eyes widened slightly. "Of the Council, and Mate?"

"Yep, that would be me."

"Forgive me, I didn't know you were coming." He hustled around the desk, using his key to call the elevator.

"Have you noticed anything strange going on here?" I asked, slanting him a glance as the elevator counted down floors.

He moved his weight from foot to foot. "Strange?" he repeated.

I turned to face him. "Yeah, weird. Strange people, unexplained issues?" I let the question hang between us.

He ducked his head before looking back at me, shrugging. "I've only just started. They found the previous guard dismembered by an animal."

My eyes rounded as his meaning penetrated. I sure as shit hadn't heard of this.

"An animal?" I repeated.

He nodded slowly. "Apparently there was a wolf sighted in the area."

The elevator dinged. "Thanks," I uttered as I stepped in, ready to cause some havoc. How fucking dare she kill on my territory? Oh wow, that was all shifter emotion and logic there. Still, it was my territory under The Council as well.

"Hey, um, should I call someone for you?"

Aww, how sweet, he was concerned.

"Nope, I got this." I hit the large P for penthouse and the doors closed between us.

My arms were crossed over my chest, fingers drumming against my forearm. I couldn't wait to get my hands on the bitch and her fucking minions.

The elevator sputtered. I reached a hand out to steady myself. She wouldn't, right? Sage wouldn't dare try and off me in an elevator.

The quick pace resumed and I again assumed my annoyed position.

The silver doors opened silently and I pulled my guns, expecting an ambush. When none came, I re-holstered, stepping into the gray and white interior.

No one greeted me.

"Sage, show yourself," I stated, not needing to raise my voice for her shifter hearing.

Behind a black piano, a figure moved into my line of sight. Dressed in a skin-tight black strapless, she sauntered into the room.

"Olivia, it's so good to see you. I hope you are having success in your wild goose chase," she purred.

I grunted, "First off, how do you know it's a wild goose chase, and second, are you admitting to setting those traps?"

She poured herself a glass of champagne, smoothing back an errant strand that had separated from her high bun.

"I know because I am the one who is growing the St. Helen Olive," she admitted proudly, taking a sip.

"What?" I was having a hard time making the jump. "You are telling me that you created the shot that can make a shifter, like you, go insta-beast?"

She nodded, a smile on her ruby lips. "Well, I really can't take all the credit. Amin, come say hello to our guest."

"Yes, my Queen," the gray-skinned djinn stated, appearing behind Sage with an arm around her waist, his lips at her neck.

"You are betraying your entire species!" I was still having a hard time with this.

"No, I am saving the shifters," she hissed. "I'd already have challenged Logan, except for you." She pulled out of Amin's embrace, stalking to me. "You are helping a dying man. Hell, now you are mated to a man with a time limit. Logan is weak, his rule with Lorraine proved that, and I am simply correcting the imbalance."

"Then challenge him," I answered with a shrug.

She laughed, "Juiced up on succubus power? I don't think so."

I narrowed my eyes. "That only works for vampires."

She cast a glance at Amin before rounding on me. "You lie, you want me dead."

"Um, yeah, duh."

"You see!" she cried triumphantly to Amin.

"You did try to kill me first," I reminded her. Something wasn't right here, and I was hoping I could use it to my advantage. Djinn were such a fucking pain to kill.

She waved her hand. "That was The Conferences. Who wasn't trying to kill you?"

"The rest of the Compass Alphas," I answered. I crossed my arms over my chest, letting my hands rest close to my guns.

"Bah, those fools! The Shifter Nation has been crumbling under Logan's reign. We are weak! Prime for the taking over by the vampires."

"Why are the vampires taking over?" I asked, honestly curious. I mean, the fact a war was coming had been dropped repeatedly, although no one was giving me an actual target.

Sage drained her glass, holding it out to Amin to refill.

"You saw it firsthand, the rogues they are creating. We need the pure beasts to compete with that."

"That was a crazed demigod named Nari, not the vampires."

She smiled at me, bringing her full glass to her full, ruby lips without breaking eye contact. "Who do you think bankrolled him?"

"What proof do you have?" I challenged, resting my hands on my hips.

Sage laughed, throwing her head back, exposing the throat I wanted to slice. "My darling girl, who do you think bankrolled me?"

I blinked at that, surprised. "Why would the vampires bankroll you to make a serum that creates a beast, if you intend to use it against them?"

She laughed. "My dear girl, you prove how poor a choice you are for Mate. The vampires only see me weakening the shifters, nothing more."

"I can't believe I am going to say this, but I don't think the vampires are that dumb."

She scoffed, "You don't think the shifters would pay for such an expensive place, do you? Oh no, they're all about the secluded, cheap, rundown, rustic homes." Her face contracted with disgust. "I deserve more than that. I deserve it all." She examined her nails. "The real trick was convincing the blood suckers to give me Amin."

"If you wanted it all, you should have challenged Logan. Challenging me does nothing to advance you with the shifters."

"No, but killing you will greatly weaken Logan." She sat regally, with perfect posture. "I can kill him then."

"Just to clarify, you aren't strong enough to kill Logan healthy, but you think you are the strongest choice to run the shifters? Please tell me you see the flaw in that logic."

"The only flaw I see is you."

"I couldn't agree more, but I do have one additional question. How did you make Amin your bitch?"

She stood, furious. "You will not speak to him that way." Regaining her composure, she said with a flourish, "He was a gift from Zachariah."

I groaned, "I should have fucking known."

"He has grand plans for you," she taunted.

I was done with this evil mastermind dialogue.

"So Amin, if I kill her, are you going to be a problem for me?"

"If you kill her, I will become your possession," he answered, his dark gray eyes watching me closely.

I grunted, "I'm not really into keeping Supernaturals as possessions."

"As if you will win!" Sage screamed, shifting forms to fight me. "Amin, I wish to be the victor of this battle."

With that, she morphed into a jaguar.

Alright, I'm willing to admit that was impressive. Her black lips peeled back, exposing sharp teeth. But what really had me worried was that wish. I'd be fighting them both when I got the upper hand.

Sage growled low in her throat and stalked toward me, before pushing off the ground, leaping at me.

I set three daggers into her soft stomach, quickly rolling out of the way as she crashed down, destroying the wood coffee table, sending splinters scattering. With a cat howl, she twisted up. Amin waved a hand and the knives fell harmlessly onto the pile of wood.

Fuck, where was that chopper when I needed it?

As if summoned by my thoughts, Sage turned, looking at the ceiling. I smiled, "That would be backup."

She snarled something at Amin. "I can't understand you in that form," he replied nonchalantly, having no concern over the life and death fight happening.

Sage snarled once again and came at me, teeth snapping. I pulled both guns, training them at her. She paused, looking at me, before charging again. I managed to squeeze off a few shots, none of which did any real damage, as she pinned me under her.

I kept shooting, emptying both clips into her chest. Her eyes widened, mouth hanging open slackly, before Amin stepped in again. The bullets dropped harmlessly from her body.

I took advantage of her hesitation, though, dropping my guns and slamming my palm against her left paws, which had me pinned down. No wonder she was willing to take such chances with her life. The fucking djinn made her a fucking god.

But I wasn't done yet.

I rolled quickly, feeling her hot breath against my neck. I pulled another dagger from my boot, launching it while I ran. I heard it clatter harmlessly to the floor. I needed to play it smart. I was losing weapons and not gaining any ground.

Claws slashed at my back and I arched, sliding around the counter into the kitchen. There goes my jacket.

I also needed to stay alive until Mark and Jerry got here, preferably in one piece.

I pulled a kitchen knife from the counter, turning and plunging it into her flank. She in turn clawed at my thigh, her claws raking deeply.

I went down in front of her gaping jaw and she fucking smiled. I yanked the kitchen blade out, thankful she kept her knives sharp. I used both hands to slam it through her brain. It wasn't silver; it wouldn't kill her.

Her surprised yelp made me smile. I left the knife, knowing I didn't have long before the djinn pulled the steel blade out. Pulling my silver dagger from the small of my back, I wheeled and wrenched the blade through her neck, yanking it to the side. She lolled to her side, half her head hanging off.

Sage rolled away from me. Following her, I slammed my blade down to sever the remaining tendons.

I wasn't moving fast enough. The djinn had removed the blade lodged in her brain. If I didn't finish removing her ugly head from her body—yes, that was jealousy—then I was done for. The wounds on my back and legs were weeping blood. I may heal fast, but not shifter fast.

The pressure against my blade disappeared and my momentum kept me going until I landed hard on top of Sage's corpse in her human form.

I sighed, leaning back, keeping my knife gripped tightly in my hand.

A door burst open and my name was screamed out.

I lumbered up, smearing blood on the quartz countertops.

"Olie," Jerry cried out, running to me.

"Nice of you to join the party," I grunted, taking a tentative step, finding it more like a limp.

"I'd like to hear it now," I continued.

"Hear what?" Jerry asked.

"I'm right, you were wrong."

Mark looked between me and Amin, not sure if he was a threat or not.

"You were right?" Mark offered uncertainly.

"Thank you. Mark, Jerry, meet Amin. He's the djinn bound to Sage." I groaned as Jerry set me down onto a white couch, where I just kept seeping out bodily fluids. I was enjoying ruining the dead bitch's furniture.

Alright, so I was jealous. But just to be clear, I was still right.

"Amin, you going to be a problem?" Mark asked.

"Only if my new mistress requires it of me," Amin replied, totally unfazed by Sage's decapitation.

"Amin, I don't want to be your mistress—" Jerry clamped a hand over my mouth.

Amin's eyes glistened with hope. "Do not free him," Jerry whispered.

I looked at him. "Why?"

"Because he will kill you."

I grunted, looking at Amin. "True or false?"

He shifted, looking mildly perturbed. "Truth, I am required to kill the one who frees me."

"That's stupid," I grunted.

Amin shrugged.

"So what happens now?" I asked.

"Make no wishes, command him to do nothing," Jerry informed me.

"Didn't I already do that?" I asked.

"No, you asked a question. He wasn't forced to answer because of how you asked it," Jerry informed me.

185

I sighed. "Amin, what would you like to do now?"

He looked at me, surprised. "Anything?"

"That doesn't involve harming humans, Supernaturals, or animals," I amended.

"But I have to stay close in case you need me," Amin stated, coming to stand closer.

"She won't." Jerry was adamant.

I pressed a hand against my stomach, feeling a little lightheaded. "Get a cell phone, Amin. I can call you if I need something and you can check in if you have any questions about the arrangement."

Jerry nodded.

"Great, now can someone stitch me up before I lose all my blood?"

Amin waved a hand and pain disappeared. I ripped open my shirt, finding my wounds perfectly stitched. "Nice work," I commented.

"Are you certain you don't need me?" he asked with longing.

"Look, Amin, I'd be perfectly happy fr—" Jerry slapped a hand on my mouth. I looked at him and he lowered his hand cautiously. "But since I can't do that, I'd like you to live a pleasant life without harming anyone."

Amin nodded, pulling a cell phone out of his pocket. "I am unfamiliar with this technology."

Jerry took it cautiously. "Here, let me show you."

After a twenty-minute demonstration on how to use a phone and a few test calls to make sure he had our numbers programmed in, Amin disappeared.

"Well, that was fun," Mark grunted.

"Not even a thank you," I added, annoyed. I leaned against the couch, my eyes drifting closed.

"You gotta see what we found, Olie," Jerry said, helping me stand.

We made it to the roof and I looked around at the hundreds of potted St. Helen Olive plants.

"No flowers," I whispered, wandering though the rows.

"What do we do, Olivia?" Mark asked me softly.

"Burn it, burn it all." I looked to Jerry. "You got enough juice for it? Everything has to be destroyed, we have to torch her apartment, too. Actually, we should probably check the entire building."

Jerry nodded, looking around.

"The rest of the building is rented. I can hear the others," Mark said, bending down to inspect a plant. "How could she have gotten these?"

"The djinn, she must have wished for it." I rubbed my temple, pulling out my phone, "The real issue is, how long has she been experimenting and how long has Zachariah been bankrolling her?"

I dialed Logan's number and he answered groggily. "You okay?" he slurred.

"Yeah, but I need to you to wake up. We have a situation."

He cleared his throat. "Go ahead."

"Sage had a djinn that she was controlling. She told me the vampires have been funding her experimentation on how to make insta-beast, Zachariah to be specific. That he was also bankrolling Nari." I paused.

"Is there more?" he asked, now fully awake.

"A roof full of St. Helen Olive without flowers."

"Fucking hell. You have to destroy it."

"Duh, Logan. Jerry is going to light it up. I just wanted to call and fill you in."

"Oh, are you hurt?"

"My leather jacket is done for," I admitted. "Amin, the djinn, who is now mine by right of my winning the death match, stitched me up."

"Wait, you have a djinn?"

"Yeah, apparently it's not a good thing."

"Take care of the plants and come home," he urged, his voice earnest.

"Will do."

"Oh, and Olie?"

"Yeah?"

"I love you."

I stopped breathing for a moment before my smart ass kicked in. "Hmpf, you should be saying I was right about her."

He laughed, "Yeah, that too."

I delayed saying goodbye, not wanting to say the L word, but needing to say something else. "How's the nanny working out?"

"Great, she even came back for my emergency call when the kids were watching Ginny. I'm having her babysit tomorrow as well."

"Good, I'm glad."

A squawk sounded.

"Alright, take care of our girl."

"Will do."

I turned to see Mark looking at me like a lovesick puppy. "Your love, it's trickling down the packs."

"I didn't say I loved him."

Mark shrugged, patting his chest.

"Whatever. Jerry, you ready to light it up?" I asked.

Jerry was looking at Mark with longing. "Can you mate mark me, Mark?"

I looked at Mark, having no idea what the answer was.

He shrugged. "I can try, but I didn't even know it worked with a succubus. I have no idea what the effects would be on a mage."

Jerry nodded. "Give me a minute." He walked to all four corners, muttering.

"Alright, let's get back into the penthouse," Jerry instructed.

Jerry repeated the same four corner muttering in the apartment, while Mark and I looked through the rest of the penthouse. We didn't find anything of interest.

"Let's get out of here," I instructed.

I leaned on the back wall of the elevator, ready to get some food and some sleep to help my body heal. I hoped I hadn't made a mistake with Amin. I knew I didn't with Sage. I groaned, now we had to fill the North Compass Alpha's spot.

"Any chance you guys wanna take over here?" I asked, closing my eyes, feeling the downward momentum.

"No," they answered in unison.

I gave a soft laugh. "Politics not your thing?"

"Have you met us?" Jerry asked.

The doorman was busy on the phone, calling the fire department.

I smiled at him. "The roof and the penthouse are going to burn. Let them."

I could feel his slack-jawed gaze following me, but I heard the phone click. Hi, I'm Olivia and I will be obeyed. Mark had an arm around Jerry's shoulders, helping him across the street as Jerry continued to mutter.

I held the door to the hotel open, following behind my shifter and mage. Oh crap, I called them mine. Like I wasn't possessive enough.

I helped Mark get his door open, following them in.

He deposited Jerry onto the sofa and he went down with a groan. "How you doing, Jerry?" I asked, rubbing his shoulders.

"Nothing some food and rest won't cure," he assured me. He pawed around for the phone, lifting it to his ear.

"As much as I'm enjoying your poor attempt at a massage, you reek," he informed me.

...

I set the spray to scalding in the shower, letting it work on the kinks in my back and shoulders.

I heard the food arrive as I finished dressing. "That was fast," I commented, running a dry towel through my wet hair.

"Impressively fast," Mark said around a wad of food.

We devoured every scrap of the food and I was giving serious thought to ordering seconds. A yawn had me changing my mind.

"Good night, guys." I hauled myself up, dragging ass back to my room. The bed felt empty without Logan. I curled up on my side, holding the extra pillow to my chest.

...

Morning came too fucking early and I rolled out to the bathroom, shuffling my feet. I could hear Mark on the phone ordering breakfast for us.

"I'm getting way too used to nicer accommodations," I grunted to myself. Crap, and I couldn't afford them.

The knock on Mark's door came faster than I expected and I hustled to get dressed. I could expense this to Logan and not feel guilty, right? Fuck, no.

The door opened and the cart rattled in. Music to my ears, or really to my stomach.

I had just tied my tennis shoes when Mark grunted, his cry of pain cut off.

I barreled into the next room. Mark was on his side, the hotel employee holding a stun gun to his neck, delivering far above the recommended dosage.

I lunged for him. He straightened up. I took out the food cart in my zeal to bring the fucker down. The cart smashed into him, hindering my takedown attempt. The taser was conveniently rammed into my neck. Clearly, not my most brilliant move.

I lost all control over my body, my muscles jerking at random intervals. I rolled, pretty sure I was drooling. That was attractive. Fucking tasers.

My vision ceased, my teeth vibrating together. I curled around myself in the fetal position.

It felt like hours later, but I was guessing it must have been a few minutes, before I regained my faculties. I batted at the white, swishing clothing in front of me, finding my arm not responding to my commands.

"Hurry, she's waking up," a voice hissed.

I wrapped my hand around the cool metal of the rolling cart I was stuffed under, finally getting my bearings before I was shoved down a steep ramp, still under the cart. I braced myself against the poles, silently cursing my idiotic captors. And seriously, what the fuck is going on with me getting kidnapped so fucking often?

I gave thought to letting my momentum take me over the edge, but I decided to wait. Look at me, having patience.

The ground finally evened out and my empty stomach lurched. Motherfuckers were going die bloody for making me miss breakfast.

A hand reached under the linen to grab me. I bit down, tasting blood. A scream greeted my ears and I released, spitting. I fell forward from the cart, rolling to get free of the linen before I got my feet under me, staying low.

Grunting, I turned on my heels, looking at my would-be captors. This whole kidnapping thing ended right here. I'd leave a bloody fucking warning for anyone else thinking I was easy prey. I scented the air and growled disgustedly. Humans. Three humans were going to kidnap me?

They at least had the decency to look properly terrified.

"I'm going to kill you all," I promised with glee.

I launched onto the closest one, my momentum carrying us to the ground. Landing my hands on his bulletproof vest, I gripped both sides, pulling him up before bouncing his head off the concrete with a satisfying crunch. Brain matter and blood spread out in a dark pool, his eyes glazing in death.

Another barreled into me, his shoulder knocking my head back. We landed with my back slamming hard against the concrete. My legs were free so I slammed my knee into his side. He huffed, his body arching away from me. Sitting up, I shoved him off.

I turned to the side, my fingers wrapping around the wrist of the bellhop, the taser hissing inches from my face.

"You're going to regret the use of that." My fingers closed until my thumb overlapped my fingers. His wrist bones pulverized in my hand. Oh yeah, that was all shifter anger and it felt fantastic.

I stood, releasing his hand with a fling.

"Back off!" a familiar voice yelled. I lifted my eyes to the back of the hotel and saw Mark barreling down the ramp toward us.

I smiled before the asshole I had hit in the side tackled me. "Motherfucker," I hissed. My arms were pinned so I kicked out, but I was on my side so it wasn't doing any good.

"Get away from her!" Mark screamed. I felt the air shimmer as he shifted and a pissed off wolf landed next to me.

"Shit," a familiar voice exclaimed. I turned, cranking my head to look back at Nathaniel standing next to the getaway van.

"Don't let him get away," I wheezed to Mark. He tore the throat out of the man on top of me before bounding over me. I heard Nathaniel go down with a thud.

Shoving the body of the dead man off of me, I stood. The bellhop, whose wrist I'd crushed, was yelling incoherently on the concrete, writhing in pain. I looked at him for a moment, deciding he wasn't going anywhere, and turned my attention to Mark.

"It's too late, the team for Logan was successful," Nathaniel hissed at me. Sage's beta. I should have seen this coming. Mark had him pinned under a massive paw, his jaws dripping drool inches from Nathaniel's face.

I slipped off the concrete pad next to them onto the asphalt.

"Sage is dead," I reminded him, leaning heavily on my knees. Those fucking tasers hurt.

Nathaniel sneered at me and Mark inched closer, blowing his hair back in a huff. "It doesn't matter. The show must go on. I may have failed here, but our other teams were successful."

"Other teams?" Jerry asked behind me.

I turned. "About time you got in on the festivities."

He huffed, "I don't have shifter hearing. I got out of the shower to find Mark a drooling mess."

I grunted, speech seemed like too much work. From the back of my head, tightness was spreading, along with sharp points of pain. I fell to my knees, my vision blacking out.

Logan, his name whispered around my head. I shook my head, pressing a hand against my forehead. Logan. I cried out, falling onto all fours, an awful wrenching twisting my insides. The air coming into my lungs was jaded with fire and I screamed again.

Where was my mate?

The torment was blinding and it wasn't going away. I had to get control over it, but I couldn't. They weren't my emotions to control. I had to stem the flow. I had promised Logan I wouldn't block the mate bond, but I had no choice. I threw my shields up forcefully, blocking myself from the rest of the pack.

Sweet relief flooded my body. I sagged against Jerry, my air whooshing out. Guilt was the next strong emotion flooding me. My mate was suffering and I wasn't sharing in it, wasn't helping him.

"Alright, Nathaniel, you have two options. One, you tell me where Logan is and I kill you quickly. Two, I slice, maim and dismember you for the information, then feed you to Logan."

Mark snapped his sharp teeth at him and Nathaniel glared at him, unfazed. I'd change that.

"Your pet doesn't scare me. I rank higher than he does as an Alpha."

Mark pushed his nose against Nathaniel's. I moved forward, resting a hand against Mark's black-with-gray flank.

"While my dear friend makes an exceptionally talented negotiator, you, Nathaniel, are all mine."

"Not to break the spell of intrigue you two are creating, but we need to go before we are seen," Jerry reminded me.

"How nice, Nathaniel, you provided transportation." I hauled him from Mark's threatening teeth and tossed him into the opened cargo van. Mark followed. I shut the door, turning to Jerry, still on the dock.

"I'll get our stuff. Call me with a location," Jerry stated, carefully moving over the piles of dead flesh. A writhing form was still on the docks.

"Hey Jerry, that guy tased Mark." I pointed at the groaning bellhop.

He stopped, looking down at the asshole's injured form with a smile.

I turned away, getting into the van, trusting Jerry to handle it. I wasn't leaving witnesses.

I cranked the engine and turned out of the downtown hotel, searching for a secluded part of Chicago to interrogate Nathaniel.

...

Thirty minutes later, I shut off the engine, looking around at the abandoned blocks of industrial buildings.

Mark had shifted back, finding a spare pair of badly fitting black pants in the back.

"I can't hear anyone around us," he announced, listening closely.

"That was faster than I anticipated," I answered, spinning around in the driver's seat.

Jerry came to a stop next to us, killing his engine. I moved into the cargo hold with Mark and Nathaniel, opening the driver's door for Jerry. He slid in, handing a wrapped leather package over my shoulder.

"Thought you would need those." I could hear the smile in Jerry's voice.

I smiled, letting my fingers trail over my knives. "You know me so well."

"And while I know you both love a good torture session, I have to ask why you don't just read his mind," he questioned.

I groaned, "Crap, you're right. I should have thought of that sooner."

I sighed, "Alright, this is going to hurt."

I dropped all my shields; at this point, I was losing track of how many I had. White hot searing pain closed down my airway. My vision gone, I could hardly feel my body.

I forced myself to see the pack structure, the golden threads that I knew were my pack.

Blackness was starting to trickle down into the threads. Shit.

Back to my current issues.

"Where is Logan?" I asked, or tried to or hoped.

Please let this work, Mark thought.

I'll never tell the bitch he's so close to her home.

I slammed my shields up, drawing a pain-free breath. How the fuck did he know where I lived?

"We're heading home. Leave the van, let's move him into the SUV."

They obeyed my commands, securing Nathaniel in the backseat with handcuffs.

"Call for backup. I have to keep the darkness from spreading."

Mark nodded, reaching out a hand to my shoulder from the backseat. Jerry was driving and I was riding shotgun. Hope glowed in Mark's eyes.

I nodded, letting my focus turn away from the physical word. I reached for Logan, feeling his agony, pain, and hopelessness.

Hold on, Logan. We are coming.

There was no answer, not even an indication he heard me. I dropped my head against my knees, drew my legs to my chest, and pulled. Blackness coated the inside of my mouth, halting my ability to breathe. Still I pulled the darkness away from Logan, funneling it into myself, letting it fill every deep, dark, crevice inside my broken soul.

I may not have much or be much, but I wouldn't let the shifters lose Logan. Even if it killed me, he would take care of my kids.

I tilted my head back, my jaw locking with the overflow.

...

"Olie," Jerry was rocking me. My body was spent. I was hanging on to consciousness by a thin thread.

"She's stemming the flow of insanity from Logan," Mark explained.

I rolled my head down, a breath hissing between my lips. It was a slow process building the walls back up until I was mildly conscious.

It took a few long blinks for me to be able to focus on the situation around me. I had been moved from the SUV and had an arm slung around Jerry's shoulder. I dropped it, standing on my own, surrounded by an impressive number of shifters. Darkness swarmed around us. Behind the imposing small army of shifters was an outdated, pea green metal building, three floors high.

"Nathaniel?" I hissed.

"He is here," Bear answered. Now that's the kind of backup we needed.

"Good, keep him alive. I want to feed him to the Alpha. How did you find this place? Are we sure Logan is in there?"

Jerry nodded. "You kept chanting 'close to home,' so we drove around until Mark heard him."

"He alive?" Caleb asked, his eyes hopeful. "I'm having a hard time feeling around your blocking."

"Yes, no one's fucking dying on my watch. Well, except for Nathaniel. And Sage."

Bear's eyes widened. "Yeah, that's another story." I rubbed my temples. "Okay, give me the situation."

"Our recon shows only humans inside. From heartbeats, maybe twenty," Caleb dictated.

I nodded, Nathaniel laughed.

"Bring him forward." My voice dropped deadly.

The shifters parted to reveal Nathaniel, his hands bound together in front of him. Bear reached and fisted the back of Nathaniel's shirt, yanking him down. He landed hard on the pavement, his head bouncing.

I stepped between his legs, applying enough pressure to get his attention.

"What are you hiding?"

He hissed, "Do what you will to me. The pain you are delivering is nothing compared to what he is doing to Logan. Since you left your mate, he's been tortured for the last seven hours. You are a pathetic choice for a partner."

I pressed my foot to the ground.

"Who is torturing him?" And bitch I just killed your partner without you so much as making an appearance. I dropped my walls and in my own ears it sounded loud, crashing around me.

Zachariah.

I shook my head from the effort to delve into his mind, building my walls back up rapidly, willing Logan to hang on.

"There's a master vampire here also," I croaked out, leaning on Jerry again. Dammit, I straightened up.

Nathaniel's eyes widened, and I leaned down, releasing my foot. "I'll make good on my promise. They will eat you alive."

I drew back from the piece of shit, forcing my spine straight. "You ready?" I asked Bear.

He smiled, nodding.

"Lead the first charge, I'll be right behind you." I wasn't admitting I was too weak to lead to this bitch.

Bear leaned closer, resting his forehead against my own. Wait until it's safe, Mate. We need you.

I smiled, relieved. "Always. Thank you." I checked my shields, finding massive holes from my exhausted state.

Mark hauled up Nathaniel. "I'll stay with you."

I nodded. Bear led the shifters into the darkness. If Zachariah was paying attention, he'd hear us. I hoped he wasn't. Caleb reached out, resting his hands against my biceps, leaning his forehead against my own.

"Stay safe, Mate," he whispered. It was a high sign of respect and I was honored.

"You as well."

I watched my pack disappear into the shadows. I wanted to lead the charge, I wanted my mate back. I needed Logan on a fundamental level.

I loved the motherfucker. Dammit all.

"They're gone, Olie, come sit down." Jerry helped me to the back of the SUV and I sat down heavily.

An explosion ripped through the air. I was up instantly, searching the building, running golden threads through my mind.

"Easy, Olie, Bear planned it."

I nodded, still watching. Still needing to be sure my pack was okay.

"Can you hear what's happening?" I asked Mark.

"Bear has shifted." He chuckled, "He apparently thinks he can take everyone out himself."

...

After fifteen minutes I followed Mark in, Nathaniel in front of him and Jerry behind me.

Bear had shifted back, a long bloody streak on his stomach healing as I watched.

"Where is he?" I asked, needing him.

Bear braced his hands on my shoulders. "Olivia." The word was loaded with hesitation and worry.

"I don't care how bad it is, Bear. He. Is. Mine."

Bear searched my face before nodding. "Follow me."

"Zachariah?" I asked.

"Gone. We never saw him."

Dammit. I needed proof he was here.

The warehouse was dark. The humans were contained. I moved behind Bear to the room where Logan was being held.

Mark backed slowly out of the room, his fear rank.

"You can't go in there," he whispered, turning wide eyes to me.

Chains rattled and pulled. A desperate howl erupted.

Resting a hand on his shoulder, I smiled. "Keep everyone out until I say."

He wanted to deny me, the fear evident in his gaze, but I was bound to the Alpha and Mark would obey me. That would take some getting used to.

As I crossed the threshold, the scent of urine and dead things assaulted my nose. Steeling my nerves, I waited for my eyes to adjust. In a dark corner where the light in the center didn't penetrate was Logan. I didn't need to see him. I could feel him just fine, pressing against the shields in my head.

Exhaling, I focused, dropping my guards. The pain was dimmed but ever-present. Zachariah hadn't had long with Logan, but it had been enough.

"Here, Kitty Kitty," I called him. Probably not my best idea to taunt him, but it was my favorite nickname and it made light of a situation that was kinda scary. Seriously, I'll never admit that. I kept my steps even as I passed through the shadows and to Logan.

He launched from the darkness, his chains pulling taut and jaws snapping. Still I moved forward. He re-grouped within the small space, turning as best he could in his lion form and bounding at me again.

His heavy paws landed on my shoulders and we went down to the concrete with a thud.

"Missed you, too," I grunted, fisting his fur to touch the skin beneath.

He roared, fangs extended. Dropping his head with force, he sank them into the skin of my neck.

"Fucking hell! You already marked me," I hissed at him, my stomach muscles contracting. Pulling my head closer to him, I stayed there, blowing out a ragged breath.

"Easy baby, I'm here," I whispered.

I wasn't gentle, assaulting him with safety and tranquility. The shifters were picking up his anger and discontent from afar through the pack bonds. It wouldn't be long before the weaker ones succumbed to pure beast.

I envisioned our first kiss, well, the first kiss I remember. His soft hands cradling my face, his long, strong body pressed against me. Warm lips slowly caressing my own before his tongue demanded entrance into my mouth. I let the feelings of peace and safety he inspired in me coat his body. The joy I felt at being included in his family gatherings.

The gratitude I felt when he helped me take care of Patricia Bellarosa. The comfort of his steadfast support when the sex tape was leaked. Everything I poured into him, and the tears showed up on their own, trickling down my face.

"Come back to me," I whispered. "I need you."

I had never uttered truer words. We might have been thrown together in this situation without full control, and without my consenting to be his mate, but I was in it now for better or worse.

The fangs in my shoulder pulled back and I felt the warm blood flowing. The popping of bones followed the brush of magic as furry Logan turned into human Logan.

"I'm here," came the faint reply, his voice rough as he leaned his forehead against my own.

"Horrible things," he whispered to me. I felt his shift of emotions flowing through the rest of the pack. I could see how each member related to him, was bound to him, and how they shared his pain.

My mind knew what to do. Before I realized what was happening, blocks were being installed around Logan's memories. Only a trickle of emotion was going to leak, enough to assure everyone he was alive but not enough to influence them.

I felt the collective sigh when I was done.

"Look at me," Logan demanded

"I have something in my eyes," I muttered, opening them so he could see the tears. "I'm so sorry it took me so long to find you," I whispered.

He shook his head back up. "How did you find me?"

"The mate bond." Well, kinda. That was the romantic answer, anyways.

"I never taught you how to use it."

"Good thing I didn't wait for you to. I had to block you for a bit, but it all worked out."

Logan moved off of me and I stood, careful of my new neck wound.

"Mark, you can unlock the cuffs and bring in the bitch."

Mark and Bear marched Nathaniel in, careful not to meet Logan's gaze.

"Meet the traitor," I told him. Well, the traitor I left alive.

"Bitch, you do not belong with us, we are stronger without your kind—" He would have continued, but I stepped up and punched him across his jaw, breaking it.

"I hope you've enjoyed your last few minutes alive." I turned to Logan. "I wanted to kill him or at least maim him, but I think that honor belongs to you."

His eyes glowing, he waited for Mark to finish with the last restraint before he pounced. I would like to say he prolonged Nathaniel's misery, but the kill was quick. The mutilation took a while.

"I have more," I announced when Logan finished. He was breathing heavily, blood staining his face and naked body. I reached out to cup his cheek with a smile, so grateful to have him back. He pressed into my touch, drawing me near.

"Follow me," Mark beckoned, moving in front of us, but not before throwing Logan a pair of sweats.

I nodded to another shifter who was placing C4 around the place to blow it sky high.

"Bombs?" Logan asked.

"Our official story is a group of fanatic shifters blew themselves up in protest to the new Alpha Queen because if I'm here, they didn't want to be."

We rounded the corner and I watched his face light up at the humans bound in rope. "It feels like cheating," he whispered.

"It's not, but I can free one if you want. I need their limbs to stay attached, but do what you want to the flesh."

Logan wanted to go but stayed close, touching me.

"I'm not going anywhere," I assured him.

He shook his head, looking down at me. "I want to be here with you."

I smiled, nodding. We moved outside, leaving and trusting the others to handle the bombs and humans.

I turned to Logan when I couldn't wait any longer. "Was it Zachariah?" I asked, needing confirmation.

Logan shook his head, his eyes clouding over. "I don't know. I never saw his face."

"Smell?"

"Wolfsbane."

"He covered his bases."

Logan put a thick arm around my shoulders.

"Let's go home."

Chapter 18

I stood at our window holding Ginny, swaying as I cooed to her. Logan was taking his time in the shower. We hadn't talked much on the short ride home. His shields were in place while mine had been dropped.

He hadn't been a captive long, but it was enough for damage to be done. I knew all about damage. I just hoped he trusted me enough to help him.

The irony wasn't lost on me. I needed to trust him enough with the broken pieces of my own soul.

I heard the door open and I eased Ginny down into her crib.

"Your mate bond is open," Logan commented, his sweat pants low on his hips.

"Yes, yours is closed to me."

He paused in shuffling though his clothing. "I know."

I moved to him, wrapping my arms around his expansive waist from behind. "I'm here, Logan. Whatever you need."

He turned, wrapping his arms around me.

"I love you, Olie."

I nuzzled into his warm chest. "I love you, too."

He pushed back, looking down at me, shocked. "What?"

I socked his shoulder. "You heard me."

With that I turned and headed for the shower, a shit-eating grin plastered onto my face.

When I got out, Logan was feeding Ginny, propped up in bed. I slipped in next to him, running a hand over her soft cheek.

"She's so perfect," I whispered.

Logan kissed my forehead. "You ready to be a mom?"

I looked up at him. "I'm not her mom, Logan. I'm her protector, her confidant, and her friend. I think we should give Lorraine supervised visitations."

"She signed the paperwork releasing all maternal rights."

"I know, but Ginny needs to know her story. She needs to know the truth."

"Nothing good can come from Lorraine being in Ginny's life."

I reached out to run my fingers over his stubbly cheek. "Okay, whatever you think is best."

He nodded, looking down to check on Ginny. "I found a house I want you to look at."

I nodded. "Sure, do you want to go today?"

He shifted uncertainly. He needed to sleep, but I knew it would be a long time coming.

"Yeah, I'll call the realtor."

...

I looked at the circle driveway and mansion behind it. Turning, I looked at Logan, who was leaning against the SUV with a knowing smile on his face.

I crossed my arms over my chest, kicking a hip out.

"Really?"

Logan smiled, and happiness tickled our link.

"Who is living with us?" I asked, waving at the monstrosity behind me.

He shrugged, turning his gaze to me. "The Compass Alphas will be here four times a year along with their betas. My parents, I'm certain, will visit unless they purchase their own home." He stepped toward me and I took a step closer to him. "The children will need a home as well."

"What?" I gasped, my heart constricting painfully.

His knuckles brushed away a tear I hadn't given permission to fall. "Let Grams have it, all of it. We will rebuild the funds of the Council. We will build another Kitten, or a Lovely Lust, or hell a combination of the two." Another fucking tear boycotted my authority. "I know this situation wasn't planned, but I don't regret any of it. Build a life with me, Olie."

I drew a tear-punctuated breath and punched him in the arm, smiling. Alright, fate, you might have won this one. "You are the best, Logan."

He didn't even rub his arm, just kept on smiling.

"Oh, and Darren asked me to tell you that Kass owns Halfling. The human and Supernatural mixer club."

"She WHAT?"

Logan laughed, "Yeah there was some debate on how to tell you, but I don't want there to be any secrets between us." He took my hands, his warm palms caressing my skin.

"I'm not sure I can give up everything to Grams. My ego is having a problem with it."

Logan nodded, his arm going around my shoulder. "Easy, turbo, your second mate mark is still healing."

He leaned down to nuzzle the spot in question and I punched him in the abs.

"Your hand okay?"

"Shut it."

He picked up Ginny's car seat, where she was sleeping peacefully, and we headed up to the house hand in hand.

Connect with Me!

Thank you for reading A Council of Betrayal! I greatly appreciate your support and I whole heartedly hope you enjoyed it. If you did, please consider leaving me some love on the platform you purchased on.

Facebook: kimbairauthor

Instagram: KimBairAuthor

Email: kimbair@proton.me

Website: www.kimbair.com

Telegram: kimbairauthor

I am always looking for beta readers to help me iron out the kinks, if you would like to join please email me at kimbair@proton.me

Thank you and happy reading!!

More books by Kim Bair:

Dead Shifter Walking, The Succubus Executioner Book 1

Demigod Down, The Succubus Executioner Book 2

A Witch's Fury, The Succubus Executioner Book 3

A Council of Betrayal, The Succubus Executioner Book 4

Death of a Succubus, The Succubus Executioner Book 5

Legacy of the Succubus, The Succubus Executioner Book 6

Creation of the Dual Shifter, The Dual Shifter Executioner

The Mel Files

Andy's Origin, The Andromalius Chronicles

www.ingramcontent.com/pod-product-compliance
Lightning Source LLC
Chambersburg PA
CBHW022100170626
46808CB00002B/529